MUTANT EMPIRE

BOOK 1

SIEGE

SPIDER-MAN: THE VENOM FACTOR
by Diane Duane

THE ULTIMATE SPIDER-MAN
Stan Lee, Editor

IRON MAN: THE ARMOR TRAP
by Greg Cox

SPIDER-MAN: CARNAGE IN NEW YORK
by David Michelinie & Dean Wesley Smith

THE INCREDIBLE HULK: WHAT SAVAGE BEAST
by Peter David

SPIDER-MAN: THE LIZARD SANCTION
by Diane Duane

THE ULTIMATE SILVER SURFER
Stan Lee, Editor

FANTASTIC FOUR: TO FREE ATLANTIS
by Nancy A. Collins

DAREDEVIL: PREDATOR'S SMILE
by Christopher Golden

X-MEN: MUTANT EMPIRE: Book 1: SIEGE
by Christopher Golden

COMING SOON:

THE ULTIMATE SUPER-VILLAINS
Stan Lee, Editor

SPIDER-MAN & THE INCREDIBLE HULK: RAMPAGE
by Danny Fingeroth & Eric Fein (Doom's Day Book 1)

SPIDER-MAN: GOBLIN'S REVENGE
by Dean Wesley Smith

THE ULTIMATE X-MEN
Stan Lee, Editor

SPIDER-MAN: THE OCTOPUS AGENDA
by Diane Duane

X-MEN: MUTANT EMPIRE: Book 2: SANCTUARY
by Christopher Golden

X-MEN

MUTANT EMPIRE

BOOK 1

SIEGE

CHRISTOPHER GOLDEN

ILLUSTRATIONS BY
RICK LEONARDI AND RON LIM
WITH TERRY AUSTIN

BYRON PREISS MULTIMEDIA COMPANY, INC.
NEW YORK

BOULEVARD BOOKS, NEW YORK

Special thanks to Lou Aronica, Ginjer Buchanan, Ken Grobe, Steve Roman, Bob Harras, Julia Molino, Stacy Gittelman, and the gang at Marvel Creative Services.

X-MEN: MUTANT EMPIRE
Book 1: SIEGE

A Boulevard Book
A Byron Preiss Multimedia Company, Inc. Book

PRINTING HISTORY
Boulevard edition / May 1996

All rights reserved.
Copyright © 1996 Marvel Characters, Inc.
Edited by Keith R.A. DeCandido
Cover design by Claude Goodwin
Cover art by Ray Lago
Interior design by Michael Mendelsohn
This book may not be reproduced in whole or in part,
by mimeograph or any other means, without permission.
For information address: Byron Preiss Multimedia Company, Inc.,
24 West 25th Street, New York, New York 10010
Check out the Byron Preiss Multimedia
Co., Inc. site on the World Wide Web:
http://www.byronpreiss.com

The Putnam Berkley World Wide Web site address is
http://www.berkley.com

ISBN 1-57297-114-2

BOULEVARD
Boulevard Books are published by The Berkley Publishing Group
200 Madison Avenue, New York, New York 10016
BOULEVARD and the "B" design
are trademarks belonging to Berkley Publishing Corporation

PRINTED IN THE UNITED STATES OF AMERICA

10 9 8 7 6 5 4 3 2

For my good friends

Steve Williams and Jeff Galin,
the Xavier and Magneto of my life.
Neither of whom will have any idea what that means.

Acknowledgments

As always, this wouldn't have been possible without the love of my wife, Connie, the laughter of my son, Nicholas, and the support of my family.

Special thanks to my agent Lori Perkins, my editor Keith R.A. DeCandido, and to Ginjer Buchanan for the tip.

A debt of gratitude is owed to all those wonderful creators who have brought the X-universe to life over the years, particularly Stan Lee, Jack Kirby, Dave Cockrum, and Chris Claremont.

Finally, profound thanks to those folks in the comic book industry who didn't hold it against me that I'd only written, God forbid, novels before. They include: Scott Allee, Steve Bissette, Meloney Crawford Chadwick, Robert Conte, Glenn Greenberg, Bob Harras, Scott Lobdell, Ralph Macchio, Jeff Mariotte, Marcus McLaurin, Mike Mignola, Jimmy Palmiotti, Mark Paniccia, Ed Polgardy, Mark Powers, Ross Richie, Evan Skolnick, Tom Sniegoski, Billy Tucci, and Rick Veitch.

MUTANT EMPIRE

BOOK 1

SIEGE

PROLOGUE

Cloaked from all detection by its extraordinary technology, the space station Avalon described an elliptical orbit around the Earth. On her observation deck, a gleaming metal platform with little ornamentation to warm the cold expanse of space, Eric Magnus Lehnsherr stood alone, gazing down at the planet of his birth with a heavy heart. He was no longer welcome on Earth. More than a man without a country, he was a man without a world. And he feared that such would be the fate of all his kind.

Eric Lehnsherr was a mutant.

He was not an uncommonly large man, standing just over six feet tall and weighing just under two hundred pounds, but there was a quiet fury about him that gave even the bravest soul pause. His eyes were the blue-grey of an impending storm, his long hair an extraordinarily perfect white. Defined by his command, of himself and others around him, he was not given to frivolous commentary or physical expression. Still, he allowed himself a low sigh, a shake of his head, and then his hand came up to stroke his smooth chin.

Lost in contemplation, in waves of hope and grim determination, he barely noticed the hiss of expelled air as a door slid open behind him. There was no danger to him, here. On Avalon, he was . . .

"Lord Magneto, you summoned me," Exodus said reverently.

Magneto felt a moment of regret for the day he chose

2

that name. In his anger, his need to present himself to the world as a being of power, he had abandoned the name his parents had given him. It had set him apart from the humans, made them fear him all the more. But it had also made it easier for them to hate. That distance, that difference, also existed in the hushed reverence with which his Acolytes treated him. Fear, hatred, reverence . . . Magneto wondered if he would ever grow used to them, or to the solitary world they had built around him.

Exodus stood silently, patiently awaiting whatever response Magneto might provide. His robes flowed around him, reminding Magneto of a purple and black butterfly, such a contrast to the hard shell of crimson that he himself wore.

"Your tone reveals your hope that I have finally come to my senses, Exodus," Magneto said. "I'm sorry to inform you that I remain dedicated to the Empire Agenda."

"My lord," Exodus gasped, "you know that I would never think to question your will. I have not . . ."

"Yes, yes, I know," Magneto assured him. "You have no fear that I will question your loyalty. Yet I know that you disapprove of this endeavor. Don't think for a single moment that I don't know, and understand, your feelings on this subject."

Magneto walked to Exodus, whose eyes were downcast, and laid a hand on the other's shoulder.

"Avalon will continue to be a haven away from Earth for those mutants who accept our invitation, our challenge to live free," Magneto said reassuringly. "And you, my friend, will continue to be the ferryman who guides those lost souls to their new lives, and the chief protector, other than myself, of all who reside here."

Exodus nodded, but did not appear relieved.

"Please, Exodus, enough of this propriety!" Magneto said in frustration. "Ask the questions that weigh so heavily on you."

"I know it isn't my place, Magneto, but it all seems so unnecessary," Exodus explained. "We have Avalon. What is keeping us from abandoning the Earth entirely?"

Magneto realized that Exodus simply could not comprehend his plans, and resolved to change that. True, Exodus would follow his orders to the letter, no matter what they might be, and he owed no one an explanation of his actions. But what good was blind obedience? Whoever followed him, Magneto had vowed, would not do so in ignorance. That was the human way.

"We are the next step in evolution," he began, and turned to look back out at the vacuum of space, and the blue world spinning below. "We are *homo sapiens superior*. It is the destiny of the species currently referred to as 'humanity' to die out, to be replaced by our kind. It is natural that they should fear us, for we are the harbinger of their doom.

"I have spent my life trying to carve a place in the world for mutants. By natural law, we ought to be the sovereign race on this world. It is inevitable. Time and again, my efforts have been thwarted by Charles Xavier and his X-Men. Mutants themselves, these so-called heroes have naively worked toward Xavier's dream that mutants and humans can peacefully co-exist."

He paused, but when he spoke again, he no longer seemed to be speaking to Exodus.

"Xavier is a madman," Magneto said, a strange sadness in his tone. "What creature ever embraces entropy? How can any rational being live side by side in harmony with the evidence of its impending death?"

"Yes, lord," Exodus agreed. "But what you say only strengthens the case for Avalon as the haven for all mutants until we are strong enough to take the entire Earth, or until the humans begin to destroy themselves. Why continue to struggle for a refuge on Earth when we have one in the heavens?"

"Why indeed?" Magneto asked himself, a wistful smile playing at the corners of his mouth. He brushed an errant lock of white hair from his face, then spun to look at Exodus once more.

"I must try, don't you see?" he asked, suddenly vehement. "That ball of dirt and water spinning down there is our home, Exodus. We have a *right* to it as the next rung on the evolutionary ladder. The Earth is *my* home, for better or worse. Every moment of happiness, every ounce of agony, sprang from its soil. To abandon it to the new dream of Avalon means putting my vision of an Earth ruled by mutantkind on hold for an indefinable time.

"That may be what is necessary for the vision to become truth. If so, I am prepared for it. But before I am able to reconcile myself to that decision, I have to make one final effort to create a haven for mutants on Earth now, today! I put the Empire Agenda in place several years ago for just such an attempt. The moment has arrived. Do you understand that?"

Exodus cast his gaze at the floor again, and nodded. "Yes, lord," he said. "I realize how foolish I was. Your courage is equaled only by your vast love and compassion for your fellow mutants. I am ashamed to have questioned you. What may I do to atone for my doubts?"

Magneto smiled now, like a proud and indulgent father. "The only thing I ask of you, Exodus, is to continue to populate Avalon with the seeds of the future of mutantkind and to protect her with your life until my return."

"It shall be done, lord," Exodus said.

"Excellent," Magneto responded. "Now, please gather the Acolytes who will accompany me to Earth, and send Voght to me immediately."

When Exodus left, Magneto's spirits had risen considerably. Though he was born there, Exodus had no interest in Earth, but Magneto had been able to make him realize what the Empire Agenda meant to all mutants. To have faith. Faith was important. Magneto intended to carve a mutant haven out of the Earth, and from there begin a campaign to gradually take the entire planet. For the mission to succeed, all of his Acolytes had to be as confident as he was.

There was a rustling behind him, like wind in the fallen leaves, and Magneto turned to see the psychically projected image of the Acolyte called Scanner shimmer into existence.

"Yes, Scanner?"

"Voght has arrived, lord," Scanner said, but did not wait for a response. Magneto watched as her psionic holo-body disappeared.

The door hissed open and Amelia Voght was there. She was a beautiful woman, with a mane of auburn hair that Magneto found quite alluring. There was nothing romantic about their relationship, yet there was a certain undeniable intimacy between them. Unlike the other Acolytes, Voght did not worship him as her lord and master. She believed in him and his vision, certainly, but when she spoke to him, particularly without the others around, it was with a familiarity that Magneto found refreshing.

"You rang?" she asked as she stepped into the observation deck.

"We will depart for Earth momentarily, Amelia," Magneto said. "I thought it best to take you aside to inform you that I have decided to appoint you field leader for the duration of this operation."

Voght was clearly stunned, and uncharacteristically speechless. The effect didn't last long, however.

"I'm grateful, Magneto," she said. "I'm assuming you've taken into consideration that the others will be less than pleased, particularly Unuscione?"

"I have confidence in you, Amelia," Magneto said. "Now, shall we begin to enact the Empire Agenda?"

"Absolutely," Voght said, her voice rising with excitement. "It isn't every day you get to hold a planet hostage, after all."

•   •   •

It was just past seven o'clock in the morning, but the Rocky Mountains were alive with activity. Birdsong filled the air, the wind whipped through the trees, and animals prowled throughout the region. In a remote section of Colorado, on one of the many large sections of land the federal government still owned, a long, open field was surrounded by a touch-sensitive electrified fence, trimmed with razor wire. Inside the fence, a tiny bull's-eye on the open field, was a two-story gray brick structure that would appear, to the uninitiated, as nothing more than an office building.

Beneath the field, however, there was something more.

A crackling sound drowned out the birds and the

breeze and the choking stench of burning rubber suddenly filled the air, and was joined by the smell of scorched grass. Though it wasn't more than seventy degrees, the air above the field warped and shimmered as if it were a summer swelter over heat-wave–baked pavement. There was a loud, echoing bang, like the crack of a rifle, and birds fluttered in flocks from treetops around the perimeter of the fence.

Magneto and the Acolytes had arrived.

"You realize, my lord, that I could have teleported us here as easily as the technology of Avalon," Voght said with a trace of annoyance.

Magneto turned, facing the zealous followers he had chosen for this mission, and nodded patiently. He wore the crimson helm that had covered his head, hidden his face, for so many years. It had come to represent terror in the hearts of so many humans, and majesty in the minds of the Acolytes.

"The last thing I want, Amelia," he said after a pause, "is for you to expend energy needlessly." He lifted his arms to include all of them. "Before this is over, each of you will be taxed to your limits. We must work together, or the dream will fail. Now, let us begin."

The Acolytes tensed, moving into offensive positions in preparation for the moment when Magneto lowered their cloaking shield, allowing the base's security sensors to register their presence for the first time. He surveyed the team he had chosen for this mission, and decided that he had chosen well. They looked organized and strong in their navy and crimson uniforms, and danger crackled in the air around them like heat lightning.

Senyaka's face was hidden, as always, behind the cowl he wore, but Magneto did not need to see his face to know the blood lust in the man's heart. Senyaka held a psionic whip, created by the power of his mind, which hummed with a paralyzing current not unlike electricity. Its every coil and snap was controlled by the Acolyte's mind and Magneto allowed himself a moment's sympathy for those who would feel the sting of Senyaka's zeal.

Next to him stood Milan, who was invaluable to the Empire Agenda. Milan stood quietly, eyes covered by a visor whose sensors helped him to process incoming information instantly. His brain was like a computer, and could access both human and artificial intelligence, flesh and machine, with equal expediency.

Magneto allowed himself a slight smile at the sight of the powerhouse Joanna Cargil, once known as Frenzy, attempting to contain her hyperactive personality. Cynical by nature, the black woman had nevertheless become one of the most devout among the Acolytes. She stood next to Javitz, who was equally powerful. At nearly nine feet tall, the gold headset and shoulder armor they all wore made him look even more imposing. The only flaw in the giant's form was the bandage he wore to cover his useless left eye.

The Kleinstock brothers, Harlan and Sven, guarded their flank. The twins had once been triplets, but the third brother, Eric, had been lost on one of the Acolytes' missions. Their power, hideous as it was, had been cut by one third then, but they were still effective. Unfortunately, the twins rarely thought ahead, and had to be kept tightly reined.

Voght was in the front—where she belonged as field leader—despite the displeased grunts with which several of the others had greeted the news of her appointment. By her side was perhaps the most dangerous of the Acolytes, and the one most startled and chagrined by Magneto's choice of Voght, Unuscione. With the psychic exoskeleton her mind constantly emitted to defend her body, she was untouchable. She was even more dangerous, however, because she could bend, shape, and extend that shell as she wished, using it to capture, crush, or pummel an enemy.

They were young, yes. Magneto had seen too many young mutants lose their lives in this struggle. But they believed with all their hearts, and he could not have asked for a more dedicated team for this mission. He was proud to stand with them, though their near worship of him must ever keep him apart from them as well. All but Voght.

"Amelia," he said softly, "on your word."

Her eyes widened, the honor of command still taking her by surprise. Then she nodded almost imperceptibly, and barked out her orders.

"Cargil, Javitz, on the point. Kleinstocks through the back. Senyaka and Unuscione on the flank and Milan with me. On my word, shields down and attack," she snarled, then paused a moment.

"Go!" Voght yelled.

Alarms shattered the air as the shields dropped. They moved as one toward the small building. Previously concealed weapons stations began to fire a tightly woven pattern of plasma bolts and laser bursts across the field. Harlan Kleinstock took several out with a plasma blast from his hands before Magneto caused the rest to simply explode with nothing more than a dismissive gesture and a light electromagnetic pulse, generated on a specific wavelength.

Javitz and Cargil didn't bother knocking, choosing instead to simply crash through the front of the building. A heartbeat later, the Kleinstocks blew the rear wall out. As Voght and the others approached, Magneto held back, waiting to see what the next move would be. At the center of the nearly destroyed building was a massive, square, vault-like structure, perhaps eight feet wide, high and deep. To the right of the doors, which resembled those of an elevator, was a slot for a keycard and a keypad, which clearly implied a combination of some kind.

"Milan," Voght barked. "Open it."

Magneto was pleased. Most of the others would have simply smashed the vault, but there might be security or defense measures that could hold them up, or it might conceivably be tough enough to slow their advance just a little. Sometimes the light touch was the best way to proceed.

Milan walked calmly to the door, his dark, angular features only intensifying the oddness of the arrowhead tattooed on his forehead, pointing down at the bridge of his nose. He reached out a gloved hand and lightly touched the keypad next to the door, but did not enter any numbers.

"My friend," Milan said to the computer. "I would be very grateful if you would let us inside."

There was a pause, and the mutant cocked his head as if listening to a ghostly voice none of the others could hear. After a moment, Milan spoke again.

"Certainly," he said. "I would be pleased to speak with you again when our business here is concluded. I know how lonely it must get."

With a rushing sound like the fall of a guillotine, the door slid open.

"Thank you," Milan said calmly, and moved into the shaft before addressing the others. "We will be taken to the main complex, but there will most certainly be guards waiting there for us."

"Good!" the Kleinstock brothers said in unison.

The lift, a large, armored elevator, dropped rapidly down the shaft and came under fire the moment it appeared in the main complex area, though the guards doing the actual shooting must have known their plasma bursts would not penetrate the lift's armored shell.

When the doors opened, Magneto stepped forward, motioning for the Acolytes to wait a moment. The predetermined schedule and his own impatience demanded that not another moment be spared. He set up an e-m field around himself, which deflected the many shots that now assaulted him. At his most imperious, Magneto raised his arms as if conducting a symphony, and each of the guards—he counted an even dozen—jumped back as their firearms shattered in their hands.

Unuscione was the first out of the elevator, in advance of Voght's signal, and he made a mental note to punish her later for that transgression. With her psionic exoskeleton forming a huge battering ram, she reached out with her mind and slammed the woman who appeared to be captain of the guard into a low cement wall and held her there.

"Listen up, flatscans!" Unuscione yelled. "As much as it pains us to say it, none of you have to die here today. All you have to do is leave, immediately and without a word, and you will live."

"You're dealing with the U.S. Army here, mutant scum," the captain croaked. "Withdraw now, or there'll be hell to pay."

"Don't you worry about us, G.I. Jill," Unuscione said. "I've been paying that bill since the day I was born."

SIEGE

The green energy that formed Unuscione's exoskeleton changed shape then, twisting, folding, and snapping the captain in two with a sickening crunch.

"Die, you mutie freaks!" a soldier screamed as he leaped for Unuscione, singling her out for her actions even though his comrades stood frozen with fear and horror. Though her exoskeleton shielded Unuscione from any such attack, Cargil stepped forward, cornrowed hair jingling with her movement, and slammed her fist into the soldier's chest, shattering his ribcage. The man crumpled to the ground, wheezing in pain. He would not live out the hour.

"Only thing worse than a flatscan," Cargil sneered, "is a flatscan jarhead."

Magneto discouraged the use of such words as *flatscan*, a derogatory term which mutants had coined for those who did not show the essential x-factor that caused mutations on their genetic charts—in other words, "normal" humans. However, since the humans had chosen to make *mutant* the dirtiest of words, he could not bring himself to correct his Acolytes when they used such terms.

Voght stepped forward into the aftermath of the violence and addressed the soldiers.

"This facility and all of its contents are now the property of the lord Magneto. As you can plainly see, you have no hope of defeating, or even injuring us. For the duration of our visit here, you will be incarcerated. As long as you do not resist, you will survive," she said, surprising Magneto, who had originally planned to simply expel the humans.

"She said we could go!" one of the soldiers howled in complaint, pointing toward Unuscione.

"That was before you decided to make our lives difficult," Voght responded. "You've already taken up more time than you are worth. It would have been more expedient to kill you. Keep that in mind, and get the hell out of the way."

Magneto smiled. Unuscione had overstepped her bounds, had taken the aspect of field leader for herself, and this was Voght's way of reestablishing her primacy without showing the enemy that there was any dissension in the Acolytes' ranks. He was proud of her.

"It's not what you think," Voght said as he approached, both of them watching the Kleinstocks herd the humans away. "I simply realized that it will be beneficial to keep our identity secret for as long as possible. If the military don't know you are here, they won't be as quick to reach a drastic decision like just nuking the whole place."

Magneto raised one eyebrow.

"Very good, Amelia," he said. "I often underestimate exactly how much they hate me."

"It isn't the hate, Magneto," she answered. "It's the fear. Anyway, I imagine my test run is over with. Your turn to give orders again."

"My turn, Amelia?" he asked, eyes narrowing. "I always give the orders."

"As you say," she answered, and bowed her head in earnest acknowledgment of her error.

"Round up the engineers and whatever other personnel are present and put them in with the soldiers," he instructed. "I'll meet you in the silo."

Magneto turned, his heels clicking on the cement floor and echoing through the chamber. He walked briskly, cape flying behind him, down the short hall that he knew led to what had once been an enormous nuclear silo. Now, it housed something far more dangerous. The silo doors were twenty feet high, the bare metal of their adamantium alloy gleaming dully in the false light. They were, of course, closed.

Magneto's stomach muscles tightened as he reached out with his heart, soul, and hands, with the complete and total mastery of the Earth's magnetic fields that were his to command, and tore the doors from their frame with the echoing screech of a tanker striking an iceberg.

A dozen more steps brought him into the silo. As he looked up, scanning the massive constructs that lined the sides of the silo, Magneto's face lit up with pleasure. For the first time in a long time, he actually grinned. Each of them was one hundred feet tall, equipped with destructive technology decades ahead of anything else in the world, the deep purple metal of their bodies gleaming in the burst of light coming from the door Magneto had torn open.

"Magnificent," he said under his breath, to no one but himself. And maybe, to them, though he knew they couldn't hear him.

Not yet. But when the twenty killing machines in that silo were activated, they would hear him. And obey.

Humanity would forever regret that they had created such monstrous robotic weapons as the Sentinels.

CHAPTER 1

S mashing through Earth's atmosphere, the starship's hull burst into flames. The planet's gravity pulled them ever faster toward the surface and the pilots struggled to slow the craft. They knew they weren't going to die. Dying was not an option. They had to reach their destination, one way or another. They had to survive to pass along the message.

Once they had completed that task, should their injuries be sufficient to take their lives, then so be it. But first, they had to regain control and guide the ship to their target location.

They had to reach the X-Men.

* * *

It was a peaceful Sunday morning on the beautifully wooded grounds of the Xavier Institute in Salem Center, New York. Salem Center was a small community in affluent Westchester County, and Professor Charles Xavier, founder and president of the Xavier Institute, one of its most upstanding residents.

Down at the lake that stretched across the center of his estate, Xavier's comrades, most of them former students, prepared for a day of picnicking, swimming, volleyball, and other, more innovative sports. There was no reason, particularly, for the celebration. It was simply that the band of mutant heroes known as the X-Men found themselves a beautiful summer day without any crisis to attend to. Such an occasion was rare enough that they put all their energy into making the most of it.

Cradling a decent-size watermelon on the tops of his thighs, Xavier gave one final shove of his wheelchair to get himself off the lawn and onto the wooden pier that jutted out into the lake. The gas grill was already on, and he caught a whiff of the tantalizing smell of hot Italian sausage, an especially spicy lamb and pepper blend that Remy LeBeau had picked up at a Greenwich Village butcher shop the day before.

"Don't do it, Hank!" Bobby Drake yelled from the end of the pier. Xavier looked up to see that Hank McCoy, called the Beast because of his extraordinary strength and agility—not to mention the dark blue-black fur that covered his body—was dangling Drake off the pier.

Xavier's first impulse was to interrupt the pair, to instruct Hank to put Bobby down. But it had been a long time since the two men had been his students. Hank was now a world-renowned biochemist (not to mention a former member of the Avengers in good standing). Bobby could stand a little more maturing, but that was their business now, not Charles Xavier's.

"My apologies, Bobby," Hank said, the teasing obvious in his voice. "Was there something you desired to say to me? Some sort of repentance, perhaps?"

"Not on your life, blue boy!" Bobby said in smug defiance. "And if you drop me, I'm not swimming all by my . . . hey!"

Hank let go of Bobby's legs, a grin showing the elongated canines in his powerful jaws. He seemed about to make another comment when, in an instant, a huge hook made of already melting ice shot up from below, snagged Hank around the waist and pulled him into the water. Just as suddenly, Bobby appeared next to the pier on a pillar of ice, his body completely covered with it. There was a reason, after all, that he was called the Iceman.

"You two will never grow up," Scott Summers said from behind the grill, where he was turning sausages and basting chicken breasts with his "Mad Dog" hot sauce. He tried to hide his amusement, ever the serious, mature field leader of the X-Men. But Charles knew Scott as if the man were his own son, had nearly raised him in his late teens, and right now Scott was doing his best not to laugh.

When Hank pulled himself onto the pier, his blue fur soaked and sticking to his body, showing just how muscular he was, Scott did finally burst out laughing, along with the rest of them, Xavier included. It couldn't be helped.

"You know," Hank said with a wry grin, "this isn't the sort of thing a reputable scientist does on his days off. I'm growing too old for this roughhousing."

"Not too old, Hank, just too serious," Warren Worthington said amicably, and Xavier was glad to hear him speak up. Warren had once been the high-flying Angel, his mutant genes gifting him with a set of beautiful white wings. When those wings had been destroyed, then amputated and replaced with deadly substitutes formed of bio-organic steel, Warren's demeanor had changed drastically. Now called Archangel, he had only recently begun to emerge from the dark cloud these events had cast over him.

"Look who's talking about too serious!" Bobby cracked, and Warren smiled. Once he might have joined in their foolishness, but for now, Xavier thought a smile was better than nothing.

"The more things change, eh, Charles?" a soft, beautiful voice said behind him. Xavier didn't need to turn to identify her. If Scott Summers was his surrogate son, then Jean Grey was a surrogate daughter. Years ago they had all come to him as his students, learning to live as mutants in a world that hated and feared them, learning to use their mutant-born abilities, and of course, simply learning.

"It's always refreshing to note that some things never do, Jean," Xavier said, as Jean took the watermelon from his lap and put it on one of the two long picnic tables. He watched her move, in that elegant way of hers, to where Scott stood over the barbecue. Her long red hair was pulled back in an intricate braid, and it swung to one side as she leaned in to kiss Scott, the man she had loved since the X-Men began.

Though the rest of the team was certain to make their way to the pier shortly, for the moment he was alone with his five original students. The first mutants to bear the name X-Men! It was a family, his family, and like every other they had their squabbles. It had grown as well, members coming and going, numbers rising and falling. But no matter what the future held, no matter how many new names were added to the roster of the X-Men, there would always be something special between Xavier and these five. There was no question that he loved the others just as much, but there was a difference.

Hank and Bobby were trying to get Warren into the water. Jean and Scott spoke softly, the sun reflecting off the ruby quartz glasses he had to wear to keep his mutant energy beams from bursting uncontrollably from his eyes. In the field, Scott wore a visor made of the same material, thus his codename, Cyclops.

Xavier leaned back and took it all in, glad to have that moment with this group. The summer sun was warm on his face and his bald pate, countered by a fine breeze and the coolness of the lake. From somewhere on the estate, he smelled freshly mowed grass, even above the scents of the barbecue.

He closed his eyes and, for a moment, Charles Xavier was truly able to remember what it had been like to be a boy. What it had been all about. Many claimed to remember, but those spontaneous moments when the past was there, just within reach, when all senses combined with the sense of childhood self to remind you what it was like . . . those moments of clarity were extraordinarily rare, and sadly fleeting.

But they felt wonderful. With all that he had experienced as an adult, Charles Xavier rarely had time to miss the innocence of his youth. Even when he did, it was usually accompanied by a wistful mood that was unlike him. This was different. This was a feeling of well-being he had not experienced in many years. Other than the day, the company, the memories, there was no tangible reason for it. That made it all the better.

Five minutes later, when Storm, Rogue, Gambit, Wolverine, and Bishop had all arrived, he had reason to be proud and content all over again.

When Rogue demanded a volleyball rematch to avenge the trouncing her team had been given the month before, the entire group was happy to oblige.

After lunch, of course.

* * *

"What do you mean, 'out of bounds,' Rogue?" Bishop growled.

"Which word didn't y'understand, sugar?" Rogue teased, her Southern accent adding a gentleness to her sarcasm that always made it much easier to withstand.

"Our serve, I believe," Storm said, a wry smile on her face as Rogue passed her the ball.

Scott Summers smiled as well. All of the X-Men dealt with the pressures they lived under differently, and it always amazed him to see how those pressures had shaped their personalities. Over time, as Cyclops, the co-leader of the X-Men, Scott had come to know them all.

Storm, with whom he shared leadership duties, was grand and as blustery as the weather she commanded in battle, yet in calmer times she was quiet, almost shy. Her chocolate skin and silk white hair combined with her regal manner to give her statuesque quality. A proud woman, she often seemed cold to those meeting her for the first time. In truth, though, Storm cared very deeply for those around her as well.

Rogue was the polar opposite of Storm's profound calm and control. Her auburn hair had a skunk trail down the center that added to her natural flamboyance. She was quick with a jab, physical or verbal, but nearly always in good humor. A humor that was, in truth, often a thin veil covering the pain she felt regarding her mutant abilities. Gifted with extraordinary strength and the ability to fly, not to mention being nearly invulnerable to harm, Rogue was one of the most powerful X-Men.

Yet, she had another power, one she could not control, which allowed her to temporarily steal the memories and abilities of an opponent, simply by touching his skin. It was often a devastating, even debilitating, experience for her. Tragically, this meant that Rogue could virtually never touch another human being without doing them harm, could never be intimate, never even share a simple kiss.

The midday sun hung benevolently in the sky above the Xavier Institute. A cool breeze stirred in the trees, and the sunlight sparkled on the tiny waves the wind brought up on the lake. Laughter filled the air, the laughter of friends, nearly family. Scott knew Rogue as well as any of them except perhaps for Gambit, and at least enough to know that a day like today would let her forget, at least for a little while, the curse of her mutant powers.

But nothing, not the most beautiful day imaginable, ever seemed to shake the grimly serious man known as Bishop. Scott watched as Storm served to Bishop's team again, prompting a brief volley from Bobby to Hank, back to Gambit then Rogue, and finally to Bishop, who slammed it out of bounds again.

"Good one, Bish!" Bobby shouted, good-naturedly mocking his teammate's ineptitude.

"You mean that was out as well?" Bishop asked in earnest amazement. "What, then, would be 'in bounds?' What a foolish game this is!"

"You realize, Bishop," Hank put in, walking across the grass on his hands, "that your protestations commenced immediately subsequent to the reversal of your team's fortunes in this contest."

Bishop gritted his teeth, his temple pulsing under the scar of the letter M that had been branded onto his dark skin. His fists tensed and muscles bunched under his sky blue T-shirt, before relaxing again. He looked down at his sneakers amidst a pause in the day's festivities—everyone seemed to be holding their breath, ever unsure of how the enigmatic man would react. Then, incredibly, a small smile crept across his face.

"Serve the ball, Beast," Bishop said. "I'm going to kick your fuzzy blue ass from here to Manhattan."

Scott laughed along with the others, as Hank assured Bishop he was more than happy to oblige. It was a refreshing moment, one of many that fine day. While the rest of them often had an edge, Archangel particularly, they were all capable of letting off steam from time to time. Until that moment, Scott had wondered whether Bishop would ever take a moment to relax.

Not that his constant alarm and grim countenance were difficult to understand. Bishop had come from a future where the X-Men were little more than a legend to which one might aspire. It was a world gone drastically wrong, where mutants had been subjugated, hounded and destroyed, and had only begun to rebuild some kind of life on Earth before Bishop was lost in time. He had been a mutant policeman there, a member of the XSE, whose job was hunting outlaw mutants.

They didn't know if the world of Bishop's time was an inevitability, but ever since his arrival in their own time, the X-Men had fought to make certain it never came about. Scott himself had often been accused of being far too serious, but he hadn't heard that criticism very often since Bishop's arrival. He hoped that they both were learning to relax when the opportunity came.

"Uh-uh, Hank," Wolverine said, his voice a low rumble as always. "It's time for the ol' Canucklehead to serve. Me an' the Cajun got a score to settle."

"Ah, indeed," Hank said with a smile, "how could we

forget the little matter of the exploding ball from our last game? By all means, Wolverine. Your serve."

"Hey, no fair," Bobby called. "You guys have been pretty strict with our team on the boundary lines. I don't think you should serve out of order now."

"What's the matter, Bobby?" Storm asked. "It's only a game."

"Maybe to you it is, *petite*," Gambit finally piped up, his Cajun patois marking every word with his New Orleans heritage, "but to us boys, winning ain't everyt'ing, it de only t'ing."

"You're such a sexist, Remy LeBeau," Rogue snapped. "I don't know why I put up with you."

"Must be love, *chere*," Gambit said with a lustful grin, rubbing the ever-present bristle on his chin. "Got to be love."

"Heads up, Cajun!" Wolverine growled, then smashed the ball across the net.

Scott watched the volley, dimly aware of Jean and the Professor behind him. He could hear nothing, but he assumed they were communicating telepathically. Charles Xavier was the most powerful psi the world had ever known, his telepathy unmatched anywhere. And he had spent years training Jean so that she was, if not gifted with as much raw power, then certainly nearly as adept at using those same powers.

The game continued, Gambit's natural agility helping his side immeasurably, though the entire team was in peak condition. Scott found Gambit fascinating, and strangely, had never been able to completely trust the Cajun. Like Rogue, he had done questionable things, his past shrouded in mystery and intrigue. When Rogue had reformed, there was no question in his mind about her sincerity. With Gambit however, a member of the New Orleans Thieves' Guild for most of his life, it was another story. Though Gambit was an integral part of the team, and Scott was as certain as he could be of the man's loyalty, there always seemed to be a hidden, personal agenda behind Remy Le-Beau's actions.

Nothing of the sort could be said about Wolverine. What you saw with Logan was what you got. His heart was as bare as the gleaming adamantium claws that burst from his knuckles whenever he needed them. None of them knew his age, his full name, or more than the most significant details of his past before he joined the X-Men. But there was no deception involved, for Wolverine himself knew little more than they. He'd been a covert operative before he was experimented upon, by whom he did not know. He'd been nearly savage then as well, but had thankfully grown less so over the years.

Unless, of course, he was pushed over the edge, into the berserker fury they had all witnessed, and found so disturbing that it was rarely discussed even when Wolverine was not around. He was fiercely independent, prone to acts and words of defiance simply to prove it, but just as passionately loyal when he was needed: As traumatic as many of his life's defining moments had been, there was not a soul among them who put more energy into having a good time—in his own way—when the opportunity arose.

"All right, Cajun, get ready," Wolverine said as Bishop made a high, arcing hit, the ball sailing lazily, well above the net. "Here it comes."

Though short in stature, Wolverine was a powerful figure. He leaped high to spike the ball down on the other side of the net, most likely directly at Gambit's face. Gambit was also aloft, hoping to deflect Wolverine's shot. Logan's arm shot forward, palm out flat, the ball inches from his hand . . .

Snikt!

Wolverine's claws popped out, puncturing the ball with a whoosh of air. He dropped to the ground in a fighting stance, ignoring the cries around him.

"What the hell do you call that, Logan?" Bobby yelled.

"Now, that can't be in the rules," Bishop said reasonably.

"Wolverine, what are you doing?" Storm asked.

"You know that's the only ball we got, sugar," Rogue laughed.

"Quiet," Wolverine snapped. "All of you. Listen."

Scott was at attention immediately, as were they all. They knew that tone in Wolverine's voice. Danger. Scott strained to listen, knowing how much more acute Wolverine's feral senses were than his own. And then he did hear something. A low whine, or whistle, almost like a bomb falling . . .

"Incoming," Wolverine said simply.

The whistle grew into a terrible, deafening screech, and all ten X-Men went on alert. Archangel, Rogue, and Storm took to the air while Bobby instantaneously transformed himself into the Iceman. Gambit uprooted one of the volleyball net posts and tore it free, prepared to use it in place of the bo-stick he usually carried.

Wait, X-Men! Professor Xavier's telepathic voice burst into Scott's head, and he knew the rest of the team heard it as well. *We are not under attack. Look . . .*

"Up there!" Jean shouted, for clearly she had sensed it too. "It's a ship!"

Scott looked up, along the angle of Jean's pointing finger, and saw it for himself. A silver dot, trailing smoke and growing larger, seemingly headed directly for the Xavier Institute. In that moment, Scott Summers was no more. He was Cyclops now, and in command.

"Storm!" he shouted over the wail of the plummeting vessel's engines, screeching as the pilot tried desperately to pull out of the dive. "Use the wind to try to slow their descent, and try to aim them for the lake! Bobby, get ready to ice down any flames on the ship."

He turned to Jean, far across the lawn from him now where she stood on the pier. Her fiery red hair shone in the sun, and she shielded her eyes as she watched the ship's deadly descent. God, how he loved her. Though he knew she was just as capable as he, often more so, he could not help feeling a twinge of concern for her safety.

Jean, he thought, knowing that the psychic bond that she had created between them would carry his words to her. *Is there anything you can do to slow the ship's descent?*

Not significantly, and not without risk. Certainly we could do no more for them than Ororo with her control of the weather. But Scott, you should know that I sense two beings on board that craft. Both are badly hurt, and I recognize their psychic auras. I know who they are, Scott! The ship, it must be . . .

"The *Starjammer!*" Scott exclaimed as the craft finally dropped close enough for a clear view. Its back end was in flames, and Storm was attempting to guide it to the lake. It was going to be a close call, but it seemed as though the *Starjammer* would crash in the water after all.

"Jean! Professor!" Hank shouted from behind Scott. "Get off the pier! It's going to be very close!"

The rest of the team gathered round, ready to extract the ship's passengers and get them to safety in case they could not stop it from sinking, or the flames were out of control. An explosion was not out of the question.

Jean had said there were two passengers, which confused Scott, and worried him. The Starjammers were a band of interstellar pirates turned freedom fighters who stayed mainly within the confines of the alien Shi'ar Empire. Their presence on Earth always meant trouble, and usually some kind of off-planet travel for the X-Men.

But there were four members of the Starjammers, not two. The X-Men had fought at their side many times, and gotten to know them all quite well. Their ranks included Raza, a cybernetic swordsman; Ch'od, a huge amphibian alien; Hepzibah, a female of the feline Mephisitoid race; and Corsair, the Earth-born human who was their leader.

But Corsair was more than just another Terran, and more than the leader of the Starjammers. His real name was Christopher Summers. Cyclops was his son.

The *Starjammer* slammed hard into the lake, sending a huge wave of water up over its banks. There was no way Cyclops could know if his father was on board. And if he was, what kind of condition he might be in. With the staccato rap of sleet on pavement, liquid ice sprayed from Bobby Drake's frozen hands, solidifying in place to form a smooth ramp to the *Starjammer*'s hull. With another burst from his hands, Iceman froze the ship's burning parts instantly.

As Cyclops pushed through his comrades and rushed

across the ice bridge to the ship, he prayed for his father's safety. They'd had so little time together, and Cyclops could not bear to think that it might be all they would ever have.

"Get back!" he barked, then let loose with a finely honed optic blast, cutting through the hull like a laser with only the power in his eyes. Despite the bright, clear blue of the sky, the peace of the day, a terrible dread came over him as he looked into the darkened inner hull of the *Starjammer*. The smell of burning rubber and fuel was heavy in the air, blocking out the scent of the forest around them, and the wild lilacs that grew not far from the lake. An errant thought skipped through his mind: Jean loved lilacs. He tried to hold the thought, to focus on it, but could not.

Cyclops wanted to rush in, to search immediately for his father, but he held back. For years he had honed his skills and instincts as a warrior and a leader. It would benefit no one were he to abandon those hard-won instincts now. The X-Men were a team for a reason, and unlike many of the others, Cyclops never forgot that. Not even in times of personal crisis.

"Bishop, take point," he called, knowing that Bishop's ability to absorb energy made him the perfect human shield. "Wolverine, with me. Scout for scents. Gambit, take the rear and check all compartments."

Then, as an afterthought, he added, "Rogue, you and Warren fly recon, make sure whatever did this to them isn't coming after them."

Bishop passed Cyclops on the bridge, barely acknowledging the team leader as he passed. Though in his time with the X-Men he had learned to relax somewhat, when danger presented itself, or a crisis arose, Bishop was all business. Fear, action, adrenaline were his world. Cyclops knew simply from observing Bishop during their missions together that the man only felt completely in control when all else was in chaos.

Wolverine appeared at his side, adamantium claws flashing silver in the sunlight. His eyes darted around in predatory fashion. Nearly a foot shorter than Cyclops, Wolverine weighed almost as much. He was broad and stout, and lightning quick. His brown hair was shaggy, swept back into two peaks like a wolf's ears.

"Stay frosty, Cyke," Wolverine snarled, an uncommon concern in his voice; uncommon at least when dealing with Cyclops. Scott and Logan had never been the best of friends.

"I can't say yet just who's inside," Wolverine added, "but not all of 'em are still breathin'."

Cyclops sniffed the air, trying to catch the scent of death that Wolverine had so obviously detected. He could not, and was glad. He set aside his fears for his father and the two mutants stepped aboard. A moment later, he heard soft steps behind them, and Gambit's low voice rasped, "Right behind you, *mon ami.*" Cyclops did not turn around.

Seen through his visor, everything inside the cabin had a dark, bloody red color to it. It was something about his daily life, his existence, the spectre of his mutant powers, that nobody ever considered. Certainly it was nowhere near the social handicap that Rogue's powers caused for her. It was also not as obvious, more easily dismissed, and painful for that.

Cyclops could not remember the last time he had seen any color other than red. His ruby quartz visor focused and controlled his optic blasts, and even in civilian garb, he had to wear glasses made of the same material. He was not the complaining type, so nobody had ever thought to ask what it was like, seeing only in shades of red.

He hated it. But he endured it. There was so much else to be thankful for.

"Cyclops, over here!" Bishop shouted from directly ahead. If Cyclops remembered the ship's layout correctly, it would be the main cargo hold. Gambit made a more complete search behind them, but Cyclops was certain that, if there were any danger in the staterooms and engine area, Wolverine would have smelled it before now.

They entered the cargo hold and found Bishop kneeling beside a pair of dead men, laid one on top of the other. They wore tight, alien military body armor. Their eyes were surrounded by tattoo-like markings, beautiful and flowing, that would have been strange to most Terrans, but were familiar to the X-Men. Where humans had hair, these aliens had a high ridge of long, thin, radiant feathers.

"Shi'ar," Wolverine said, and Cyclops only nodded.

"High charge plasma burns," Bishop said succinctly, indicating that the pair had been dead long before the ship had crashed to Earth.

"Keep moving," Cyclops ordered, and they went up through the companionway that led to the forward section of the ship, the main cabin and the cockpit.

At the top they were met by a sealed hatchway. Bishop reached out to open it. He grunted in surprise as a burst of electricity shot through him with an audible crackling noise. He was blown back against the wall, but did not fall down.

"Bishop?" Cyclops asked in surprise. With Bishop's

power to absorb energy, it had to have taken quite a jolt to create such an intense reaction.

"I'm all right," he answered, shaking his head and raising his eyebrows in appreciation of the shock he'd gotten. "Intruder security, so the ship wouldn't be looted in case of a crash just like this."

"Better you than me," Wolverine said, without a trace of a smile.

"Very true," Bishop answered. "Now I can use the same burst of energy, multiplied many times over, to short the whole system."

The broad-shouldered man slid past Cyclops again, planted his feet and slammed his hands down on the hatchway. What emerged from those hands was not exactly electricity, but something else, something completely different that had been metabolized by Bishop's body and returned in a highly destructive form.

The hatch blew in, tearing right out of its frame, and clattered to the metal floor of the cabin ahead.

Bishop stood aside for Cyclops, who had begun to walk forward when Wolverine said, "Get back!" and dove ahead of them.

In a flurry of white fur, arms lashing, claws slashing, a small alien beast fell upon Wolverine in a rage. Cyclops was stunned, watching Wolverine try to beat the thing away, and so for a moment did not recognize it. Then, as Wolverine reached a hand behind his head and tore the thing from his shoulders, cocking back his right hand to tear it open with his claws, Cyclops finally did realize what, or who, the little beast was.

"Logan, no! It's Cr+eeee!" he shouted.

Though he could not hold back the momentum of his slashing fist, Wolverine's reflexes and instincts were far faster than those of mere humans. As his blow fell toward Cr+eeee's head, his adamantium claws retracted, snapping into place as the skin healed instantly over the holes they left behind.

Cyclops breathed a sigh of relief as Wolverine held Cr+eeee at arm's length, the little beast still chattering away but no longer attempting to harm them. It must finally have recognized them as well, Cyclops reasoned. Cr+eeee was from the distant planet Lupus, and had been with the Starjammers since long before their first contact with the X-Men. The creature was a constant companion to Ch'od, who claimed to understand its chittering language, and that it was as intelligent as any other sentient being they had encountered.

"Cr+eeee, what happened to the Starjammers?" Cyclops asked.

The little alien reached a furry paw up to scratch at his long, pale proboscis.

"You t'ink maybe he pilot de ship, *mon ami*?" Gambit purred, his sarcasm unwelcome and ill-timed.

"He understands," Cyclops said coldly.

"Maybe so," Wolverine added, "but will you understand him if he answers?"

Cr+eeee cocked his head to one side, listening to this exchange, then dropped to the ground from Wolverine's shoulder and raced to the cockpit door. Bishop was already there, prepared to endure whatever defense mechanisms the space pirates had built into the passage. When he reached out a hand, Cr+eeee started to screech wildly, and Bishop paused a moment.

"I don't think he wants us to go in there," Bishop said, studying the alien with new appreciation.

"I don' t'ink it matter what he want," Gambit said, striding forward.

"Gambit, wait . . ." Cyclops began, but Wolverine stood in front of both of them, his claws popping out with a clang.

"Door's mine," Wolverine said, just as Cr+eeee leaped from the floor, sank his claws into Wolverine's flesh and clothing, then bounded onto a nearby control panel. His claws began to tap out a numbered sequence on the keypad even as Wolverine's adamantium claws raked a gaping hole open in the cockpit door.

A shock ran through the metal claws and up his arms. Every muscle in his body tensed with its power. Wolverine bared his teeth and a low growl emitted from deep in his throat as he shook with the energy of the door's protective field.

Cr+eeee finished entering the code, and Wolverine seemed to deflate slightly, a hiss of air coming from his mouth. He kicked through the torn apart cockpit door, then turned to look at his teammates, motioning toward Cr+eeee as a bemused grin lifted one side of his mouth.

"Furball's not as dumb as he looks," Wolverine said with a chuckle, then entered the cockpit.

"Damn!" he swore softly. "Looks like we got a situation here."

Cyclops steeled himself against what he would find, then went in, Bishop and Gambit following quickly behind. The grotesque tableau that awaited them filled his heart with a nauseating mixture of dread and relief.

Ch'od lay slumped across the ship's instrument panel. The steering column had broken off, and its shaft impaled the Timorian's scaly, reptilian hide. A pool of green, brackish liquid had formed under his seat, and a darker, sticky looking green lay at the center of several charred wounds on his back.

Raza, the Shi'ar cyborg, looked even worse. He lay on his back on the cold metal floor, one hand covering a gaping wound in his belly. There was a laser-clean slice in the cyborg side of his face, and his biomechanical left arm was nowhere to be seen. Only a sparking, smoking stump remained, emitting a noxious chemical smell and the sickening sound of gears that ground on despite his unconsciousness.

Cyclops was deeply concerned for them, but the dread and relief he felt came from the same bit of information. His father, Corsair, was not among them. For the moment, at least, he forced himself to take that as good news.

"If dis green stuff is blood," Gambit said in wonder as he crouched next to Ch'od, "den de big guy seem to 'ave lost an awful lot of it."

His words spurred Cyclops into action. Wolverine and Bishop were attempting to lift Raza in order to carry him back through the hold.

"No time for that," he said sharply, then focused his fear and uncertainty into an optic blast that took out the entire glass observation shield at the front of the cockpit. It exploded into shards and he shouted for Iceman to get a ramp up to them immediately. Only then did he notice that the ship had sunk so far into the lake that the cockpit was mere inches from the surface of the water.

Cyclops reached for Ch'od, and Gambit began to pull on the nearly quarter-ton reptilian alien.

"No, Gambit, wait," he said. "We pull him off of there now, and whatever blood he's got left is likely to pump out at our feet."

"We goin' to leave 'im 'ere, den, Cyclops?" Gambit snapped.

"Relax, Remy. We just have to take it another way."

Cyclops focused his optic blast into a tight beam, the thinnest of lasers, and burned through the shaft of the steering column where it met the ship's controls. Ch'od slumped back in his seat, no longer hung on the stake that had impaled him. Then Iceman was at the blasted hole in the front of the cockpit, slippery ramp ready to get the wounded Starjammers to land. Wolverine and Bishop took Raza out, and Iceman came inside to help with Ch'od.

As they lifted him, muscles straining, Ch'od's eyes opened. Cr+eeee, who had been watching the proceedings in silent fear, begin to chitter with pleasure that his friend was not dead. Ch'od's gaze seemed to waver, unfocused, and then suddenly found the face of Cyclops.

"Scott . . ." he croaked softly. Cyclops tried to shush him, but Ch'od forced himself to go on. ". . . must get . . . Corsair before . . . his execution."

Then his immense, amphibian head fell back and Ch'od slipped into unconsciousness once more.

CHAPTER 2

Inside the government installation that was home to Operation: Wideawake, silence reigned. Magneto stood in the control center, built into the silo wall, and looked down at the fleet of Sentinels that would soon be at his disposal. He could not help but recognize the irony in his plan, to turn humanity's terrible, ultimate weapon against mutants back upon themselves. Rather than being amused by this irony, however, Magneto was profoundly unsettled. The Sentinels were one of many signs that, just as he had always said, humans and mutants could not live in peace.

Yet in the war of philosophies that he had waged with Charles Xavier for so many years, Magneto had never wanted to be proven right.

The Acolyte called Milan, whose mind communicated directly with technology, sat in silence at the command station—the main computer terminal linked to the installation and the Sentinels. His chin lay slumped down onto his chest, the goggles that covered his eyes hardwired into the terminal through a jack at his left temple. His mind was in cyberspace, the ultimate in virtual reality, and Magneto wondered, idly, what would happen if Milan were simply unplugged.

Which would, of course, never happen. Magneto would not allow it.

"It's chilling, don't you think?" a voice echoed inside the control center, and it took Magneto a moment to realize it was an audio link, piped into the room from the silo below. Senyaka and Unuscione were there, on guard, in anticipation of more soldiers arriving; and they would arrive, eventually. Senyaka had asked the question.

"What is?" Unuscione answered, her tone betraying the arrogance that was her deepest flaw.

"Being here, among them," Senyaka answered, clearly not as sure of himself now. Magneto watched the cowled man turn from Unuscione, and walk deeper into the silo, looking up at the Sentinels towering over him like an ancient forest.

"We've come to take these weapons for ourselves," Senyaka said. "But they have proven deadly in the past, to mutants. Knowing that the sole purpose of their creation was the destruction of our kind . . . Unuscione, as strange as it sounds, though not a spark of life or intelligence exists in them at the moment, I feel as though they are watching me. Biding their time. It is chilling."

Unuscione uttered a low, dismissive chuckle. Had it been anyone else, Magneto knew the woman would have spoken her thoughts aloud, said the word that was no doubt in her mind, the word *coward*. But Senyaka was as dangerous, as uncontrollable in his way as she was. If they were to battle, Magneto would have to step in. He could not afford to lose them both.

The Lord of the Acolytes looked up at the motionless faces of the Sentinels, the smooth metal surfaces, the slitted sockets inside which sensor eyes lay dormant. Dormant, yes perhaps, but Magneto discovered that Senyaka was right. It felt as if the murderous robots were watching him. The effect was quite chilling indeed. The silo was a ghost town, a place of death. The effect was even eerier with Milan slumped, corpse-like, in his chair.

The feeling, Magneto finally decided, was neither completely unpleasant, nor inappropriate.

Voght appeared suddenly in the open doorway behind him, and Magneto motioned her forward, glad of her company.

"All the humans have been corralled, Magneto," she reported. "Javitz and the Kleinstocks are watching over them, and Cargil has gone topside to keep watch."

"Thank you, Amelia," he answered. "You may be at your leisure until reinforcements arrive. Everything seems under control."

Voght nodded, then walked quietly to the long window overlooking the silo. All was quiet below once more, Senyaka's attempts at communication rebuffed by Unuscione's harshness. Years before, Unuscione's father, known as Unus the Untouchable, had been one of Magneto's followers as well. The man's mutant powers had eventually killed him, leaving the young woman terribly bitter. One day, Magneto hoped she would end her grief. For her sake, and that of the other Acolytes.

"Maybe it's not my place," Voght said, turning Magneto abruptly from his thoughts, "but I would imagine the programming for the Sentinels, for the entire base, would be buried in complex encryptions and decoy files. And once we're there, you'll have to reprogram the mecha-Godzilla rejects out there yourself. Even with Milan's abilities, we could be here days."

Magneto raised an eyebrow, a bemused smile lifting one side of his face. "Your point?" he asked.

"I don't know about you, but I don't guess there's much by way of pizza delivery way out here," Voght said with a shrug. "I guess I just wonder what we're all going to eat."

"My dear Amelia, you must have faith," Magneto said. "I'm sure there is enough to eat in whatever sanitized galley the American government calls a kitchen to feed us for today. That will be long enough."

He could see that Voght still did not understand, and though he was loath to explain himself to his Acolytes, he found himself making increasingly frequent exceptions for Amelia. She had become, strangely, his confidant.

"You have been involved with the politics of mutantkind longer than most of the other Acolytes, even those older than yourself," Magneto began. "Surely, you remember a group of wealthy, power hungry mutants called the Hellfire Club?"

"Of course," Voght said. "But what has that got to . . . ?"

"The Hellfire Club was ruled by an inner circle," Magneto interrupted. "Their ranks were fashioned after pieces on a chess board, and there came a time when they were lacking a White King."

Voght's eyes widened with surprise. "You?" she asked. "I'd no idea."

"It was a short-lived relationship but, as you will soon realize, a fruitful one. Though the Black King, a mutant named Sebastian Shaw, always struck me as a braggart and a fool, he spent most of his time making allies. He was a politician, not a leader; there is a vast difference. He wanted me on his side, and so took me into his confidence. That Shaw was a mutant was not publicly known. In fact, his military industrial empire was inextricably tied to the federal government. Profoundly."

"Operation: Wideawake," Voght realized aloud, and Magneto nodded.

"The single time Shaw took me into his confidence," he said. "He had buried a secondary program into the Sentinels, which could be accessed and activated with the use of a single password: *empire*. Once Milan has befriended the main computer and has found the backdoor into the Sentinel command program, that code word will give me total control of the Alpha Sentinel, and through it, the entire fleet."

Magneto walked to where Milan still slumped at a rapidly changing computer screen, laid a hand on the unconscious mutant's shoulder and knelt to watch the binary numbers flashing by. When he looked back at Voght, his smile was triumphant.

"If your stomach is growling, Amelia, feel free to scout us up some breakfast. But trust me, we won't need to worry about dinner."

Voght returned his smile, and Magneto felt just a single moment of the calm he hoped all mutants would be allowed once they were provided with a haven from humanity's yoke.

* * *

Soles slapping the marble floor, muscles tense, Valerie Cooper tried not to let her anxiety show as she hurried toward the Secretary's office. Even in times of crisis, when her expertise or her team was needed, it was rare for the 'boss' to request a face to face. Either her team, the government sanctioned mutant strike force called X-Factor, to which she was attached as federal liaison, had completely blown their diplomatic mission in Genosha, or something worse had happened.

Though at the moment, she couldn't think of anything worse than that. Particularly since she'd only just arrived in her office when the call from the Secretary's aide came. She hadn't even been able to gulp down a cup of the godawful mud that was passed off as coffee to government employees. She was, suffice to say, somewhat on edge.

Opening the heavy oak door, she crossed the carpet of the impeccably decorated outer office and was waved in by the Secretary's secretary, the mere thought of which confounded her. Valerie Cooper had never been a morning person.

"Ah, Ms. Cooper," the Secretary said in his perfunctory manner, motioning for her to close the door behind her. "I believe you two know each other?"

Two? Val was so relieved by the lack of hostility in the Secretary's voice, which of course meant X-Factor hadn't screwed up after all, that she'd barely acknowledged the presence of the third person in the room. Now, however, as the stiff-looking, auburn-haired man turned toward her, his face was marred by an incredulity and disgust that she knew was but a mirror of her own.

"Gyrich!" she said in revulsion.

"What the hell is she doing here?" the man, Henry Peter Gyrich, snapped in anger.

"You forget yourself, Mr. Gyrich," the Secretary said, and Val wanted to warn the older man to be careful. Gyrich might answer to him for the moment, but he had many powerful, invisible friends in the intelligence community. Through all her dealings with him, Val had yet to find a single commendable thing to say about Gyrich, except perhaps that he was a snappy dresser. The man was a master manipulator who used every assignment, public or clandestine, to further his personal agenda.

"My apologies, Mr. Secretary," Gyrich soothed. "I just didn't expect to see Ms. Cooper here. This is omega-level clearance subject matter after all."

"Valerie *has* omega-level clearance, Henry," the Secretary said, admonition in his tone. "Please do sit down, Valerie, we have much to discuss."

"Thank you, sir," she said. When she took her seat to Gyrich's left, he glared at her silently before turning his attention back to the Secretary. His frustration gave her great pleasure.

"Earlier this morning," the Secretary began, "we failed to receive a report from one of our sensitive facilities. Communication has yet to be established. We must assume a security breach, and I look to both of you to counsel me regarding immediate action on this crisis. The facility in question is the Colorado base of Operation: Wideawake."

"No!" Gyrich gasped in astonishment.

"It's never over, is it?" Valerie said softly, shaking her head.

"What's that?" the Secretary asked.

"We're going to destroy each other, aren't we, sir? Mutants and humans, I mean. It just doesn't end," Val sighed.

"It's your job, Cooper, to see that it does end. And soon. Now, my first inclination, of course, would be to send in X-Factor . . ."

"Oh, perfect!" Gyrich exploded. "The mutie freaks have found a way to take off-line our number one defense against their plans to dominate humanity, and you want to send them reinforcements! That's beautiful!"

"That will be *enough*, Gyrich!" the Secretary shouted, his booming voice rattling picture frames on the office walls. "Another outburst like that and you will be relieved of your responsibilities pertaining to Wideawake. Are we clear?"

Gyrich's eyes hardened. Val wanted to tell the Secretary he'd just made a dangerous enemy, but she didn't dare.

"Yes, sir," Gyrich said slowly. "But I would recommend that you not allow my vehemence to disguise the truth of the words."

"Mr. Secretary," Val said, ignoring Gyrich, "Mr. Gyrich has never been very good at covering up his bigotry, or the personal agenda he has had for becoming involved with Wideawake. His comments about X-Factor, government operatives themselves, make it clear that he is not rational on the subject of mutants."

"Enough of this, both of you," the Secretary snapped, losing his patience. "If I didn't know Henry was less than clear-headed on this subject, I wouldn't have called you in as consultant on this, Val. I am the Director of Wideawake, after all. Now, can we just get down to business, please?

"Henry, if you'd been a little patient, I'd have informed you that X-Factor is on a diplomatic mission in Genosha, and so are unavailable for at least the next four days to help with the Colorado situation. Therefore, I have already made the decision to send troops in to recapture the facility, if it has, indeed, been breached. And we have no reason to think it has not. The question is, do either of you have any idea . . . any reasonable idea, who might have been capable of and interested in finding and capturing this facility?"

Val could see Gyrich struggling with the question.

She knew he probably had dozens of suggestions, hundreds even, but few of them with any valid reasoning. Unfortunately, she had the same problem. There were too many possibilities, though fewer than Gyrich imagined.

"Sir," she said finally, as Gyrich studied her intently, "might I suggest you contact Professor Charles Xavier for his input as well. His expertise might have . . ."

"Come on, Cooper," Gyrich hissed. "That mutie lover would be number one on my list. He's been in deep with the freaks since day one."

"You know, Gyrich," Val said wistfully, "I can honestly say I've never met anyone as paranoid as you."

"That will be all," the Secretary said quietly. He stood and walked around his desk, then folded his arms across his chest.

"Henry, the troops are already mobilized. Once they have arrived, they will be under your command. Valerie will be your consultant, and you *will* consult with her. That's an order. She will make regular reports to me, and will include any objections she has to your course of action.

"In the meantime, Val," he said thoughtfully. "I seem to recall Professor Xavier was instrumental in helping to set up X-Factor. It couldn't hurt to at least get his opinion, especially once we find out exactly what kind of fox has snuck into the henhouse."

Together, Val and Gyrich rose and walked from the Secretary's office. Gyrich even held the door for her on the way out. Once in the hall, however, he spun on her, his face etched with fury.

"Stay out of my face, Cooper," he growled. "And maybe, just maybe, you'll still have a job in D.C. when this is all over."

Val Cooper smiled sweetly.

"You don't seem to get it, Henry," she said pleasantly. "The Secretary has just given me license to put my claws into you deep. And I plan to."

The smile left her face then, and was replaced by a hatred even more pure in its way than Gyrich's.

"You'll excuse me, now," she said with a withering look. "I have an important call to make."

* * *

Moving through the partially collapsed shell of an old tenement building, Gambit at his side, Hank McCoy did his best to keep his mind on the situation at hand. He felt a certain distress as he realized that, despite his years of training and combat as the Beast, he still was not completely able to shut out other concerns.

Perhaps, though, he was exaggerating the problem. Despite the smell of fire-blackened beams, the shattered glass and torn carpet that decorated the floor and the flickering of fluorescent lights that reminded him of the New York City morgue, everything around them was false. It was a cybernetic and holographic construct, created by computer intelligence using advanced Shi'ar technology that had been a gift to Professor Xavier from his lover, the Shi'ar empress Lilandra Neramani.

Nothing they were seeing was, technically speaking, 'real.' But that did not mean that he and Gambit were not in danger. Otherwise, they could not have called the place the Danger Room. Still, as merciless as the computer could be, depending on the level of difficulty the program was set to, it could never be truly devious. That took humanity. So from time to time, instead of the X-Men facing the Danger Room, they used it to stage their own war games, facing one another.

The Beast was paired with Gambit because they were unused to working together. The opposing 'team' was chosen for the same reason. And the game? A simple one, really, one every child knew: Capture the Flag. They had already found the flag, but that was only half the contest. The other half was getting it out of the tenement. The opposing team would, of course, try to stop them.

The startlingly red kerchief was impossible to miss against the deep blue of the Beast's fur, where he had tied it around his wrist. That was one of the rules, too. It had to be prominently displayed, rather like painting a bullseye on your forehead. Hank motioned for Gambit to take the point, then fell in behind him as they stepped around a large hole that looked as though it had been left behind when a stairwell had collapsed. There was no exit that way.

At the end of the hall, past several darkened doorways that might well have sheltered Cyclops or Rogue, there was a large window with jagged glass like fangs jutting from its frame. That would be their exit, Hank decided. Even if he had to climb down the outside of the structure with Gambit under one arm.

"Cover the doors," he whispered. "I'm going for the window."

Gambit nodded. With the deftness of a magician, the Cajun fanned half a deck of playing cards out in his left hand. Hank hadn't even seen him reach inside his coat for them. Then five others appeared in his right hand, a royal flush, Hank saw, and wondered if it could be a coincidence. Gambit's powers allowed him to give any object an energy charge that would cause it to explode on contact. In his hands, then, even playing cards could be deadly.

Cards held before him like the lethal weapons they could become, Gambit began to run down the hall with a whispery footfall that the Beast envied. Hank was right behind him, not even attempting stealth as he rushed for the shattered window. He expected an attack from one of the doors, or from above, but the faster he moved the better.

Incredibly, Gambit reached the end of the hall unmolested, then turned to guard Hank's back. The Beast slammed his palms against the floor and thrust himself, feet first, out the window.

"This is way too . . ." he began, but then all the breath was knocked from his lungs as Rogue flew at him, fists slamming into his belly. She'd been waiting for him outside, an option he hadn't even considered! Maybe his mind was elsewhere after all.

Rogue drove him halfway back along the hall then slammed him into the floor.

"You weren't goin' to say, easy, were you, sugar?" she said with a laugh as she yanked the kerchief from Hank's wrist. "Don't go gettin' cocky on us, ya hear."

Though Rogue and the Beast were fairly evenly matched in the strength department, they each had their advantages over the other. Hank was far more agile, and faster. Rogue, on the other hand, could fly. Neither would be much help in such closed quarters. But before Hank could even regain his footing to go after Rogue, an explosive royal flush knocked her off her feet.

They rose at the same time, and Rogue dove at Gambit with a disgusted scowl on her face. The Cajun dodged her attack and slammed his right elbow into the back of her head. Before she could move he was sitting on top of her stomach like a schoolyard bully. He held a playing card, charged and glowing, half an inch from her left eye.

"Maybe you de stronger one, *chere*," he taunted, "but Gambit is far more dangerous."

Rogue still held the kerchief, and Beast was about to take it from her when he heard the crunch of glass in the hallway ahead of them, and realized he'd made a terrible mistake.

"You boys are getting sloppy in your old age," Cyclops said, though there was no humor in his tone.

With a crackle of energy and the barest scent of sulfur, he blasted Gambit with a low intensity optic blast. Gambit cursed and slammed backwards into the Beast, throwing them both half a dozen feet and leaving the Cajun barely conscious.

"I 'preciate the save, Scott, but I coulda taken these two guys anytime I wanted," Rogue said, and Hank wasn't sure she was wrong. She was nearly indestructible, after all, an advantage he hadn't considered a moment ago.

"You might have gone a bit overboard there, Slim," Hank said, using Scott's nickname from their earliest days under Professor Xavier's tutelage. "Remy's pretty shaken."

"I'm fine, McCoy," Gambit said angrily, getting shakily to his feet. "I don' need you watchin' out for me. Gambit's a big boy, eh?"

Cyclops approached silently, then stopped next to where Rogue stood holding the kerchief. Her satisfied grin was the total opposite of his angry countenance.

"Game's over, folks," Cyclops said. "Gambit, you know by now that we don't put our fellow X-Men's lives in jeopardy, even in the Danger Room. We give no quarter in hand-to-hand combat, because we can't afford to, but you could have blinded Rogue just now, or worse."

In the relatively brief time Gambit had been a member of the X-Men, the Beast had become accustomed to his usual modus operandi. Whenever there was an uncomfortable moment, a question of his judgment or an incipient challenge from another member of the team, Gambit would play the innocent, using his incisive sarcasm to defuse the moment. This time, though, perhaps because of his nascent (if hesitant) relationship with Rogue and Cyclops' suggestion that he might have hurt her, Hank could see that it wasn't going to be brushed away so easily.

"I like you, Scott," Remy began. "So I hope I only need to say this once, me. Just because you don' have real control over your own power, don' assume the same for me, *vous comprendez*? I don' like it."

"End program," the Beast said aloud, and the tenement around them became sleek metal and plastic alloy. It began to deconstruct around them, lowering itself back into the floor and withdrawing into the walls. In moments, they were standing in a bare room that looked more than a little like a metal gymnasium.

Gambit strode to the door and slammed his palm against the lock release. As he left, Rogue turned to Cyclops.

"I understand your point, Scott," she said calmly. "But you're outta line. You know Remy wouldn't do nothing to hurt me. And even if he did, I can take care of myself better than most of y'all. It's only 'cause I know you're worried 'bout your Daddy that I don't get mad at ya myself. Maybe you should work out alone for a bit."

Cyclops was quiet a moment, and Hank certainly wasn't going to butt in. Finally, Scott said, "Thanks, Rogue. I appreciate the understanding and the suggestion. I still think Gambit was out of line, but I did overreact."

"Don't you worry none, sugar," she said. "I'm gonna have a little talk with *Monsieur* LeBeau."

When she had gone, Hank turned to Scott and said, "I find myself decidedly cheered by the knowledge that my surname is not LeBeau."

Finally, Cyclops smiled. "You and me both, pal," he said and put a hand on Hank's shoulder. "Dial me up a solo session from the control room, will you? Something challenging."

"As you wish, my friend," Hank said, and went out the door and up the narrow stairwell that led to the Danger Room's command chamber. Once there, he programmed a scenario that he knew would keep Scott's mind off his father, and sat to watch a moment as his old friend worked out his anxiety and aggression.

When the door hissed aside and Professor Xavier slid in on his hoverchair, Hank was glad to see him.

"Ah, Henry," Xavier said, "I saw that the Danger Room was in operation and thought I would take a few moments to observe whoever was training. I didn't expect to find you here."

"Several of us were training, Charles," Hank replied, "but Scott seems to require some solitary time."

"I see," Xavier said, nodding.

"How do Raza and Ch'od fare? Any developments?"

"Thanks to the Shi'ar technology in the medi-lab,

they're recovering quickly, particularly Raza," Xavier said. "But they haven't come around yet. You might want to look in on them yourself this afternoon."

Hank nodded, then looked back out at Scott in the Danger Room.

"It's peculiar, Charles," Hank said. "Maybe I *am* growing old, but I never thought I would experience nostalgia for our old Danger Room training sessions. We spent so much time there, but now it's mostly for exercise and sparring."

"In those days," Xavier replied, "training was a necessity. Unfortunately, these days it has become a luxury. How often are any of you actually here to use the room? I'm beginning to get empty nest syndrome, I think."

"Oh, please!" Hank laughed. "There is ever a new generation of mutants who need you, ready and willing to take our places."

"To join the cause, Hank," Professor Xavier said with a fatherly smile. "Never to take your place. Nobody could ever take the place of any of you."

"Not to be morbid, Charles, but one day that may be a necessity," Hank said gravely. "Human society hates and fears us more with each passing day. Anti-mutant legislation is part of the campaign agenda for innumerable politicians, and it ensures votes. Even the liberals would prefer to focus on the quandaries of racism and sexism. Mutant bias is too volatile an issue."

"I know it's hard to believe, Hank, but we can make a difference," Xavier said. "It's when times are darkest that we have to fight the hardest not to let the dream of peace between humans and mutants disappear."

Hank was about to reply when Bishop's face appeared on the telecomm screen that was a part of the rear wall of the Danger Room's command center.

"A Valerie Cooper on the line, Professor," Bishop said. "She says it is priority omega, and that you would understand."

Hank watched in concern as Xavier's face became clouded with anxiety.

"Indeed I do, Bishop," the Professor said. "Put her through immediately."

A moment later, the face of Valerie Cooper, the liaison between the federal mutant strike force called X-Factor and the government, appeared on screen. She was an attractive woman, in her way, the Beast had always thought. Or would have been if it weren't for the harsh way the woman's hair was pulled back from her face, and the hard edge of her demeanor. At the moment, her voice and manner were even more intense than usual.

"What is it, Valerie?" Xavier asked sharply.

"A crisis, Charles, and one that you will likely want to be involved with. I've told the Secretary I would contact you for your advice, so I'll need something to tell him. In the meantime though, you'll want to scramble your team for Colorado."

"Slow down, Valerie," Xavier said. "What's in Colorado? What on Earth is going on?"

"I'm keying in the coordinates as we speak, Charles," she said. "We don't know who's behind it yet, because we haven't been able to get inside. Someone has taken over the federal installation in Colorado where Operation: Wideawake is headquartered."

"Are you telling me that someone is stealing your Sentinels?" Xavier gasped in astonishment.

"That's exactly what I'm telling you," Valerie said.

The Beast's eyes widened and he said softly under his breath, "Oh my stars and garters."

CHAPTER 3

A web of lasers moved through the Danger Room, trying to pinpoint him, but Cyclops was completely focused, moving on sheer instinct. A trio of mini missiles streaked around the room, trying to home in on him. He could easily have taken them out with an optic blast, but that would defeat the purpose of the program Hank had created for him.

A laser flashed from nowhere, newly added to the web, and he dodged to one side and rolled. He could hear the buzz of one of the missiles as it neared his back, but Cyclops wasn't about to lose this one. A forward somersault brought him around to his feet and he vaulted into a dive that took him through the intersection of three slowly moving lasers. The hole was too small, and his shoulder was slightly scorched, but the little buzz bomb that flew after him was caught in the web and exploded.

Then there were two.

It didn't matter that nothing in the Danger Room could really hurt him. Scott Summers had learned as a teenager that you always played for keeps. Which meant focus and discipline. As he moved through the program, he was able to push his concern for his father from his conscious mind, but that didn't mean the anxiety wasn't consuming his subconscious. Otherwise, he wouldn't have overreacted after the Capture the Flag program.

This was different. This was his father. He'd already

lost Corsair once, as a boy, only to discover years later that he was alive. Scott didn't think he could handle it again.

A crackling hum filled the air. At the far end of the room, laser beams began to crisscross the floor, barely leaving a spot for even a child to put his foot down without getting burned. A wry chuckle escaped Scott's lips as he glanced up toward the Danger Room's command chamber. The Beast was really giving him a workout, just as he'd asked. Hank McCoy was an old friend, the best. He knew Scott as well as anyone except for Jean. He knew exactly what Scott needed at a time like this. Distraction.

The laser grid shot across the floor, and Cyclops raced toward the other side of the room, dodging mini-missile buzzers and lasers at the same time. He didn't have far to run, though. In a moment, there would be no floor to stand on. He wasn't as agile as Hank, nor even Gambit for that matter, but he was no slouch. Still, unlike Archangel, he didn't have wings, and that's what he would need to avoid having some very singed ankles in about three seconds.

Cyclops looked up, hoping to find some kind of hand hold on the wall, but the current program had not allowed him that luxury.

Then he saw it. Through his ruby quartz visor, the otherwise invisible infrared beam was a shimmering phantom that crossed the room from the momentarily safe side to the already impassable areas. It seemed, Cyclops realized, to be the spine upon which the laser grid hung and intersected.

An observation, a moment, an idea. Cyclops turned and stood his ground. The grid advanced, shooting like wildfire across the floor, and the pair of mini-missiles converged on the spot where he stood.

Scott? came Jean's telepathic voice in his head, through the psychic rapport they shared.

A moment, Jean, he thought in response, and then the missiles were buzzing toward his chest. Cyclops ducked, and before the missiles could respond to follow him, he grabbed them both mid-flight, hoping they would not simply explode in his hands. The little buzzers were powerful, but he used their own momentum against them, rolling forward on the floor and releasing them straight at the small opening from which the infrared beam issued.

They could not turn away, and the small explosion of their impact was enough to deactivate the infrared, shutting down the floor grid and leaving only the laser web that flashed through the room.

What is it, Jean? he asked as he awaited the program's next challenge, for surely the lasers wouldn't be enough to occupy him.

I'm in the medi-lab. Raza and Ch'od are awake.

"End program!" Cyclops snapped, and the lasers disappeared. The Danger Room door slid open as he approached it, and he ran for the medi-lab.

* * *

Storm was waiting outside the door when he arrived.

"Ch'od is unconscious again, but Raza is still awake," she said. "Rather energetic, actually. It's amazing what the Shi'ar technology can do, particularly with alien physiology."

Cyclops mumbled his agreement, and Storm stepped aside to let him pass.

"Scott," she said, admonition in her tone, "the Beast

has done a wonderful job of healing them, but they are both still rather weak, regardless of how Raza appears."

"Thanks for the reminder, Ororo," he said, and put a hand on her shoulder. "Now let's find out what's happened to my father and Hepzibah."

Ch'od's huge form lay sprawled on a platform that was constructed from a soft material which conformed to the massive shape of the patient. A strange, sibilant noise came from his mouth, and Scott assumed it was some kind of snore. Raza was a different story.

"Ky'thri be praised!" Raza said harshly. "Finally thou hast arrived. We must hie to the *Starjammer* at once. Corsair and Hepzibah are to be executed without delay. I wilt not have their blood on mine hands!"

"Raza, calm yourself," Cyclops snapped. "We're talking about my father, here, remember? Archangel, Bishop, and Iceman are working to repair the *Starjammer*, but they'll need your help on the finishing touches."

"Why didst thou not simply say that?" Raza asked, snarling at Jean and Ororo. He swung his legs over the edge of the platform, his feathered ponytail swinging behind him, its rainbow colors a distraction. He tried to stand, then fell, off-balance, back toward the platform. Storm helped to lay him back down. Unfamiliar with Shi'ar biology as he was, Cyclops couldn't help thinking Raza looked somewhat nauseous.

The cyborg's nearly Shakespearean dialect was a distraction unto itself. Corsair had explained it to Scott once, grinning. Apparently, Raza grew up in a remote area of the Shi'ar Empire, where an archaic form of the Shi'ar language was in use. When the cyborg portion of Raza's brain translated Shi'ar into English, it used an archaic form of English as well, believing it the most appropriate translation. At times, he had difficulty following the cyborg's words.

"I must hie to the hangar, to see to the ship's repair," Raza insisted weakly.

"It is too early for you to be up. A few more hours of rest and you might be able to get to the hangar bay," Jean said, and looked at Scott. Their eyes met. Even without their psychic rapport, he would have understood much from her glance. Her love, support and concern for him, confounded by her worry for the health of the Starjammers, and the lives of their two missing members.

"In the meantime, Raza," Scott said, sitting on the edge of the platform. "Don't you think you should give us the details. Who is going to execute Hepzibah and my father and why? How did this all come about?"

"Well doth thou all know that mine people, the Shi'ar, be a pious lot," Raza began. "Yet with piety doth often come terrible arrogance and intolerance. Upon the Shi'ar Empire conquest of the Kree peoples, many Shi'ar considered it a mercy that yon Kree homeworld, called Hala, wast not simply destroyed.

"Despite the initial plans, or the presumably good intentions of Majestrix Lilandra, destroying Hala might have been a mercy in itself. For instead, Lilandra hath placed her sister, the dangerously insane woman called Deathbird, in power as Viceroy of Hala."

Cyclops and the others were momentarily paralyzed with their astonishment.

"Thy faces reveal that this is news, indeed," Raza said, nodding unhappily. "I will merely say that, in deference to mine respect for Lilandra, it must have seemed an excellent idea at the time. Most assuredly, however, it wast not. Rather than assuaging the fear and anger of the once-proud Kree, the naming of a tyrant such as Deathbird to the position of Viceroy hath done nothing but foment rebellion.

"Mayhap, it will be some time before yon rebellion becomes a revolution, but an extraordinary black market business doth thrive on Hala. Well dost thou all know that once the Starjammers were little more than pirates, smugglers at best, mercenaries at worst. There was a Kree/Shi'ar halfbreed smuggler, a woman called Candide, with whom we often dealt in those early days.

"Several days ago, by Terran reckoning, we had word that she had been captured smuggling contraband onto Hala. Deathbird's law be swift and unrelenting. Well we knew that such an accusation wouldst most certainly mean quick execution. The engines were barely functional, despite all the repairs Ch'od had made, and the nearest stargate wast in the next quadrant. It shouldst not have worked, but it did. Made we the trip to Hala in less than twelve hours. Corsair kissed Ch'od's scaly face, calling him a miracle worker.

"Though the war had ended months previous, yon planet looked as though it wast under siege. An entire armada of Shi'ar vessels wast in orbit, meant to discourage any attempt to reclaim Hala.

"As we cruised at low altitude toward yon appointed landing area, we wast all deeply disturbed by the devastation the war hadst wrought. Worst for me, though. As I looked at yon toppled buildings and the scarred and starving Kree, smelled the sulfur stink of chemical fires that didst linger in the air even after so long, and then saw, on the horizon, the gleaming spires of the new Capitol Building that the Shi'ar hast built amidst the rubble of the capitol city of Kree-Lar . . . verily, I wast ashamed of myself. Ashamed that Deathbird and I doth share the same race.

"Upon our arrival at the Capitol Building, Corsair and Hepzibah wast granted an audience with Deathbird, whither they wast supposed to proclaim Candide's innocence. On the nonce, Ch'od and I didst infiltrate the old dungeon that wast the foundation for the Capitol Building in an attempt to retrieve Candide."

Raza fell silent, grimacing slightly with pain and the remembrance of the botched rescue effort. Cyclops wanted to be patient, but found it beyond him at that moment.

"What went wrong, Raza?" he pressed.

"What dost thou think, young Summers?" Raza said ruefully. "Fools all, were we. Complete and utter imbeciles. All the times that we had assisted in Deathbird's various defeats, and we never stopped to wonder why she wouldst so easily grant Corsair and Hepzibah an audience! Mayhap we did not care? That's the Starjammers' way. Do it because it must needs be done and damn the consequences!

"Candide wast not in her cell. It wast what thy father would call a setup. We had no psi or locator to tell us differently, and so Ch'od and I walked into a trap, as didst Corsair and Hepzibah when they reached yon throne room. Ch'od and I escaped only because we were closer to the ship and our weapons hadst not been taken—we were not supposed to be in the building at all. Ch'od and I fought our way out. Or, rather, after I had lost my arm, he didst tear a path of escape through our enemies. If not for him, I wouldst be dead several times over."

He paused and looked across the room at Ch'od's snoring form.

"He shall recover?" Raza asked.

"He'll be right as rain," Jean answered, and Scott could feel her empathy in his mind and heart.

"Thank Ky'thri," the Shi'ar cyborg said softly. "The ship wast badly damaged breaking through the armada in orbit. On the communications module we didst receive the broadcast of Deathbird's announcement that Corsair and Hepzibah had been captured and wouldst be executed for crimes against the Imperium. With that imperative in mind, we had but one course of action. During the time of her exile, Lilandra wast one of us, a Starjammer. She didst give the ship the necessary codes to override all Shi'ar stargates, and a good thing it was, or we wouldst likely all be dead now."

"You know how dangerous the use of the stargate is, Raza," Storm interrupted. "With its every power burst, we risk the destabilization of our sun. As much loved and valued as Corsair and Hepzibah are, they are two lives held against billions."

"Wouldst thou want me to believe that thou wouldst not do the same for thine own comrades, Storm," Raza snapped. "I hath spent enough time with the X-Men to know differently."

"Maybe I'm not being objective here, Ororo," Jean said, "and you do have a point—the stargate is dangerous. But if we're not willing to risk everything for two lives, how can we claim to care about the billions?"

Cyclops was torn. Corsair was his father, and yet the thought of putting so many lives in danger was painful for him. He would brave any danger, bear any burden, to save his father. But to have the lives of a solar system on his conscience was too much to even consider.

"Storm is right, Jean," he said, and they all looked at him in shock, Raza most of all. "At least, partially right. Using the stargate is not a choice to be made lightly. However, the statistics on its potential destabilization factor are extraordinary, moving into tangible danger levels only when it is used too often and with too little lag time in between passages. In any case, and as much as I want to rush off immediately to save my father, we are obligated to look for other solutions."

"Agreed," Storm said. "And I see only one other possible solution."

She was interrupted by the hiss of a door sliding open, and they all turned to see Professor Xavier gliding his hoverchair into the room.

"Your timing is impeccable, Charles," Storm said. "We have a crisis that needs resolution. You may be the only one who can help us."

After they had given Xavier an abbreviated version of Raza's story, he merely nodded, fingers steepled under his chin as he considered it all. Finally, he looked at Raza.

"Did you have any opportunity to contact Lilandra through all of this?" he asked.

"That is the other solution I had considered," Storm confirmed.

"Our ship wast in distress when we didst emerge from yon stargate, but still did we manage a subspace call on her private comm-link," Raza admitted, but Cyclops knew from his tone that the news was not good. "She vowed to do what she couldst to delay the execution of our comrades, but stood firm on pursuing it any further. She believes that, because Deathbird's actions be well within the law, her position as Majestrix couldst be undermined by confronting Deathbird on such a public level."

"That doesn't sound like Lilandra," Jean said distantly.

"Professor," Cyclops began, "you are Lilandra's royal consort. Is there anything you can do or say to convince her to intercede?"

Xavier seemed to slump in his chair ever so slightly.

"I'm sorry, Scott," he sighed. "Lilandra and I have not been communicating very often or very well for some time. While I am still the royal consort, her entire being has been consumed by the demands of the empire. If I can reach her, she may speak to me, but I doubt I will be able to change her mind."

"Anything you can do, sir," Cyclops said quietly.

"Of course," Xavier answered. "But now, unfortunately, I have more bad news of another crisis which demands immediate attention. All of you please meet me in the ready room in five minutes, suited up. If I haven't reached Lilandra by then, I'm certain I won't be able to reach her for at least a day, far too long to wait.

"Five minutes," he repeated.

* * *

Ch'od seemed slightly disoriented, but against the Beast's advice and despite their incomplete recovery, he and Raza had managed to get out of bed and join the X-Men in the ready room. Cyclops was glad they had made it. It was comforting to have them near, because he knew in his heart that, reservations about the stargate or no, there would be no avoiding a trip to Hala. And though the logical, practical side of his brain would never have allowed him to admit it, he would have it no other way. His father was going to be executed. That was all the argument necessary.

When Professor Xavier finally glided into the ready room, Cyclops was relieved, despite the grim cast to his mentor's features.

"All present and accounted for, Professor," he said. "Were you able to contact Lilandra?"

Xavier glanced around at the men and women gathered in the hangar. Cyclops thought he caught a flicker of anxiety on the older man's face, which was somehow made more expressive, and often more severe, because of his complete lack of hair.

"I did reach Lilandra," he finally said, with obvious resignation. "Unfortunately, it seems she was not able to speak freely. She did tell me that she was sending an envoy to Hala to witness the executions, and that they would not take place until that envoy arrived. It is clearly her way of stalling. Only because I know her so intimately was I able to see the pain which this situation has brought to her.

"Scott," Xavier said softly, "I'm sorry I could not do more."

"We know you did all you could, Charles," Jean said, even as she wrapped her arms around Scott's waist. "The question is . . ."

"What now? Yes, of course," Xavier nodded.

"You spoke of another crisis?" Cyclops asked, impatient to be away on the *Starjammer*, en route to his father's rescue or funeral. But he had an obligation to the X-Men and to Professor Xavier, an obligation that had become, over the years, the definition of his life and identity.

"Hank?" Xavier said, and the Beast stepped forward.

"Simply put," he began, then paused a moment to

determine how, indeed, to put it simply, something Hank McCoy was not always able to do. "Simply put," he began again, "some person or persons, likely possessing either supranormal powers or nouveau tech weaponry, has seized a federal facility in Colorado that is the focal point of Operation: Wideawake, which manufactures and commands the Sentinels."

"Beautiful!" Iceman said, his sarcasm unwelcome. "Just what every household needs, the mutant equivalent of mechanical dog catcher!"

"I don't see what the big deal is, Charles," Archangel said calmly. "If someone has taken Wideawake from the government, we'll just shoot out there and take it back. We'll be back in time for dinner."

"It's hardly that simple, Warren," Storm began, but Bishop cut her off.

"You don't see what the big deal is, Worthington?" Bishop said curtly. "Haven't any of you paid attention to what I've told you of the future, the world that I lived in before I traveled back in time and ended up with you? Are you all deaf? Once the Sentinels are unleashed upon mutantkind, it's the beginning of the end!"

He stopped, fuming a bit, and glared around at the others, several of whom would not meet his gaze. Cyclops did not turn away, fascinated by what he observed was not anger but fear in Bishop's eyes. Though after the tales the man had told them of the America of his birth, his fear came as no surprise.

"Whatever's happening out there, we need to stop it," Bishop added, then lapsed into silence, awaiting Xavier's instructions like the soldier he was.

"Storm was accurate, however," the Beast said into the silence. "It is hardly that clementary. We have no idea who might be inside the facility, and the U.S. military is en route to the site as we speak. We must approach this matter with the utmost diplomacy."

"Bring the Cajun along, Hank," Wolverine rasped. "He's such a people person, a natural born diplomat."

"I can't help it if I'm too charmin' for my own good, me," Gambit said with a mischievous grin.

The conversation erupted in earnest, opinions flying back and forth, but Scott and Jean only stood at the edge of the group, waiting patiently for Xavier's decision. In the field, Cyclops was leader, with Storm as his second or as leader herself in his absence. But here at the Institute, the X-Men answered to only one voice.

"Quiet," Xavier said softly, using both his physical and his mental voice. Silence fell.

"You must leave immediately for Colorado," he said. "Your gear should already be stowed on the *Blackbird*, if you've all been keeping up with protocol."

Immediately, Cyclops began to stammer a stunned response. "Pro-professor," he said, "I don't think I can . . ."

"Please let me finish," Xavier said with a raised hand. "You will be split into two groups, one to investigate and if necessary act on the situation developing in Colorado, the other to accompany Raza and Ch'od back to Hala to effect rescue of our allies, if at all possible. Both endeavors will likely require diplomacy, or at least expediency.

"Scott will, of course, lead the Hala mission, while Ororo will lead the Wideawake recovery team," Xavier concluded, nodding first at Cyclops and then at Storm. "I'll want Hank with Storm, but the rest of you can make up your own minds. While we don't know what waits for us in Colorado, we are certain that the Hala mission is extremely dangerous. If you are caught, you will share Corsair's fate and there will be nothing I can do for you. Lilandra will not help."

Cyclops looked at Jean, met her eyes, and that was all that was necessary to reaffirm their commitment. He didn't need a verbal or psychic cue to know that she would be coming with him. He turned to look at the team once more, and found himself face to face with Rogue, the white streak in her hair startling against its deep, dark red, a sparkle in her eye.

"If y'all are guaranteein' trouble, you know that Remy and I'll cover your backs," she drawled, then turned to Gambit. "Won't we, sugar?"

"*Chere*," Gambit grinned, "I guarantee it."

"I will go with Storm," Bishop said grimly. "The Sentinels must never be unleashed."

Iceman began to speak up, opting for the Hala mission. Cyclops was grateful for his friend's support. Bobby knew it was more dangerous, and yet his concern for Scott and his father was more important. He wondered if there wasn't also an element of bravado. Bobby had always been considered one of the less powerful X-Men, and Cyclops often worried that Iceman wanted so badly to prove himself that it might one day get him killed.

"Forget it, Drake," Archangel said, stepping in front of Iceman. He took another step toward Scott, and spoke quietly. "If you have to go against Deathbird, old friend, you're going to need me."

Cyclops nodded.

"Excellent, then it is done," Storm said. "An even split: Iceman, Beast, Wolverine and Bishop with me; Gambit, Rogue, Jean and Warren with Cyclops." She turned to the Beast. "Hank, Bobby, fire up the *Blackbird*. We dustoff in five minutes."

Cyclops watched the 'home team,' as he had started to think of them, prepared for their mission, even as his 'away team' gathered round. Professor Xavier began to glide toward them, but Cyclops realized there was far more to their plan than merely making a decision. He scanned the room for Ch'od and Raza, uncomfortably aware that he hadn't even noticed their withdrawing from the debate. Finally, he saw them, conversing quietly at the base of the long entry ramp of the ship. He signaled to them, and the two aliens walked back to where the remaining X-Men stood with their benefactor.

"How is the ship?" he asked.

"You people have done an excellent job," Ch'od said happily. "She's as ready to fly as the day I first laid eyes on her."

"She wast a vile monstrosity when thine eyes first lay upon her!" Raza snapped, and Cyclops was glad to see that the pair were back to themselves again.

"Still," Raza continued, "I suppose she shall suffice for the nonce. At least to get in. It may be that we shall all die trying to leave Hala, if we doth survive even that long."

"You always this glum, fella?" Rogue asked.

"He de life of de party, Rogue," Gambit said, one eyebrow arched.

"In fact," Jean said, "compared to his usual demeanor, I'd say Raza was almost effusive today."

"If I was a little less friendly," Ch'od said happily, "I'm sure Raza would not be quite so angry. But I cannot help myself. It's my nature."

"That's what I keep trying to tell them," Warren said,

but barely cracked a smile at his own humor.

"Scott," Professor Xavier said, "could I have a moment, please, before you depart?"

"Certainly, sir," Cyclops answered, but already his mind was consumed by the journey ahead, and thoughts of what might lie at the other side of the stargate.

He took a few steps away from the rest of the team, and Xavier glided at his side.

Believe me when I say I understand your feelings here, Scott, the Professor began. *Yet I know how you get in times of personal crisis. Often you try to deal with such things yourself, and I know you'll be tempted to cut the others, particularly Jean and Warren, out of the picture, to keep your pain to yourself. But you need them, Scott, and not merely as backup.*

I know that, Professor, Scott responded mentally. Though he had no psi abilities himself, Xavier could read as well as project thoughts. *It's just that, well, I already feel as if I'm endangering all of their lives for my own reasons. It's not . . .*

They go where they will, Scott, the Professor interrupted, and Cyclops knew from his tone that the subject was closed. He hoped Xavier wasn't too frustrated with him.

"We must avoid an incident between Deathbird and Lilandra at all costs," the Professor said aloud. "You won't have any backup out there."

"Do we ever, Charles?" Jean asked as she came closer, and Xavier merely raised his hands in defeat.

* * *

The *Blackbird* had long since fired her engines and shot into the western sky toward Colorado. As the *Starjam-*

mer performed its vertical liftoff, then began her journey in earnest, metal shrieking as she climbed ever higher into the sky, Charles Xavier shot an errant thought out into the void of space after them.

Godspeed, my X-Men. Come home safe.

Chapter 4

In the galactic region known by Terrans as the Greater Magellanic Cloud lay the Pama planetary system. Once upon a time, the planet Hala was the jewel of the Pama System, the proudest of planets, the center of an extraordinary empire. Entropy destroys all things, but in the case of Hala, destruction was not left to nature and time. The Kree homeworld was, instead, undone by its own leader, the artificial life form known as the Supreme Intelligence.

That wondrous being conducted a terrible experiment with its own people, manipulating their war with the Shi'ar so their most hated enemy would use the dreaded nega-bomb against them. More than twenty-nine billion Kree lost their lives, and many of those who lived underwent startling, often terrifying, sometimes fatal mutations. Exactly as the Supreme Intelligence had planned.

The survivors lived, for the most part, on the ravaged surface of what remained of Hala. Only the capital city, Kree-Lar, had been rebuilt to any semblance of its former glory, and then only to trumpet the superiority of their savage new Viceroy, Deathbird of the Shi'ar royal house of Neramani. In time, many had begun to overlook the betrayal of the Supreme Intelligence, to ignore the proof that the Shi'ar had been manipulated. None of that mattered, when they lived as serfs on a world controlled by a tyrant.

The gleaming spires of the new capitol building

stretched higher than anything else still standing on Hala. It was a beautiful sight, but one hard to appreciate in light of the poverty, disease, and squalor outside the gates. The new capitol had been built on the remains of the old, the centuries-old foundation still solid. Deep beneath the surface of the planet was the dungeon of Hala, which held more prisoners now under Deathbird than they ever had during the height of the Kree Empire.

Four of Deathbird's most elite soldiers guarded the approach to the cell where three condemned prisoners awaited their execution. Two more stood immediately outside the door to the cell. One, recently promoted to the elite corps, winced as yet another piercing wail of agony escaped the cell.

The screaming continued.

• • •

Candide stopped screaming. Mercifully, she had fallen unconscious and now hung limply from the metal cylinders which entrapped her hands. The top of her head, her eyes and the bridge of her nose were covered by a copper colored metal helmet the function of which was simple: to destroy her will, and her mind if necessary.

"Enough, Deathbird!" Corsair snapped, straining against the cylinders which paralyzed both hands and feet, a torture in itself. "If Candide had anything to tell you, surely you would have heard it by now."

Deathbird put one hand against the wall and leaned close to Candide's face. With the talons of her other hand, she plucked the helmet from the smuggler's head and turned slowly toward Corsair. Her golden skin and white eyes, with the extraordinary markings around them, combined with the mauve feathers that grew from her head and spread around her shoulders like human hair, ought to have made her beautiful.

Instead, they made her more horrible. Deathbird was a genetic throwback, even among her own people. The Shi'ar had characteristics of both Earth mammals and birds, but as a race they had lost their wings to evolution. Deathbird had been born with wings intact under her arms and lethal talons at the end of each finger.

But those things were not what made her so terrifying. It was as simple as the cast of her face, the sickly light in her eyes. At different times Corsair had thought her purely evil, then completely insane. He had finally realized that she was a combination of both. Her mere presence sickened and unnerved him.

But he'd be damned if he'd let her know that.

"If you're going to kill us, lady, why don't you do it and get it over with?" he snarled.

Their torturer floated lithely across the room, smiling at Corsair, a predator sighting her prey.

"Away from him, stay, little bird!" Hepzibah growled, and Corsair turned his head hard to the right to get a good look at his lover. She'd been born on Tryl'sart, under Shi'ar Imperial rule, spent some time in prison on Alsibar, where Corsair had first met her.

The Shi'ar Emperor D'Ken, the long dead brother of Lilandra and Deathbird, had destroyed Corsair's life as Major Christopher Summers, had murdered his wife, Kate. D'Ken ordered Corsair imprisoned on Alsibar not long after that. It was there, cowed and broken, that he had met the Starjammers. Ch'od's entire race had been wiped out by the Shi'ar; Raza was a prisoner of his own people; and, taunted and tortured by the guards, Hepzibah . . . Hepzibah was simply beautiful.

With their courage as example, and his attraction to Hepzibah growing, Corsair rebuilt his sense of self, his pride. Heartened by their presence, he regained his humanity. He aided the trio in their escape, and eventually, became their leader. And Hepzibah's lover.

Like all members of the Mephisitoid race, Hepzibah resembled nothing so much as a humanoid cat, with the colors of a skunk. Most human males would shrink in horror at the sight of her, but Corsair could only see her beauty and grace.

And now her pain.

Deathbird lashed out with the talons of her left hand and slashed Hepzibah's arm, drawing blood and a hiss from the female's mouth.

"You're wasting your time, witch!" Corsair shouted. "You can say whatever you like to rationalize our deaths, but you'll never get your confession."

"Fool," Deathbird said with a shake of her head and the rustle of feathers, "I don't need your confession to execute you for smuggling. What I want are your contacts with the Kree rebels. I want names, Corsair. Give me the leaders of this Kree insurgency, and perhaps I will be merciful to you and your female companions."

"Forget, you do, Deathbird," Hepzibah said before Corsair could answer, "familiar, we are, with your so-called mercy."

"None of which means a damn thing," Corsair added. "We don't know anything about any Kree rebellion. Candide is a smuggler, pure and simple, selling to whomever is buying. Hepzibah and I came only to free her from your bizarre version of justice. Though I pity anyone living under your rule, I have no special love for the Kree, and no desire to lose my head for them."

Deathbird's eyes narrowed and she glared at them both, ignoring the unconscious Candide. After a moment she sucked in air, as if she'd been holding her breath, then shrugged her shoulders in almost human fashion.

"As you wish, Starjammers," she said. "Continue your denials but you will neither convince nor dissuade me. I will have those names . . ."

"Paranoid bitch," Corsair interjected, exasperated.

"Enough!" Deathbird barked, and backhanded him across the face with such force that she nearly broke his neck. Corsair was grateful she hadn't used her talons. With that strength, she might have torn his face completely off.

"It seems the torture must continue," she said with mock sadness.

"You may drive me mad, but that won't get you the answers you're looking for," Corsair said.

"Oh, but it isn't your turn yet," Deathbird replied, then reached out to clamp a hand on Hepzibah's jaw while she lowered the copper helmet to the Mephisitoid's head. Almost immediately, Hepzibah began to scream. Corsair had experienced the psionic torture of that device only once thus far, but that was enough to feel a terrible nausea at each shriek or whimper that issued from his lover's mouth.

Inside her mind, he knew, she was experiencing the worst physical and emotional torture that her own mind could conceive of. The thing tapped into both her imagination and her pain receptors to create false events and mingle them with actual pain.

Deathbird merely smiled as he ground his teeth together, then made her way from the cell, the guards locking the door behind her. Hepzibah's screams were loud enough that, just as the first tear slipped down Corsair's cheek, Candide began to wake.

The smuggler was a Shi'ar/Kree halfbreed, which for years had made her an outcast in two empires. Corsair had known her a long time, had once been a little sweet on her, but there had never been anything but friendship between them despite her great beauty. It occurred to him that, in most cases he'd seen, halfbreeds were generally more attractive than either of their parents' races. A message of harmony, he might have thought if he wasn't so cynical.

Hepzibah howled again, and Corsair could not keep his mind off her any longer. There was nothing he could do for her. Whatever torture he might endure when that copper helmet was placed on his head, it could not be worse than listening to his lover, a strong and stubborn woman, cry out in agony. Deathbird knew that, of course. Corsair cursed her under his breath.

"Corsair?" Candide asked tentatively, her pain obvious.

He did his best to face her, despite the lack of mobility in his arms and legs. He thought it might help if he smiled, but he couldn't bring himself to do it.

"I'm here, old friend," he answered grimly. "I've got nowhere else to go, after all."

"What?" she asked, raising her voice to be heard over Hepzibah's cries.

"God!" he shouted, ignoring Candide now, enraged by the surreal quality of his situation. "Enough now! Let her be!"

It had been decades since he'd prayed, years since

he'd even considered it. This was different. There would be no mercy from Deathbird, no mercy but the blade that would separate their heads from their necks. Corsair reached out with his mind, heart, and soul to Hepzibah, to the universe itself.

He didn't know whether it was mere fate, or some divine intervention, but Hepzibah finally succumbed, falling unconscious within her restraints. Just in case, he mumbled a soft thank you under his breath.

"Why doesn't she just kill us?" Candide asked quietly.

"She thinks we're part of some Kree insurrection, that we can provide her with names," he said, still astonished by the concept. "She's insane. Most of the Kree hate the Starjammers as much as they do the Shi'ar or the Terrans. If we knew anything about the rebellion, doesn't she think we'd tell her?"

Corsair's mind was swirling with pain and wonder, so at first it didn't strike him as odd that Candide did not reply. After a moment, though, her silence became a distraction.

"Candide?" he said. "Are you listening?"

He turned to look at her, but Candide would not face him.

"Candide?" he asked again.

Finally, his old friend looked up, tears streaming down her face. And then, of course, he knew.

• • •

Though he was far from unintelligent, Gladiator never aspired to become a ruler himself. His race were singularly powerful amongst their galactic neighbors, but he had been raised a loyal soldier to the Shi'ar Empire, just as all of his people had. Everything that defined him was wrapped up in his position, which at one time had seemed unattainable for a being not Shi'ar by birth. And yet, despite the odds, he had become Praetor of the Shi'ar Imperial Guard.

It was testament to his loyalty to the throne and his objectivity that Gladiator had maintained his position throughout the despotic rule of D'Ken Neramani, the tyranny of Deathbird, and the relative peace and prosperity of Lilandra. Three vastly different leaders, all from the same family. Gladiator and the Guard had served them all. He was not dedicated to a single ruler, but to the empire itself. It was his life and his blood.

Or so he told himself. There were times, however, in moments of what he would call weakness, that he would admit in his private thoughts that Lilandra was the best and rightful Majestrix of the Empire. At certain moments it was difficult to remain impartial. While Deathbird had been Majestrix he had served, had done his duty, but at his core Gladiator had been less than pleased.

His duty brought him to Hala, into the court of Deathbird. A small part of him, a blasphemous voice in his head, wondered if accepting the position as Praetor was a wise choice. Though he had fought against them more often than he had fought by their side, he did not want to see the two Starjammers executed. But the law was the law. He was happy that, though she clearly had reservations about the sentence, Lilandra was not going to challenge Deathbird. It would be unwise and, in the eyes of many, unjust.

Gladiator knew that his traveling to Hala as envoy, with Oracle, Starbolt, Titan and Warstar of the Imperial Guard, was Lilandra's way of delaying the executions, and he was forced to wonder what she hoped to accomplish by such tactics. But he didn't wonder long. The conclusions he would invariably reach could be unhealthy for all involved.

His heels clicked on the polished stone of the hallway, an honor guard to either side and the four Guards who had accompanied him bringing up the rear. They marched down a long hall where Deathbird's men insisted that the rest of the envoy stay behind while he went ahead to meet with her. He would have liked to resist, but an order was an order. The Viceroy could order him to do anything she wished so long as it didn't go against the Empire or the direct instructions of the Majestrix.

At the door to Deathbird's private aerie, the honor guard stood aside to let him pass and it hissed shut behind him. He scanned the room, the ingenious natural lighting and odd geometry, the cascade of feathers down one wall, and the diaphanous curtain that separated the foyer from an interior area. Deathbird was nowhere to be seen, but a moment later her voice floated to him from deeper in the room.

"Dear Gladiator, do come inside," she said.

Wary of her, as he instructed all the Guard to be, Gladiator pushed his way through the curtain and stepped down one warmly appointed hall to a large chamber. Inside, Deathbird lounged on a chaise covered with white fur, sipping a blue liquid from a fluted glass.

"At ease, good Praetor," she said sweetly. "Enjoy a brief respite after your journey. Share a glass with me."

Gladiator almost laughed, but his training would not have allowed it under any circumstances. Still, it was both unnerving and amusing to see Deathbird attempting the role of seductress. There were many creatures in nature, Gladiator knew, that lured their mates to passion and death. He vowed to stay far away from the clutches of this one.

"Greetings to Deathbird, Viceroy of Hala, sister to the Majestrix Lilandra Neramani, from her very august personage, the ruler of the many peoples of the Shi'ar Empire," Gladiator said stiffly, making the formal introduction expected of him on behalf of the Majestrix.

"Hmm," Deathbird mused, not rising to respond formally. "I had forgotten how strictly you adhered to official convention. I suppose when I was Majestrix I had other things on my mind."

Gladiator lowered his head in appropriate respect, eyes never losing their focus though all they could see was the crimson and sable of his uniform and the dim light reflected off the hard floor. Deathbird's words suggested many things, not the least of which was nostalgia for her days as Majestrix. She would not dare say something treasonous in Gladiator's presence, though. He would take her into custody immediately, and he was certain she knew it.

Still . . .

"Ah, such a pity," Deathbird sighed and finally rose to stand half a dozen feet from Gladiator, arms crossed and wings blocking his view of her gossamer clothing. "What is your message, then, honored envoy?"

"You have no doubt received word from the Majestrix that the executions of the prisoners Candide, Mademoiselle Hepzibah, and Corsair, was to be delayed until the arrival of this envoy," he said. "The Majestrix, your loving sister, respectfully requests that you be absolutely certain of the charges against the condemned prisoners before they are executed. To allow you time to consider this request, the Majestrix orders a stay of the executions for one standard day."

"Don't you think I know what is going on here?" Deathbird laughed. "My sister has a soft spot for the pirates, particularly Corsair. After all, it was they who came to her aid when she was an excommunicant from the empire. She thinks she will discover a way to stop their deaths without the empire seeing her actions as a weakness."

Gladiator did not respond as Deathbird moved closer to him. She touched his cheek, lifted his chin and looked him in the eye.

"It's not going to happen, Gladiator," she said. "They are going to die. Oh, don't be overly concerned. I will wait the day as instructed, and so will you and the rest of the envoy, and stay to be witnesses to the execution. I order it, an instruction you cannot deny unless you have previous orders from the Majestrix?"

Gladiator nodded, once.

"I thought not. Therefore you will stay, and watch, and report back to the Majestrix all you have seen. These are criminals, likely involved with a planned rebellion in which the Kree hope to have their revenge on the Shi'ar Empire. I do the Majestrix a great service in their execution, as I'm sure you will soon see."

She turned away from him and picked up her glass again. Gladiator did not move. He stood, hands crossed at his back, his face gravely serious. After a moment, Deathbird faced him again, sighed in contempt, and barked: "Dismissed!"

Gladiator turned on his heel and left her chambers, trying his best not to think about politics, diplomacy, and their consequences. He was a soldier, after all. He had never wanted to be more.

• • •

Cyclops sat silently in the back of the *Starjammer*'s cockpit, mind lost in the nebulous space outside the ship's view shields. The infinite stars glowed pink to his ruby-covered eyes. Ch'od and Archangel sat at the controls and their technical conversation was little more than a drone to his ears. They would be approaching the stargate shortly, and he tried not to consider the possibility that he was endangering faceless billions, and many of his loved ones, for the life of one man.

That was foolishness, he knew. If they thought the stargate's destabilizing effect would blossom out of control because of the random passage of a vessel as small as the *Starjammer*, they wouldn't be going at all. His father would be left to die.

"Scott," a voice came at his ear, startling him.

"I'm sorry," Rogue said, clearly surprised at his reaction. "I was just hopin' you could be of some assistance back here. Jean an' I don't seem ta be havin' much luck."

"What's the problem?" he asked.

"Testosterone's the problem, if ya ask me," she said, frustrated. "Gambit an' Raza haven't really been gettin' along since we took off. It's only gettin' worse."

Cyclops left his uncomfortable perch in the cockpit and followed Rogue back into the main cabin. Jean sat at a holo deck studying the layout of Kree-Lar and its new capitol building. She caught his eye, and there was a question there, but he ignored it for the moment.

"Thou wouldst dare question the honor and integrity of the Starjammers? Thou art a fool, Terran!" Raza roared, poking a finger into Gambit's chest. "Countless times have we have aided the X-Men in battle."

Gambit held a ragged paperback book in his right

hand, and even as Cyclops entered the cabin, it began to glow with explosive power. He wondered a moment if Gambit was even aware of it, and was disturbed when he concluded that the Cajun was completely in control of his powers.

"I tell you how I dare, me," Gambit said angrily, his Cajun patois heavier than ever. "De Starjammers been pirates from de beginnin', sellin' to de highest bidder. Maybe you backed up de X-Men a coupla times, but don' you try to claim you always on de right side, 'cause we all know it just ain't true."

Raza looked prepared to tear Gambit's head off, but before he could open his mouth, Gambit held the charged up book next to Raza's neck.

"You put dat hand near me again, cyborg, an' you gonna draw back a bloody stump!" he said.

That was it. Raza leaped at him, knocking the book to the floor of the cabin as the two tumbled to the ground.

"Jean!" Scott shouted, all that was necessary for her to pick up on his instincts. The paperback exploded at the center of the cabin, but Jean had to have surrounded it with a telekinetic shield in time because it did no damage other than to shred itself into fine confetti.

As a young man, Scott Summers was called "Slim." While in excellent physical condition, muscles finely honed, he still looked relatively wiry. Appearances are often deceptive, however. With Rogue at his side, he strode over to where Gambit and Raza were about to truly get into it, and his anger was only matched by his concern at what might happen when Gambit's powers and Raza's cyborg strength were turned to a pitched battle in the heart of a spacecraft.

SIEGE

"You idiots!" he shouted, as he pulled Gambit away from Raza and lifted him off the floor. Despite his cyborg enhancements, Raza was no match for Rogue's sheer power.

"What in God's name is the matter with you?" he asked. "This childishness endangers our mission and the lives of everyone aboard this craft. If we all make it out of this alive, you two can tear each other apart if you like. Until then, this feud is over or you'll both answer to me. Let's not forget that we're all here for the same reason."

He caught Gambit giving him a sidelong glance that spoke of wounded pride and eventual payback. He moved close, so that only the Cajun would hear, and said, "I'm a rational man, Remy. But trust me, it's a mistake you don't want to make."

Gambit smiled disarmingly, showing off the charm that was just another weapon in his arsenal.

"Don't worry 'bout me, Scotty," he said warmly. "You know I de president of de Cyclops fan club. I jus' don' like gettin' my toes stepped on, *mon ami*. You understand, eh?"

Raza tried to shake loose of Rogue, but could not and began to curse her instead. With a look, Scott signaled her to let go, and he pushed away in anger.

"Thou art a man of honor, Cyclops," he said through half a sneer. "Thy father, scoundrel though he may be, is also honorable. Mine loyalty is to him. Thou wouldst be wise to ensure that those whom thou doth lead are equally loyal."

Raza headed for the cockpit while Rogue spoke quietly yet sharply to Gambit. Cyclops sighed, grateful that he'd averted the crisis. Gambit had always been a bit of a problem; a lifelong loner thrust into a team situation. Often, Scott wondered why he stayed. He supposed it was partly due to loyalty to Storm, who brought him to the team, not to mention his obvious affection for Rogue.

His ruminations were interrupted by Archangel, who came in from the cockpit, leaving Raza and Ch'od to their usual copilot status. "Approaching stargate," he said. "Everyone get strapped in. Ch'od says we're in for a rocky ride."

"You seemed to be doing pretty well up there, Warren," Jean said, and Archangel smiled. Despite the shocking contrast between his blonde hair and eyebrows and his blue skin, he was still as handsome as the day he first joined the X-Men. He'd been through a lot, Cyclops knew. They all had. And they'd stuck together. He was lucky to have them.

The five X-Men in the *Starjammer*'s main cabin strapped themselves into form-fitting seats, all of which faced forward, toward the closed door of the cockpit. Just as Cyclops snapped his belt in place, the ship seemed to pause a moment, as if it had been thrown straight up and was waiting that heartbeat before gravity took hold and brought it crashing down again. It was an eerie, almost nauseating feeling, but not nearly as bad as what came next.

The stargate had offered a moment of resistance, stalling the ship in place despite its thrusters. When that moment ended, the ship was not thrown but yanked forward with impossible strength and speed. The material of his seat seemed to fold around his back and shoulders, his neck and the back of his head, nearly bursting with the raw force of the stargate's pull against the gravity of real space they were exiting.

For a moment, he couldn't breathe. The lights in the

Starjammer dimmed, then went out. A moment later auxiliary running lights cast a ghostly gloom across the cabin. The pressure relaxed gradually, though the sensation of speed did not lessen at all. It wasn't the first time Cyclops had passed through a stargate, but he didn't think he would ever be used to it. The speed was at once almost unnoticeable and terrifyingly disorienting.

"I don't know 'bout y'all," Rogue said with a nervous laugh, "but this ain't the kind of thing I'd like to do every day."

"You're not kidding," Archangel added. "At least we can be grateful that getting out isn't as hard as getting in."

"I hope that's true of this mission as a whole," Jean said. "With what Raza told us about an armada waiting in space around Hala, I'm not exactly feeling confident about our chances here."

The *Starjammer*'s engines began to whine loudly as Ch'od fired the backward thrusters and the ship started to fight the stargate's natural velocity. Cyclops planted his feet firmly on the floor and held on tight, every muscle fighting the shattered momentum caused by the vessel's braking. They were getting ready to exit the stargate. It all seemed to have happened much faster than he remembered. Or perhaps the trip to Hala was simply shorter than the one to Chandilar, the Shi'ar throneworld.

"I wouldn't worry much about our arrival, Jean," Archangel said haltingly, the pressure of braking getting to him as much as it was the others. "After all, Ch'od's rigged the ship so that the moment we exit the stargate and enter Hala's orbit, we'll be cloaked from all detection. I think we're going to sail right through this mission and make it home in time for *The X-Files*."

Then the ship was traveling normally again. They began to unbuckle themselves as Raza emerged from the cockpit.

"Prepare thyselves, X-Men!" he said. "Ch'od shall place the *Starjammer* in cloaked, autonomous orbit, thus can we all teleport down without fear that she'll be discovered. But yon planet awaits, and whither . . ''

A thundering crash boomed up the companionway from the cargo hold, and the auxiliary lights flickered several times.

"Shields!" Raza yelled, then turned back toward the cockpit.

"What was dat you say 'bout cloaking, 'angel?" Gambit asked sourly.

And with good reason. The *Starjammer* was under attack.

CHAPTER 5

Miles of green slipped by beneath the dark whisper of a plane that was the X-Men's *Blackbird* (so named because it was modeled after the SR-71 *Blackbird* jets). From the pilot's seat, the ground looked like nothing so much as a great quilt of brown, yellow, and green squares, with the occasional string of river, highway or mountain range snaking over its surface. The American Midwest held an extraordinary majesty from the air, where one could forget that the poisons of city industry and city life had long since begun to seep into rural life.

Where Dr. Henry P. McCoy could forget, just for a moment, that he was a member of that elite race known as *homo sapiens superior*, a mutant. With the claws, fangs and indisguisable blue fur that were the hallmarks of his mutation, of the genetic x-factor that made him the Beast, Hank McCoy would not have been able to walk a block in the Midwest without being the object of fear, revulsion, and hatred.

The same might be true of New York or L.A., he realized, but somehow it seemed worse when the magnificence of nature surrounded him. Perhaps because in the city there were so many other eccentric and frightful things happening at all times, while in the country, he could almost understand the feelings of so-called "normal" people toward mutants. Almost. If he ever reached the moment when he could completely comprehend their bigotry, that would be the day he retired from society all together.

A red light popped into life on the control panel, accompanied by a high-pitched beep, alerting him to an incoming call on the *Blackbird*'s vid-comm unit. While the *Blackbird* was loaded with as much high-tech as they could fit into her innards, the size of his hands and length of his claws made Hank's preferences for the control panel decidedly low-tech. To answer the call, he flipped a green toggle switch just to the left of the vid-comm screen. The picture snapped to life: a split-screen view with Professor Xavier on one side and Valerie Cooper on the other. A three way link-up that Hank hadn't been expecting.

"Professor. Valerie. Has our strategy been modified?" the Beast asked, concerned creasing his furred brow.

"Hank, Valerie and I have been talking and I know how cautious you and Ororo are, but I just wanted to emphasize how delicately this must be played," Xavier said.

The Beast watched the image of Xavier onscreen. They had known one another for a long time, and Hank had learned to read the man fairly well.

"What is it, Charles?" he finally asked. "I appreciate that we're confronted with a lot of unknowns here, but that isn't what's perturbing you, is it?"

"I'm afraid the knowns are more my concern at the moment, Hank," Xavier answered. "Valerie, will you tell Hank what you told me, please?"

The woman was all business as she told him of her concerns, of the immediate problems they would face even before the one they had set off to confront. Hank appreciated Valerie's directness, especially in this time of crisis.

"What I'm really getting at," Valerie said, "is that you can almost certainly expect federal troops at the scene when you arrive. I'd hoped you would get there first but that doesn't look like it's going to happen. I've no idea how they'll react to your presence, so just watch your step."

"I don't comprehend, Valerie," the Beast replied. "If the government sanctioned your preliminary contact with the Professor, why can't we merely say that he apprised us of the predicament?"

"That would be the logical thing to do, Hank," she said grimly. "But we're not dealing with logic, or rationality here. We're dealing with a man to whom hate is sustenance. Or have you forgotten how much Gyrich hates you all?"

"Gyrich," the Beast repeated, lips curling back in distaste. "The man simply can't wait to be king. Who expired and left him in dominion?"

"The director has placed him in charge of this operation," Valerie said with obvious remorse.

"Valerie," Xavier interjected, her name itself a question, "you have still yet to tell me who the director of Operation: Wideawake is."

There was a silence on the three way call, which was quickly interrupted by the cockpit door clanking open behind Hank. The Iceman, Bobby Drake, poked his head in and, as was his way, started jabbering immediately.

"Hey, Hank, any room up here?" he asked. "A few more minutes with Mr. Depressing Bishop and I think I'll . . ."

"Just a moment, Robert," the Beast said quietly, and Iceman fell silent.

"I'm sorry, Charles," Valerie said at last. "There are some things that just aren't worth the price that is put on them. This is one of those things. Believe me when I say you don't need to know. It isn't important who the figurehead is, only the arms and weapons are your concern."

"Do you truly fear for your mortality, Val?" Hank asked before he could stop himself.

"There was a time, when I first gained high-level clearance, that I basked in the glory of secrets, and thought how silly and paranoid people were about the government," she said. "I've grown up a lot since then."

"Thank you for your help, Valerie," Xavier said.

"I do what I can, Charles. Always," she said. "As for you and your team, Hank, all I can say is watch your asses out there. Just because the dog never bit before, doesn't mean it won't."

In a blip, Valerie disappeared from the screen and all they could see was the chiseled features and gleaming bald pate of Charles Xavier.

"Keep me posted, Hank," Xavier said.

"Roger that," the Beast replied, and signed off, leaning back in the pilot's seat and letting out a heavy sigh with a breath he hadn't been aware of holding.

"Duuuuuude!" Bobby said in his best surfer-speak. "That Cooper babe is such a downer, man."

"Utterly," Hank agreed, smiling again at his old friend's ability to make light of anything and get away with it.

"Seriously, Hank, what's up with that?" Bobby asked as he dropped down into the co-pilot's seat, strapped in and ran a finger over the instruments, checking that they were all functioning correctly. "What's got the Prof and Val so spooked?"

"It appears as though we have unfortunately entered into a contest to see who can best resolve the developing situation with the Sentinels. A contest that may forthwith evolve into a conflict, as the other contestant is none other than Henry Peter Gyrich," the Beast said unhappily.

"Oh, great!" Bobby said, holding a hand to his belly. "There goes my lunch. Just talking about that guy could ruin anybody's day."

"A flawless exemplar of our tax dollars toiling vigorously," Hank said, and they both laughed. As little as he would have liked to admit it, Hank knew that there had always been people like Gyrich in government, and there likely always would.

They were quiet for several minutes after that, the way old friends can sit together silently without feeling the pressure of having to keep a conversation going. Both had built reputations as wiseguys over the years, the Abbott and Costello of the mutant set. They were constantly 'on.' But there was never a need for that when it was just the two of them.

There had been a time when it would have been the three of them, including Warren Worthington, now called Archangel. He was just the Angel way back when, and maybe they were the Three Stooges instead of a vaudeville duo. But things had changed. Warren's natural mutant wings had been destroyed and later replaced with his lethal artificial ones by one of their deadliest enemies. The Angel's mind had changed with his body, putting a distance between him and his old friends that was only now beginning to dissipate.

As he sat there in comfortable silence with Bobby,

Hank felt that distance from Warren acutely. A low wispy spider's web of clouds hung above them, but the sun shone brightly in the cockpit and the sky was a pure, icy blue where it was free of that webbing. Several thousand feet down, a passenger jet was flying a similar path, but they passed it as if it were in reverse.

"It's never going to get any better, is it Hank?" Bobby said suddenly, without looking away from the sky outside the window.

"What isn't?" Hank asked, but he thought he knew already.

"All of it," Bobby answered, his tone filled with an uncharacteristic gravity and maturity, as well as a resignation that surprised Hank. "I mean, I know we're not fighting for the here and now, that we're fighting for the future, for our children. But that's part of it, too.

"I mean, God, other than Scott and Jean, none of us can sustain a relationship for more than a year, so chances are, most of us aren't likely to have children to begin with."

Hank didn't know what to say, and so he said nothing. Bobby was right, but there was so much more to it than his frustration would allow him to consider. Finally, Bobby looked over at him, raised eyebrows in place of an actual shrug. His body had filled out from the time he'd joined the X-Men as a teenager. These days he was muscular and fit. But Hank figured that tousled brown hair and open, genuinely handsome features would make him look like a college boy forever.

"Say something, Hank," Bobby said, giving vent to a exhalation that was half sigh and half laugh. "Usually I can't get you to shut up."

"We didn't request this existence, Bobby," Hank said

finally. "You're correct about that. We didn't ask to encounter one catastrophe after another, to be the focus of the world's malice and repugnance, and the attacks of mutants with perverted priorities."

"You can say that again," Bobby nodded. "It keeps getting worse, Hank, that's what I'm saying. In the old days, it all seemed like this big adventure, Huck Finn meets James Bond or something. But people have died, Hank. Thunderbird, Doug Ramsey, Candy Sothern, Illyana. The whole Phoenix thing is part of it, and everything that's happened to, well, to Warren . . ."

"I was pondering that as well," Hank admitted, realizing finally that what had been bothering him had also been eating at Bobby. "But I believe he's improving, don't you? Not so reserved?"

"Maybe," Bobby said, flopping back against the leather co-pilot's seat. "But I have this fear that he'll never be the same, that all the days we have behind us—as original X-Men, as members of the Defenders and the Champions, even just as friends, period—that everything we built in those days is just crumbling down around us. Warren is just part of it."

"You recognize that your notoriety as a jovial, light-hearted fellow is in jeopardy, here, I trust?" Hank said, hoping to lift Bobby's spirits, and was unsurprised when he felt ice form tightly around his huge feet, freezing them to the floor of the cockpit.

"I'm being serious, here," Bobby said.

"Apparently not wholly," Hank replied and pulled one foot after another out of their frozen shackles, sending shards of ice tinkling to the metal floor. "In some ways, we are fighting a war on many fronts. Tragically, in war there is no time for luxury. Simultaneously, we are fortunate to have Charles Xavier to offer us such a distinct focus, an objective which is not merely valorous, but essential for the entire world. And we have one another, not just you and I, but all of the X-Men and our extended family."

"I love you too, furball," Bobby said with a chuckle, then he shook his head. "Sometimes it gets overwhelming, though. It's nice to be needed, believe me, but at the end of the day, does that really count for much?"

"What do you think?" Hank asked.

Bobby really, truly smiled at that, as if a cloud had passed across his face and was gone now.

"You're no psychiatrist, McCoy," Bobby said. "But I guess you're right. I guess it counts for something after all. It's enough, I suppose."

"It must be," Hank said quietly, and they fell back into that reflective silence, blue sky whipping by and sun shining warm on their faces.

* * *

Despite her wealth of experience, and the proud, almost regal air that combined with her white mane of hair and her height—she was nearly six feet tall—to make her heartstoppingly beautiful, Ororo Munroe was a young woman. She had to remind herself of this from time to time, because she thought of herself as having lived so long, done so much. She was wise enough to believe in her own wisdom. Jean had once said she had an "old soul," and perhaps that was true.

Then again, perhaps the woman she was today had been created by the many other lives she had led within her current lifespan. She had been orphaned as a child, left to fend for herself in the dirty streets of Cairo, Egypt, and became a thief. An excellent thief. As she grew older, she wandered the continent of Africa.

When she developed her mutant ability to control the weather, when she became Storm, she also became a goddess. For most women that was wishful thinking, but for Ororo it was true. When Professor Xavier had approached her about joining the X-Men, she had become a deity for a small African tribe who called her "beautiful windrider." It was a name she cherished as she cherished the memories of Kenya and Tanzania, the grassy plains and the wide open sky.

The open sky most particularly. It was not until she was forced to confront the problem that she realized she was severely claustrophobic. Even now, sitting in the *Blackbird*, with the open sky only feet from her, she felt the walls closing in, the air rushing from her lungs. She fought it with every passing heartbeat. They had no idea what they might encounter when they arrived in Colorado, so it would be foolish of her to expend her energy by attempting to fly along with the plane. No matter how much she hated being inside it.

"You're a barrel o' laughs, Bish," Wolverine said caustically, then moved away from where he and Bishop had been talking and came toward Storm.

"I thought I was the life o' the party, 'Roro," he said as he dropped into the chair beside her, "but Bishop's got me beat, no contest."

"You cannot blame him, Logan," Storm said quietly. "He was born into a world where all of us had already died, where the word 'Sentinel' evoked the same horror as the word 'Nazi' does for us. The thought that whatever is happening in Colorado might set the world on course for that future must be terrifying for him."

"The thought don't make me jump for joy, either, but I get yer meanin'," Wolverine admitted.

SIEGE

Storm smiled. Of the "second generation" of X-Men, only she and Logan remained. John Proudstar was dead, and the others had all gone to other teams, or other ideologies. She cared deeply for them all, but there was a bond between herself and Logan that she would never have imagined when she first arrived at Xavier's mansion.

He had been more feral then, an angry man looking for a fight, and never happier than when he found one. These days, Wolverine was as dangerous as ever, but he had become a bit wiser himself. As for older, it was hard to tell. Other than his incredible senses, and his enhanced speed and agility, the gift he had received from the mutant x-factor in his genes had been invaluable, and unique. Wolverine had a healing factor that not only made him nearly impossible to kill because of how quickly wounds disappeared, but also slowed his aging tremendously.

How old was he? Storm couldn't even begin to guess, but if she had to, she would probably have started with a century and worked her way up. He'd had even more lives than she—soldier, spy, wildman, tavern owner, a million other things—but somewhere in the middle of it all, his life had been taken away. His memories had been erased, replaced, complicated, created. Then, of course, there was the adamantium.

Under the guise of the Weapon X project, a group of scientists had found a way to fuse the most powerful, unbreakable metal in the world with Wolverine's skeleton, making his bones themselves unbreakable and giving him claws that popped out from between his knuckles on instinct or command. He was a cunning, savage fighter, the best there was at what he did. But as he was so fond of saying, oftentimes what he did was not very nice.

There was more to him than all of that, though, as Storm had learned over the years. They had been X-Men together, had traveled some hard roads together, just the two of them. In his years he'd learned to offer respect due to ability rather than age, and so he was more of a brother than a father figure. They'd loved and lost, and stood by each other. Though he projected the image of a loner, needing no one and having a true distaste for being needed by anyone, that couldn't be further from the truth. His love for and loyalty to his friends was as fierce and unbending as his will.

"How you holdin' up?" he asked, referring to her claustrophobia. The others all knew, and assumed she was dealing with it, which she was. Logan was the only one who could tell when it was getting to her.

"I'm all right," she answered, and found that she was.

Wolverine looked at her a moment, then nodded, accepting her response. For no reason other than the tilt of his head, the narrowing of his eyes, she was reminded of a time they'd been to dinner together in Manhattan. Even in the melting pot, they made the oddest of couples, she with her milk chocolate skin and silver white hair, and he, more than half a foot shorter and *very* Caucasian. She was young, slender and stylish, while he was obviously older, with a mess of black hair and mutton chop sideburns, in leather jacket, jeans, and pointed toe cowboy boots.

If anyone in that restaurant had been able to simply look in their eyes, however, they would have seen the most important similarity: these were dangerous people. Storm wondered when that had happened to her, when she had become one of the dangerous people.

She didn't wonder why, though. The answer was all around her, every day, and had been since the moment she met Charles Xavier. As Logan might put it, there were "things needed doin'," and they did them.

"Logan, let me ask you something," she began, suddenly thinking of something that had struck her as odd earlier that day. "You know that Cyclops and his team could have used you on Hala. Why didn't you volunteer for that mission?"

"I been to space, Ororo," Wolverine answered. "Ain't nothin' special. Anyhow, way I got it figured, Scotty and the gang know exactly what they're goin' up against. They get smoked anyway, won't be nothin' I could have done for 'em."

He leaned back and put a cigarillo in his mouth, then pulled out a silver lighter. They all hated the stench of the things, which looked like something out of an old Clint Eastwood western, but Wolverine insisted on smoking them. Besides, his healing factor negated any dangers. He bit the end off, spit it onto the floor as Storm rolled her eyes in disgust, and the lighter flared to life.

"The other hand," he said, smoke puffing from his mouth with every word. "We got no idea what's happenin' here in Colorado. Plus I ain't been out here for a while and I surely do love the mountains. Not to mention could be Bishop's right about all this, and we gotta put a stop to it. If you're headin' for trouble, I'd like to be there to back your action.

"Then again, it don't hurt that I'd rather call you 'boss' than Scott. He sort of expects it, but it surprises you every time, boss," he said, and smiled with the cigarillo pinched between his teeth.

Storm couldn't help but laugh, the grin looked so

silly. She knew that all of his reasons were at least partially true, but decided that none of them mattered. She was just happy he had chosen to come along.

They heard the whine of the landing gear beginning to descend, and Bishop snapped to attention, stood and shouldered an enormous plasma rifle that was merely one of the weapons he had brought along. He reached a hand up and held on to the *Blackbird*'s frame, nearly quivering with the tension in his muscles.

"I'm concerned about him," Storm said softly.

"Him an' us both," Wolverine answered, his voice a low growl. "Guy's wired to blow, Storm. We gotta watch that doesn't happen, or at least that nobody gets caught in the shrapnel."

Storm walked down the exit ramp even as it descended from the belly of the *Blackbird*. Wolverine and Bishop flanked her, then set about scanning the perimeter of their landing zone as she waited for Iceman and the Beast to emerge from the plane. It was still early afternoon in Colorado, and the day was cool and breezy. Almost perfect.

Hank and Bobby were talking quietly as they hurried down the ramp to the high grass of the field. As soon as his feet touched earth, Bobby iced up, and Storm couldn't help noticing how his once smooth ice-form had changed, gaining jagged edges and sharp icicles that represented his hair. There'd been a time when those changes would have looked foolish on Bobby Drake, but inside the shell of his humor and boyish charm, even Iceman had hardened somewhat over the years.

"Report, please, Hank?" Storm asked calmly.

"Mission objective is on the other side of that expanse of forest, perhaps half a kilometer," the Beast answered. "The aerial view reveals it to be surrounded by some form of energy, likely a force field. There do appear to be mutants within, but something from the base is jamming the mini-Cerebro unit on the *Blackbird*, so we can't pinpoint their energy signatures specifically enough to ascertain who it might be."

"Mutants?" Storm asked, taken aback by the news. "If they're mutants, this might not be a theft attempt as much as a sabotage mission, a mutant terrorist attack."

"Mutant Liberation Front, you think?" Iceman asked, also curious.

"There are too many candidates to contemplate," the Beast answered. "We haven't been confronted by Sinister for some time. It might well be him, or any number of others."

"We won't know until we get there," Storm said. "Any sign of the military?"

"There's definitely something happening in the woods outside the fence, but that jamming signal I mentioned defeated every endeavor to pin down details," Hank answered, stroking the blue fur at his chin. "We must presuppose that they've arrived before us, particularly since Val Cooper has informed us that she believed they would."

Storm considered his words, but there was really only one way to go about this operation with prudence.

"Bishop, Wolverine," she called, and in a moment the two had returned to the center of the clearing in which they'd landed. "We move out now, as a unit, non-threatening. Shoulder that weapon, Bishop. Bobby, power down. Logan, take point but only by a few yards. If the army is here, we want at least the opportunity to cooperate."

"And if they don't accommodate us with that opportunity, Storm?" the Beast asked.

"Simple, Henry," she replied. "We assert ourselves."

The Beast hung his head, sighed and said, "I was afraid of that."

"Wind's at our backs," Wolverine said as they entered the forest. "Could be anything up ahead and I wouldn't smell it."

"Lions and tigers and bears," Bobby said softly, to which Hank replied, "Oh, my."

Though there was no real path, they kept very rigidly to the trail blazed by Wolverine. Less than ten minutes later they could see the brightening of the sun that told them they were approaching the open field where the installation that housed Operation: Wideawake lay. Beyond the sunlight, there was a dim green glow that could only be the energy field the Beast had warned them about.

Without warning, Wolverine stopped dead in his tracks.

"Logan, what is it?" Storm asked.

"Wind's finally shifted," he answered. "And just in time. We got a sizable welcome wagon up ahead, Ororo."

Without a word, Bishop slung the plasma rifle off his shoulder and ratcheted back the safety. It was the kind of reaction Storm had both dreaded and expected.

"Shoulder that weapon, Bishop," she said, spinning on him. "Were you not listening when I said we'd go in non-threatening?"

His eyes scanned the woods ahead for a moment longer, then snapped toward Storm. He tried to stare her down but she knew he would capitulate. He'd been a soldier and a lawman in his future, so authority meant something to him. Add to that the fact that, in his lifetime, the X-Men had been nothing more or less than wondrous legends, and she knew his loyalty was unquestionable.

His ability to remain calm, on the other hand, was unpredictable.

"Move together," she said, and as a group, they walked into the lion's den. At the last minute, she began to worry that their welcome wagon wouldn't be the military at all, but part of the group that had taken over the base. She said nothing, however. It was too late for such concerns, and her gut told her that her first instinct was right.

It had to be the army.

And it was.

Wolverine stepped out of the woods a half dozen yards from the fence and energy field that surrounded the base. To their great surprise, it was little more than a shattered one-story concrete structure, and they realized that the base itself must have been underground.

Less of a surprise was their greeting. As they followed Wolverine into the clearing, they were surrounded by armed soldiers. In seconds, a pair of troop transports came around either side of the compound and skidded to a halt in the scrub only feet away. The transport to the west was followed very quickly by a fast-moving tank.

A man in the front of the eastern transport stood with a bullhorn in his hand, and began to address them just as the clattering of dozens of weapons being cocked and readied for firing echoed off the trees behind them.

"Attention X-Men," said the man in the transport, "this is Colonel Tomko, United States Army. You are trespassing at a top secret federal facility. Throw down your weapons and surrender or you will be fired upon."

"Seem a little anxious to shoot a couple mutants, don't they?" Wolverine said under his breath, but Storm put a hand on his elbow to prevent any reaction.

Out of the corner of her eye, she saw Bishop begin to bring his plasma rifle around to firing position.

CHAPTER 6

Magneto was aware of the presence of the U.S. military outside the perimeter fence. But he was unconcerned. Granted, they had arrived roughly half an hour earlier than he had expected, but that was well within the acceptable parameters for the Empire Agenda. The magnetic force shield with which he had surrounded the base was performing its function admirably, and the jamming signal Milan was broadcasting from the computer seemed to be working, for none of the radio contact they had tapped into amongst the troops signaled any knowledge of who had captured the facility.

For the moment, he was content. Soon, he would have the means at his disposal to attain the goal he had worked toward for so long: mutant domination of humanity. He would prove to Charles Xavier once and for all time whose philosophy was not only the best, but the most pragmatic. The next twenty-four hours would be glorious, the weeks, months and years afterward, nothing short of utopian. For mutants, of course.

Xavier would see the light at last. That was important to Magneto. Once, they had been the best of friends, but their divergent dreams tore them apart. Ever the idealist, Charles would argue with him hour after hour, day after day, until finally Magneto realized he must act to make his dream real, rather than simply debate its finer points.

The last time they had parted as friends, at peace

with one another, the argument had reached new heights. In the heat of the Israeli summer, desert sand flying in the sweltering wind, bodies baking inside uncomfortable clothing as their Jeep bounced on rutted unpaved roads, their already-tattered friendship was torn asunder. Finally, Magneto had insisted that Charles recognize the primary flaw in his philosophy.

"And what might that be?" Charles had asked, eyes narrowing at this new approach to the debate.

"It's so obvious, Charles," Magneto had answered. "You see it around you every day, in every newspaper, in every city. It's something I learned in war that you have yet to accept. Human society needs someone to hate. There must be a bottom rung on the ladder. Right now, mutants are it, and I don't see anyone else climbing up after us. Therefore, as long as human society exists in it's current form, humans will hate and fear mutants."

Charles was quiet for a long time after that, his face darkened by the shadow of his consternation. When he met Magneto's gaze again, he seemed unsettled, yet determined.

"There are certainly humans who need to hate," Charles began. "But I do not believe that is true of humanity as a whole. Humans and mutants can live in peace, Magnus. I will never believe otherwise. Never."

That stubborn quality had blinded Charles from the beginning, and Magneto believed that it still did. But not for long. In one day he would teach Charles Xavier what he had not been able to in all the long years since they had first met. In one day. Today.

Magneto was alone in the Sentinel control center, except for Milan, who could hardly be counted as his consciousness was completely integrated into the computer core at the moment. He was still slumped like a corpse over the console, jacked into cyberspace, and his presence gave an almost ghostly feel to the room.

"Lord Magneto," Voght's voice crackled suddenly from a speaker nearby. Magneto walked to a comm-console near the observation window of the command center and slapped a yellow button before talking into a speaker on the wall.

"What is it, Amelia?"

"In the forest outside the perimeter fence," she said quickly, obviously alarmed, "the X-Men are approaching."

"Thank you," he said calmly. "Please keep me up to date."

"Yes, Lord," she replied calmly, but it was clear that Magneto's reaction had surprised her. He had, of course, expected the X-Men, or one of their splinter groups, to make an appearance during this operation. He was prepared for that eventuality. Voght should have known better than to think he could be taken by surprise.

"Now then, Amelia, report to the control center at once," he said in his normal voice. No additional urgency was required for his commands to be carried out. He was their Lord, after all.

* * *

As she made her way to the Sentinel command center, Amelia Voght wondered, not for the first time, how she had ended up an Acolyte of Magneto when she had turned down a similar role in the life of Charles Xavier. Perhaps, though, the answer lay in the manner in which she had phrased the question. As an Acolyte, Magneto was her lord and master. Xavier had been her lover. When he began to build the foundations for the X-Men, their relationship became . . . well, competition was the only word she could think of.

If she had wanted to continue her relationship with Xavier, she would have had to throw herself wholly into his dreams for the X-Men. Voght hadn't been prepared to do that. She had known, better than any of them, what would happen. Xavier would gather his X-Men—like-minded individuals or young people whose opinions were not yet fully formed, whom he could then sculpt to his needs—Magneto would do the same, as would others she was certain would pop up eventually.

It was asking for trouble, she had thought then. She knew better now, knew that hiding her head in the sand was not the answer, that she could not live in fear and shame simply because she was a mutant. But then she had been afraid, and her fear had made her self-righteous and indignant. Xavier had chosen his path, irrevocably, and Voght did not wish to follow it. It had ended that simply.

Years later she had realized it was too late to make a choice. She was afraid again, but this time, there seemed only one way to survive, and that was to fight back against the swelling tide of human loathing. Mutants had to prevail. Magneto was the living essence of that conviction, and therefore Voght had thrown in with him.

Though she thought him foolish, she still had a soft spot in her heart for Charles Xavier, a nostalgia for the innocence of their first days together in India, he only newly crippled, and she his vigilant nurse. That modicum of good feeling did not, however, extend to the X-Men. They were hopeless fools all, seduced by romanticism and wallowing in ignorance. Amelia Voght would be more than happy to teach them the error of their ways.

The command center door slid aside with a hydraulic hiss. Magneto stood at the observation window staring out at the fleet of Sentinels that would soon be his to command. Milan was still psych-surfing the net, out like a light. Voght waited a moment, but Magneto did not turn to address her.

"You rang?" she said finally.

He started slightly, as if he hadn't heard her enter, then turned slowly to face her.

"Ah, yes, Amelia," he said absently. "I'm sorry. I was just running over the Agenda in my head. Everything seems to be running perfectly well, but there are a couple of things we need to be wary of. Including, of course, the arrival of the X-Men."

"You don't seem too concerned," she said. "I had hoped to keep our presence here unknown for as long as possible, but it seems I have failed."

"Not necessarily," Magneto answered. "It is entirely possible that they know of the Sentinels kept at this location, and mean to prevent *anyone* from possessing them."

Voght realized that Magneto was right. At least with the Sentinels in the hands of the federal government and Operation: Wideawake, the X-Men knew what they were up against. Better the devil you know, as they say. Xavier would have sent them to investigate no matter what the circumstances or the identity of the potential thieves.

"Do you want us to engage them?" she asked, but suspected she knew the answer.

"Not at all, Amelia," Magneto said with a benevolent

smile. "It will take quite some time for the X-Men to resolve their presence with the particularly hostile attitudes of the American military forces arrayed outside this base. Even then, they've got to break through our force shield. At that point, you may be required to engage them. As such, please find Senyaka, Unuscione and the others and prepare."

"You said there were a couple of things we need to be wary of," Voght reminded him.

"Indeed," Magneto agreed, nodding. "While most of the Acolytes will see your orders as a direct communication of my will, that is a lesson Unuscione may need to be taught. Were I you, I would watch my back during battle, ever a convenient time to be rid of competition."

Voght was silent. She expected nothing less of Unuscione, but felt it remarkable that Magneto should deign to mention it at all. She knew she held a place in his life as a confidant, but she hoped there was no romantic interest involved. She had already once given her heart to a man incapable of accepting the responsibility. She'd be damned if she'd do it again.

"I appreciate the heads-up, Magneto," she answered finally. "If Unuscione gets out of hand, you can be certain my retribution, or reprimand if you prefer, will be swift."

"I had thought it might," Magneto said. "The Empire Agenda can ill afford to have my orders questioned."

"Don't give it another thought," Voght said. She turned and marched from the command center, wondering if Magneto was purposely maneuvering Unuscione and herself into a confrontation. She would not put it past him, but if that was his goal, Voght was mystified as to its purpose. No matter, though. If Unuscione came after her . . .

"I'll take her down hard," Voght said under her breath, eyes narrowed and with a grim set to her jaw. Life as a mutant was becoming an ugly business. But then, she had always known it would come to that.

* * *

With mixed feelings Magneto watched Voght set off to prepare for battle. He had every confidence in her ability, both to lead and to withstand Unuscione's backstabbing tendencies, but he did not wish to see their conflict undermine the Empire Agenda. He considered for a moment that it might have been unwise to place Voght in charge for this mission, and then brushed the thought aside. The two women were on a collision course, and there would be no avoiding that fact. Best to be done with it, and move on.

A loud thump made him whip his head around, entire body taking on a defensive posture, wondering if the X-Men had somehow devised a way to enter the base unnoticed.

"Apologies, my Lord," Milan said, for it had been his open palm on the metal desk that had made such a noise. He sat, still slightly hunched over the console. Milan no longer looked dead; now he simply looked as if he were dying. Sweat ran down his forehead and cheeks in droplets and he wiped them quickly away. He stood and stretched, arched his back with a crackle of popping muscles.

"We're ready, my Lord," he said with great deference, then sat back down at the console. "All we need to do now is enter your password, and we will be online and ready for reprogramming."

Milan's exhaustion and satisfaction were evident in his features, though obscured by the visor he wore and the tattoo on his face. For a moment, Magneto wished he did not have to disappoint one of his most faithful Acolytes, but there was no avoiding it.

"I'm sorry, Milan, but I must take over from here," Magneto said.

"My Lord?" Milan asked, astonished at his master's words. "Have I offended you somehow, Lord? What may I do to salve whatever wrong I have produced? Surely, there must be . . ."

"Please, Milan, be still," Magneto instructed, and was obeyed. "You have done no wrong."

Magneto crossed the control center, his footsteps echoing heavily on the metal floor, a dead hollow sound that only served to amplify the lifeless, haunted atmosphere of the base. It was a cold place, and Magneto greatly anticipated the moment when they might quit Colorado and move on to their ultimate goal.

Milan waited, head tilted slightly downward, as Magneto approached, and only stood when his master had laid a hand on his left shoulder. When he had vacated his seat at the console, Magneto replaced him there, where his mind had labored tirelessly to navigate layer upon layer of computer security. Now that Milan had breached that security, had found the backdoor that Sebastian Shaw had built into the Sentinels' programming, Magneto knew that he must take over.

"Please sit down, Milan," he said, motioning to a chair several feet away. "Sit by me now, and you will see that I have done nothing but save your life."

On screen, the console displayed only one word, a request: "PASSWORD?" Magneto typed E-M-P-I-R-E, and hit the return key. The resounding, grinding noise of generators coming to life filled the facility. Giant engines churned with sudden purpose, like dozens of jets preparing for takeoff simultaneously.

"What is that sound, Lord?" Milan asked, hands over his ears.

Before Magneto could respond, the console began to change. Where it had been a very modern computer system, it now unfolded like a lotus flower, blossoming into a thing of much greater technological promise. The screen widened, and glowed with a pink hue that made Magneto think, absurdly, of cotton candy. The top rolled back into itself and a new apparatus was born from inside it, consisting of a long gray box with a six inch opening at one end and another, strangely shaped construct.

"*Name?*" asked the computerized voice of the command center.

"Eric Magnus Lehnsherr, called Magneto, White King of the Hellfire Club," Magneto said. Though the latter bit of information was no longer true, it was part of the identification that Shaw had programmed into the system.

"*Password?*"

"Empire."

"*Voice pattern analysis confirms identity. Please proceed with fingerprint and genetic analysis.*"

Magneto removed the glove from his right hand and slid it into the long, gray box on top of the console. He breathed deeply as the computer scanned not only his fingerprints, but the lines of his palm as well. That completed, he grimaced in pain as fine lasers sliced off a small swatch of his skin for testing.

"My Lord, you are in pain," Milan said, and Magneto almost laughed at the simple childlike wonder in the man. Though it was possible devout piety and childlike wonder were too often confused.

"In answer to your question, that sound is the arming and ignition of all Sentinel systems," Magneto said, knowing it would be several seconds before the computer confirmed his genetic pattern and realizing that Milan had probably forgotten he'd ever asked the question. "Now that Shaw is dead, if anyone other than myself were to attempt to enter the system in this fashion, the Sentinels are programmed to destroy that person."

"Fingerprint and genetic analysis confirms identity," the computer announced. *"Begin retinal scan."*

For a heartbeat, Magneto wished he could witness the enormity of it from Milan's point of view. The very idea was foolish and impossible, and he chided himself for it. Magneto placed his face against the contoured edge of the Retinal Scanner and a reddish light bathed his eyes. He tried not to flinch from its brightness. After all, any machine is capable of errors, and an error here would mean failure at best, possibly even death.

"Retinal scan confirms identity," the computer voice said. *"Welcome, Magneto. Please run system self-diagnostics before downloading alternate priority program from restricted memory."*

"Run diagnostics," Magneto said.

"Running."

Magneto looked at Milan, who sat in silent appreciation of his master and the technology that was about to become enslaved to their needs. The Master of Magnetism took in a deep breath, sweet with relief, and leaned back in his chair, content to wait while the soldiers of his empire began to learn their new duties.

• • •

Val Cooper was getting stonewalled by Gyrich's secretary, and was considering putting in another call to Xavier, as the Professor was the only other source of information regarding the Colorado situation that she had at her disposal. Gyrich was hardly following the Secretary's instructions, and he'd pay for it later, no doubt. But Val knew that the bastard couldn't care less about later if it meant not having to deal with her, now.

That's what she was thinking, anyway, when her office door crashed open and Henry Peter Gyrich stormed into the room.

"Cooper, I've got a major crisis on my hands, and I wonder if you can shed some light on it for me," he said, not caring enough to even begin to disguise the hostility in his tone and manner.

"Really?" Val asked, all innocence. She had no idea what he was referring to specifically, but loved the disgusted look on his face and the pain it must have caused him to come to her.

"What can I do for you, Henry?" she inquired, and then allowed the venom to seep into her voice. "Seeing how cooperative you've been, you know I'll help where I can."

"Back off, Cooper," he snarled, then dropped into the soft leather chair in front of her desk. "I want to know what the X-Men are doing traipsing all over the Colorado site. Somehow, I expect you'll have an answer for me."

"If you're implying that I . . ." she began, bursting with mock fury.

"I imply nothing," Gyrich interrupted. "I'm far too direct for implication, don't you think?"

"So it's an accusation, then, is it?" she asked rhetorically. "Let me tell you something, you sanctimonious bigot, unlike you, I follow orders. The Secretary instructed me to call Charles Xavier. I have done that. No more, no less. Simply because you cannot even conceive of following instructions is no reason to believe those around you share your faults."

Gyrich's eyes narrowed and his lip curled back. A pulsing on the side of his cheek revealed that he was grinding his teeth, and Val was absurdly pleased. It was to her great displeasure that Val Cooper had known far too much hate in her life. Most people, she imagined, knew too little love. That was par for the course.

Hate was completely different. It was a disease, and an infectious one at that. Still, she lived in Washington, so the choice was between hatred and self-loathing. Val Cooper thought she was pretty decent, overall, so she chose hatred.

Even in the spawning ground for heartlessness and cruelty, Gyrich was something special. Val was fond of saying that when he died, Hell wouldn't take him for fear he'd take over the joint. It always amazed her how few people laughed at that line. But they were right. The truth was never funny.

Gyrich exhaled and sat forward slightly in his seat, attempting and failing to produce a benevolent smile, which instead became the foolish grin often reserved for infants, senile relatives, and the mentally ill. In itself, it was an insult.

"Let me be specific, and official," Gyrich said slowly. "Did you inform the X-Men of the situation in Colorado?"

"No."

"Then we can only assume, as I have long believed, that Professor Xavier is directly tied to the X-Men," he said, leaning back with a nauseatingly self-satisfied air.

"Speak for yourself," Val said, just as calmly. "That's not what my report will reflect."

Gyrich raised an eyebrow. "Explain," he commanded, though she ignored his tone for the moment.

Val was thinking fast, but the basic gist of this story had already been concocted with Charles Xavier hours earlier. The last thing Xavier needed was to have Gyrich on his tail at all times. It would seriously impair the X-Men's ability to function as a team. Still, though prepared, she spoke slowly and thoughtfully to make it appear as though her reasoning was being developed on the spot.

"We know Xavier is friendly with Dr. Henry McCoy, aka the Beast," she said. "We also know that, at times, McCoy has been seen with the X-Men. Therefore, it is more likely that Xavier told McCoy, and McCoy passed it on. Even that is unlikely, however. Xavier has too much to lose in the fight for mutant rights if he were to lose the favorable opinion of the current administration. He wouldn't jeopardize that by revealing the content of what was obviously a high-level-clearance conversation."

She could see from the moment she began that Gyrich wasn't buying word one of the story. In the end, that hardly mattered. It was less important that Gyrich be dissuaded from connecting Xavier to the X-Men than it was that he be dissuaded from connecting Val herself to the X-Men. Not only would she lose her position and everything associated with it, but if he could show that she knowingly invited outside agencies in to deal with restricted federal operations, she could, and certainly would, be prosecuted to the full extent of the law.

"It just doesn't make sense," she said finally.

That woke Gyrich up from his predatory daydreams.

"You're right," he said smugly. "It doesn't make a damn bit of sense. But hey, Val, if that's your professional opinion on the subject, then I'm willing to take your word on it, of course. Only thing is, that leaves me with a bit of a conundrum."

"How's that?" she asked.

"Well, it's really quite simple," Gyrich said, nearly licking his lips with anticipation. "You claim you didn't contact the X-Men directly, though of course we both know you have the capacity to do so, since several members of X-Factor actually used to *be* X-Men. You also insist that Xavier isn't directly tied to those mutie terrorists, and wouldn't contact them even if he were. You see where this leaves us?"

"I'm not following you," Val said, but she was lying. She was following Gyrich's logic very closely, and it disturbed her deeply.

"Well, if you didn't call them, and Xavier didn't call them, then it must be the X-Men themselves who have taken over this facility," Gyrich said, almost leering now with the pleasure of the spot he'd put her in.

"That's ridiculous!" she said. "You have no reason to think . . ."

"I have every reason to think that is the case, and unless you care to tell a different story, we both know how the Secretary will feel," Gyrich said smugly. "You can file your little reports to your heart's content, but it won't change the outcome. The X-Men have been confronted by the U.S. Army on federal land. Though they have, as yet, made no hostile move, we must assume they are the culprits, and that they intend to rendezvous with teammates inside the facility."

The red-haired man leaned forward and plucked her

desk phone from its cradle. He punched in a numerical sequence that gave him access to the safe line she had used to call Xavier. It swept itself for bugs or other surveillance every thirty seconds, and automatically disconnected if the receiving line began a trace.

Gyrich then dialed a brief code number.

"What are you doing?" Val asked, though suddenly she thought she knew. She felt as though she'd been punched in the stomach, and bile rose in her throat.

"This is Gyrich," he said. "Get me Colonel Tomko."

Leaning over to speak into the phone, Gyrich looked around the room. Eventually, his eyes found Val's, and he smiled at her with genuine warmth, a first for the man. But she knew the smile was not for her benefit, it was his uncontrollable reaction to a moment of personal triumph.

"I'll ask you again, Gyrich," she said angrily. "What the hell are you doing?"

She reached for the cutoff button, to disconnect his call, but Gyrich stood and slapped her hand away.

"Move an inch toward that phone and you're done in D.C., Cooper," he snarled. Then his demeanor changed completely and his smile returned. He leaned back on her desk and spoke grimly into the phone. "Hello, Colonel Tomko," he said. "Under my authority, you are hereby ordered to place the X-Men in custody. Should they resist, you will instruct your men to shoot to kill."

"No!" Val shouted. "Gyrich, are you out of your mind? They may be the only people capable of preventing disaster out there! You're blowing your ace in the hole, you blind lunatic!"

Gyrich was ignoring her. Instead, he seemed to be having trouble with Colonel Tomko on the line.

Gyrich's face had reddened, and his nostrils flared as he spoke louder and more slowly.

"I'll say this only once more, Colonel," he declared. "You answer to me and only to me. I have given you your orders, and you will carry them out. I expect that when you next contact me, the X-Men will be your prisoners or dead, and the facility will be back under our control."

Without another word, he hung up. Val knew the horror she felt must be etched on her face, but could do nothing about it. Gyrich seemed not to notice, however. He was too happy with himself.

"Now, maybe we can finally deal with these mutie freaks once and for all," he said. "And if Tomko fails, it will only prove that Wideawake is a necessity that must be put into active use. One way or the other, it's a win-win for me, Val. Which means you lose."

When Gyrich slammed her office door, Val could only shake her head. Sometimes she thought he was merely a miserable, evil man, and other times she had to believe he might be slightly insane. For the first time, she began to actually hope that the latter was true. If it weren't, she just didn't know if she would be able to stay in Washington anymore.

Nerves frayed, Val locked her office door and retreated to her desk. She used her safe line to place yet another call to Charles Xavier, and silently asked herself if she would ever be in a position where she might be the bearer of good news. It would be a pleasant change.

CHAPTER 7

As their ship emerged from the stargate, Ch'od was, for the second time, awed and unnerved by the fleet of war ships in orbit around Hala. He had witnessed military gatherings of such magnitude before, several even larger, but more often than not the *Starjammer* was escaping capture or destruction, and it was not easy to get a decent, panoramic view of vessels in pursuit of your own.

Over the years he had learned to be thorough, so he checked and double-checked that the *Starjammer* was cloaked from Shi'ar and Kree sensors.

"Raza, make sure the X-Men are prepared to 'port planetside in two," Ch'od said absently, wishing that he could join the extraction team that would save Corsair and Hepzibah from execution, or die trying.

Of course, the latter part of it held no allure for him. Ch'od did not relish the idea of dying. But since there was no way he was going to allow himself to lose, he didn't have to worry about dying. Of course, the whole question was moot. Someone needed to stay behind in order to teleport the extraction team back to the *Starjammer*, and get them into the stargate before the fleet could begin their pursuit or blow them out of orbit.

It was going to be a long day.

Raza lifted the safety bars that held him in the copilot's seat. He stood and headed for the main cabin, and then all hell broke loose.

"Ky'thri!" Raza cried, as an intense blast at the defense shields rocked the *Starjammer*, and alarm bells clanged to life around them. Raza fell to the ground and held on to the base of his chair as a second blast caused the ship to veer sharply off course. Ch'od reached one large hand down and wordlessly lifted his comrade from the deck. Behind them, in the tiny closet that served as his "quarters," the furry being called Cr+eeee chittered in fear.

"Shields are burning out!" Raza shouted over the alarms and the rising hum of the failing defense shields. "I hadst thought we were cloaked!"

"We were!" Ch'od responded, his gentle shell giving way to bare fury as he looked over the ship's control panels. "We still are!"

The two beings, longtime friends and allies, one half of the Starjammers, froze simultaneously. Slowly, with looks of frustration and disbelief, they turned to face one another.

"Thou hast got to be kidding me," Raza said, an expression he'd picked up from Corsair long ago. The *Starjammer* shook violently as it was struck yet again.

"It's the only answer," Ch'od replied, then leaned over the control panel and brought a massive fist down on top of a bank of lights, one of which glowed green to signify that the ship was, indeed, cloaked.

It winked out.

Ch'od roared with a myriad of emotions, from anger to amusement, just as a final blast crashed into the ship and the high pitched buzzing whine of the defense shields simply stopped.

"'Twould seem we have a problem," Raza said drily, and Ch'od could only laugh. They were probably going to die, and the absurdity of it all had come to him suddenly. The cloaking systems had been offline all along, but a shorted signal had told them the opposite. They weren't cloaked, and now they weren't shielded either.

"Get the X-Men and go!" Ch'od shouted, the moment of laughter over.

"But thou canst not . . ." Raza began, then stopped when he saw that Ch'od was ignoring him.

Ch'od wrapped his scaly fists around the stick and banked into a one-hundred-and-eight-degree rolling turn. A massive Shi'ar battle cruiser appeared on the vid screen and Ch'od nodded. He preferred to face his enemies head on. The cruiser fired a pair of plasma missiles, but with them dead in his sights, Ch'od's finely honed skills as a pilot took over. He dove under the missiles, pulled up immediately and began strafing the underside of the battle cruiser.

The missiles followed, but he had gained on them. Ch'od decided to test an age-old wisdom, which said that the shortest distance between two points was a straight line. He jerked the stick backwards and passed within meters of the battle cruiser's engines. The *Starjammer*'s bottom hull was bathed in the furnace of flames that were belched from the other ship's core.

The missiles would most certainly have performed the same move. There was no way he could outmaneuver them. But if he was correct, he wouldn't have to. Ch'od bore down on the stick, snapping back into place along the same trajectory he'd followed before dodging around the battle cruiser. His position above the ship matched perfectly the missiles' position below.

When the battle cruiser exploded, the *Starjammer* received a huge speed boost, and shot toward Hala's atmosphere without any additional effort. The shortest distance between two points. He guessed it was true after all. Unless you counted the stargate.

SIEGE

The battle cruiser's destruction had already brought attention, as the *Starjammer*'s sensors indicated that several of the fleet's smaller vessels were hurrying to investigate. He hoped that the cruiser hadn't had time, or didn't think they were enough of a threat, to report the *Starjammer*'s emergence from the stargate. The way their luck had been running, he'd have had to assume that the odds were stacked against them.

He kicked in the hyperburners for a count of ten, changed course and skimmed along the outer edges of Hala's atmosphere. It was going to be close.

"Raza, what's taking so long?" He yelled, and in the moment of silence that followed, he noticed Cr+eeee's chittering for the first time and began to make a low clucking noise that he knew would calm his old friend's nerves.

Finally, Cyclops stepped into the cockpit.

"Ch'od, we don't have time to go through it, and Raza only laughs when I ask him what's happening, but I have one request for you," Cyclops said quickly.

"I only hope I can fulfill it," Ch'od answered respectfully.

"When the time comes for us to radio for dustoff, please be alive and have this ship in good enough shape to get us out of this place," the leader of the X-Men said, and Ch'od merely nodded.

Cyclops hit a comm-badge that was clipped to his breast, and asked, "Is this thing working?" His voice came through on the *Starjammer*'s comm-link, so Ch'od gave him the Terran thumbs up sign that Corsair had taught them all. When Cyclops had retreated to the main cabin, his voice came back through the link.

"Six to beam down, Ch'od," Cyclops pronounced over the link.

"Beam down?" Ch'od asked, befuddled.

"Teleport us down, Ch'od," a new voice said. Ch'od thought it was that of the Archangel. "That's what it means. Teleport us . . ."

Ch'od was no longer listening. He was about to come under fire again, and had only seconds to 'port the extraction team to the surface of Hala. In a heartbeat, it was done, but too late.

Without any defensive shields, the *Starjammer* took a massive hit. A different set of alarms went off, but Ch'od did not need them to see the problem.

There was fire in the cockpit.

* * *

At its best, teleportation is a physically disconcerting experience. When the ship doing the teleporting is under fire and preparing to leave orbit, and the job is done hurriedly, the experience can be far worse. There was no elegance to the X-Men's arrival on Hala. They did not shimmer into existence in the midst of a sprawling community as if glorious gods were arriving from another dimension. Rather, they were dumped unceremoniously into the war-ravaged remnants of a once-proud suburb of Kree-Lar.

Cyclops felt nauseous as he rose to his feet, then reached down to help Archangel do the same. A merciless sun burned high above the planet, and its intense light made the destruction around them all the more vivid. They stood in what had once been a town center, perhaps a marketplace. Water bubbled under a mound of shattered crystal, and Cyclops assumed it had been a beautiful fountain once upon a time, before the war with the Shi'ar.

Still, despite the destruction, the place was hardly

abandoned. Several women were attempting to get water from the crystal-showered spring without doing themselves irreversible injury. Dozens more were in the process of rebuilding, while five ragged-looking Kree elders cooked some kind of meat on a fire pit built into the bare earth.

"I t'ink we in the wrong part o' town, Cyclops," Gambit said uneasily.

"It isn't what it seems, I'm afraid," Cyclops answered, even as Jean and Rogue moved closer to hear their exchange.

"Where are we, Scott?" Rogue asked.

Cyclops was about to ask Jean that question, to see if she could pinpoint the distance from their location to Kree-Lar, when Raza interrupted.

"This be Ryn-Dak," Raza said, unholstering his plasma weapon as he scanned the area. "Once it didst symbolized the quality of life that the Kree young aspired to. Then came the war."

"Kree middle class, eh?" Archangel asked, intrigued. "What was here that the Shi'ar wanted to destroy so badly? Some kind of base or factory?"

"Do not play the fool, X-Man," Raza said bluntly. "The Shi'ar didst choose to destroy Ryn-Dak, but 'twas not for its military significance. They destroyed it for the peace and ideals it didst represent."

"Just like on Earth," Jean interjected. "These are the victims of war: children and the aged, civilians with no interest in battle."

It was true, Cyclops saw. Other than two burly Kree men, one with blue skin and one with pink—for Kree came in both colors—all those left in Ryn-Dak were quite young or very old. The blue-skinned Kree male, who was working metal over a fire, obviously a smith of some kind, looked in their direction for the first time. Cyclops noticed a long scar on his right cheek, but he also saw the immediate hostility on the Kree's face.

"So that's what has you all heated up," Rogue pointed out, motioning toward Raza's drawn weapon. "We've just been dumped into a place where, more'n likely, since you're Shi'ar, everybody wants you dead."

"There's more to it than that, Rogue," Jean said quietly. "Historically, the Kree haven't exactly loved humans very much either."

"I hate to break this up, folks," Cyclops interrupted, "but we're beginning to draw a crowd. I think we'd best move on."

"Thou art right, Cyclops," Raza said. "Also, we must needs not forget that, since the *Starjammer* wast being tracked 'ere we beamed down, 'tis likely they will have pinpointed our teleportational trajectory as well."

"So what you really sayin', *mon ami*, is dat pretty soon we get some unwelcome visitors, eh?" Gambit said with a laugh. "In dat case, I'm with Cyclops. *Allons!*"

"That's a first," Cyclops said, and Gambit nodded at him with a wink.

The metalsmith, along with the burly pink-skinned Kree and several younger people, both male and female, pink and blue, were approaching now, and the time for chatter was over.

Unconsciously, Cyclops touched a hand to the translator plug that sat in his left ear like a tiny hearing aid. Save for Raza, who spoke Kree and Shi'ar fluently, they all wore the device, which would allow them to hear any galactic language as if it were English, and would translate their words for those around them. It gave him a certain sense of security, and almost convinced him to attempt to speak to the gathering crowd.

But that would be folly, he knew. They needed to find a place to get their bearings, and some clothes that would make them blend more readily with the locals. And fast. Corsair wasn't getting any younger sitting in Deathbird's dungeon, and Scott feared that if they didn't hurry, his father would never get any older either.

"Here, birdy, birdy!" The pink-skinned man was chanting, obviously trying to taunt Raza with derogatory references to his feathered head. "Come, little bird, I will fold your wings and make you fly."

"Move, people, now!" Cyclops ordered, and they began walking briskly in a tight group out of the center and into the back streets.

Some houses still had their first stories, but most of their entrances were blocked. Charred craters might have been due to explosions or particularly nasty firefights. Rank odors crept from one huge pile of rubble that might have been anything before the war. None of them wanted to consider what was causing the stench.

Archangel flew recon, low above the ruins, watching for any sign of approaching Shi'ar soldiers. Thus far, they had been lucky. The mob from the center of Ryn-Dak had not followed them more than a few yards, and neither Warren's recon nor Jean's psi scans had picked up anyone else following them. A small percentage of the city's original population still survived, barely, in dwellings that were little more than hovels. Cyclops found it profoundly disturbing and terribly haunting to be among so much death.

With Archangel darting in the air above, showing them the general direction of the gleaming spires of Kree-Lar that were their destination, the five of them walked side by side when possible, on down to single file when they had to force their way through blocked streets. They picked up articles of clothing here and there, ragged cloaks and mismatched boots, remnants buried in rubble or clutched in the hands of the dead. Soon they looked at least as poor as the surviving Kree.

"Stop," Jean hissed, and they all obeyed instantly.

What is it? Scott thought, knowing Jean's telepathy would pick up the question.

We're surrounded, she responded, her mental voice filling his head. *More than a dozen. No immediate urge to attack, but definitely hostile.*

Cyclops considered their options, and realized there was only one. He motioned for the other X-Men and Raza to stand back, and took several steps forward.

"We know you're out there," he said, his voice calm and confident. "Show yourselves and state your business. Only cowards hide in the shadows."

Immediately, there came a roar from the shattered second story of a building to their right. Three thudding footfalls resounded in the otherwise empty street and then the huge blue-skinned Kree metalsmith from the city center appeared above them. He vaulted from the second story and landed on his feet with a grunt just a few feet in front of Cyclops.

"The Kree do not suffer cowards to live," the man said, lip curling in disgust. "Or humans for that matter."

Yet, despite his threat, he made no move to attack them. Cyclops knew that the others, particularly Gambit and Raza, could not necessarily be counted on to restrain themselves. He held up a hand, a signal to them that they should make no move.

The Kree noticed it as well. He whistled loud and long, and in the periphery of his ruby-shaded vision, he saw other figures, pink and blue, some badly deformed, emerge from the structures on either side of the street. Most of them were armed with plasma rifles, but several had crude battle axes or clubs. One carried a taser gun, which fired electrified projectiles—a formidable weapon. They formed a rough circle around the X-Men, but still Scott would not allow his team to react. He never took his eyes from the face of the metalsmith, undoubtedly the leader.

"Humans are not welcome on Hala," the metalsmith said evenly, the threat implicit and genuine, and therefore unembellished by detail.

"We have no quarrel with you," Cyclops declared. "Deathbird has several of our friends and plans to execute them. We plan to stop her."

There was a rustling amongst the Kree. A whispered argument erupted behind him, he thought between Gambit and Rogue. Presumably, they were arguing about the wisdom of his revealing their cause so readily, but their dissent would be seen as a sign of his, and their, weakness by the Kree.

Silence, both of you! Jean chided them mentally, and Scott breathed a sigh of relief. He tensed a moment, expecting Gambit to made some comment to prove that he was not afraid to fight these Kree, but it never came. Perhaps, Cyclops mused, he had underestimated the Cajun after all. There were times when Gambit appeared to be even more clever than he boasted, and that was saying quite a bit.

"Why should I believe you?" the metalsmith asked.

"Tell me why we shouldn't kill you, now, since your goals benefit us not at all."

"One of our friends is to be executed because she has been accused of smuggling weapons to the Kree rebellion on Hala," Jean said, and though they both paid close attention to her words, Cyclops and the Kree leader continued to stare at one another.

"Her name is Candide," Jean continued. "We travel to Kree-Lar, in disguise, and offer our own lives to prevent her execution."

"Yon Kree art a prideful race," Raza said, and this time the metalsmith did look away from Cyclops, to focus eyes blazing with hate on their Shi'ar companion.

"Do not speak again, birdy!" the metalsmith snarled.

"If Candide doth take part in thy rebellion, thou art honor-bound to do all that is practical to prevent her death," Raza proclaimed, heedless of the metalsmith's threats. "If she is not, thou art equally bound not to allow an innocent to die in thy stead."

The metalsmith considered Raza's words, looking down a moment before facing Cyclops again.

"What makes you think we are part of the rebellion?" he asked, a small smile coming over his face. "Or that we have ever heard of Candide."

"Are you going to prevent us from reaching Kree-Lar, or assist us in freeing our friends?" Cyclops asked, his patience waning. "I do not brag when I say we could have destroyed you several times over rather than waste precious minutes in debate. But your assistance could make our mission that much easier."

Cyclops knew such threats were a risk. But his words were perfectly true. They had no more time to waste with these rebels, if rebels they were.

SIEGE

The metalsmith's eyes narrowed, and Cyclops heard Jean send him some brief, cautionary words in his mind. The Kree took a step toward him, and the circle around the X-Men began to close. Cyclops was prepared to attack, and as he watched the metalsmith clench his fists at his sides, he realized that battle was inevitable.

"Kam-Lorr!" a voice shouted, and they all turned to see a pink-skinned Kree boy running down the street toward them.

"Kam-Lorr!" the boy shouted again, and Cyclops realized it must be the metalsmith's name. "They are coming. The soldiers are coming."

Kam-Lorr cursed viciously, then turned to Cyclops, his face showing every ounce of hatred he had for the Shi'ar army that ruled his homeworld.

"Follow me, fast, in single file . . ." he sputtered into silence as Archangel appeared above the building to his left and glided to the ground beside Cyclops.

"How many are there, Warren?" Cyclops asked calmly.

"More than fifty," Archangel answered. "Well armed, too. It's one thing if we have to fight our way out, Scott, but if we have to fight our way in, we've probably already lost."

Cyclops nodded, put a hand on Warren's shoulder in a gesture of thanks, and turned back to Kam-Lorr.

"Lead on," he said.

For a moment, Kam-Lorr looked from Cyclops to Archangel, still startled by Warren's sudden appearance. Scott could see that the Kree had a sudden and grudging respect for these strangers to his world. As they entered one of the crumbling buildings and descended into a sub-basement there, Cyclops realized that respect might be just the thing to keep them all alive a little longer.

* * *

Deathbird lay in peaceful repose on a chaise in her private aerie. She stretched her body and spread her arms out straight from her sides, natural wings fanning out beneath her. There was a slight chill in the breeze blowing through the vast open window of the turret room, and a delicious shiver went through her.

It might have been the breeze. Just as likely, she derived her pleasure from the knowledge that Lilandra was incensed and powerless. Certainly, the prisoners had to be executed for their crimes and their likely connection to the growing rebellion. But Lilandra's concern for Corsair and Hepzibah would make their executions that much sweeter.

A tinkling of chimes alerted her that someone was at the door to her aerie. Deathbird sighed, considering the burden of leadership, and rose to greet her visitor. When the door slid aside, Captain Lyb'Dyl nervously entered the chamber.

"I can see from your quiver that you bear bad tidings, Captain," Deathbird said. "My first guess would be that you did not retrieve the rebels who had the audacity to teleport onto Hala in the midst of a battle. However, you'd best be done with it. Give me your report and I will decide whether or not to let you live."

There was no threat, nor even hostility, in her tone. Rather, she knew she must have sounded somewhat bored. She was used to the type of deference Captain Lyb'Dyl gave her, and to the punishments that she was too often forced to mete out.

"Viceroy," he began rather breathlessly, "we

searched all the inhabitable sections of Ryn-Dak but found no trace of the incursion force."

He waited, head down, to see if Deathbird would maul him to death on the spot. When she did not strike, he continued, with an air of relief about him.

"We did, however, get full descriptions from several citizens, which were confirmed by our spies in Ryn-Dak," Captain Lyb'Dyl said proudly.

As he described the newly arrived rebels, Deathbird's calm amusement began to dissipate. In moments, she was transformed, hands hooked into savage talons and eyes narrowed in predatory fury. Captain Lyb'Dyl barely noticed, so pleased was he with the detailed descriptions he had obtained.

When Deathbird's left talon wrapped around his neck, claws biting skin, his eyes bulged in shock. Her right talon drove into his chest, tearing through flesh as she got her grip. The Captain shrieked in pain and terror as Deathbird lifted him above her head and carried him to the turret window of her aerie. She looked up into his eyes. Blood dripped from his neck onto her face.

"You fool," she said in quiet rage. "The X-Men have come to Hala, and you failed to even locate them."

Then she dropped him. Deathbird shook her head in disgust as Captain Lyb'Dyl plummeted, screaming, from the window. She licked his blood off her talons and went out the door, his screams diminishing but still audible in her chambers.

"Get me Gladiator!" she commanded. "Have the Imperial Guard report to me at once."

* * *

The sub-basement in Ryn-Dak had a hidden tunnel that opened into a virtual warren of such passages. Cyclops had the feeling they had been there long before the Shi'ar took power on Hala, perhaps the lair of some criminal element. Now, however, the tunnels were home to a literal underground rebellion.

They had followed Kam-Lorr in silence for the better part of an hour, in what Scott believed to be the general direction of the capital city. Then they had come upon a large cavern whose dimensions, according to Scott's natural talent for spatial geometry, were something like twenty-five feet wide by thirty-seven feet high. There they had rested, replenished their supplies, and moved on to what appeared to be a natural fissure.

They found a set of crude stairs cut into the stone, and followed them up and into a bustling marketplace. The majority of the war's survivors had camped as close to Kree-Lar as they could get, living off the scraps of life the city left behind.

"All de hagglin' and tradin', plus de smells of so many differen' foods cookin' remind me of de French Market in New Orleans," Gambit said quietly.

For Cyclops, the market was more reminiscent of the Egyptian bazaar he had seen when he and Storm had been in Cairo some years back. It wasn't just foods they smelled, but incense and perfumes, and less pleasant smells including animals and their offal. The combination was not completely repulsive, but Scott had no nostalgic fondness for the place the way Gambit did.

They gathered in the dimly lit back room of a small shop where Kam-Lorr sold the things he had made at his forge. It was uncomfortably small, which only fueled the tension in the group, but after a moment, Kam-Lorr sighed and began to speak.

"To say nothing of the Shi'ar who accompanies you, to whom none of us will speak, Kree have long held a hatred for Terrans," he began gravely. "The humans our race has encountered have ever stood in the path of Kree destiny, despite that they are far lesser beings."

"Hold on there, sugar," Rogue said. "Don't start playin' victim now that you had your butts whupped. You all were tyrants long before this latest war, and us 'Terrans' didn't have anything at'all ta do with that."

"You go, *chere*," Gambit muttered under his breath.

Cyclops cringed. All of the X-Men knew the value of diplomacy, but each of them had their own limits as to how much crap they were willing to take, even for diplomacy's sake. Perhaps because he, Jean, and Warren had been at it so much longer . . .

"We're wasting time," Warren said, cutting off Cyclops' conciliatory words before he could even voice them. "Shall we cut to the chase here? We're going in. If you're the rebels we've heard so much about, and Candide's one of yours, we were hoping for some assistance. If you don't plan to help, why don't you just point us in the right direction and get out of the way?"

Cyclops dropped his head and his eyes darted over to Warren, who stood as if to leave. Archangel glanced at him and shrugged.

"Sorry, Scott," he said. "But it's your father we're here for. We just don't have time for this tiptoeing around."

"Your father?" Kam-Lorr asked in surprise. "Who is your father?"

"Corsair, leader of the Starjammers," Cyclops replied, his voice and countenance hardened by Warren's blunt words. Archangel was right. He'd been trying to do things by the book, not let his emotions regarding his father make him lose control and ignore common sense and caution. But maybe, he thought, maybe there were times throwing caution to the wind was the only sensible course of action.

"Starjammers?" Kam-Lorr snarled, rising to his feet. "The Starjammers were part of the Shi'ar effort to unleash the nega-bomb. And you want us to help you free this man?"

Before Cyclops could move, Raza had launched himself across the table with surprising speed, knocking Kam-Lorr to the ground.

"Stay thee back!" he yelled, holding the gleaming sharp edge of his sword under the Kree rebel's throat even as the X-Men took up defensive positions.

"Raza?" Cyclops said tentatively.

"A moment, young Summers," Raza said, then leaned in and spoke softly to Kam-Lorr, venom dripping from every word.

"Thou know as well as I, blue-skin, that the Kree Supreme Intelligence wast ultimately responsible for the nega-bomb's use," he began. "I be Raza of the Starjammers, and I wast one of those who didst reluctantly shepherd the nega-bomb. So wast Hepzibah, who is a captive of thy current ruler. Corsair, however, wast not among us that day. Thou wouldst do well to remember this. Remember also that, no matter the sides we didst choose in a long-ended struggle, now doth we share an enemy, and a cause in common."

Raza sheathed his sword and offered his hand to Kam-Lorr, who looked at it with loathing. He rose to his feet without Raza's aid.

"If you will vow to rescue Candide as well as your comrades," Kam-Lorr announced, "though the idea of helping you nauseates me, I will show you how you may enter Kree-Lar undetected."

Cyclops was about to offer his thanks when he heard a crash outside and the scuffle of running feet. Several people shrieked and there was a pounding on the door.

"What is . . ." he began to ask.

"Everybody outside!" Jean cried. "Move!"

Gambit was at the back of the pack. The shop exploded in a burst of flame and ash, throwing him a dozen yards. Rogue caught him and went down hard in the street.

"Surrender, X-Men, or be executed where you stand!" a deep voice boomed above them.

Cyclops searched the sky for the source of the command. He saw Starbolt, and realized it was he whose power had destroyed the shop. Even before he saw Gladiator flying through the rising smoke, he knew the danger the X-Men faced.

"Imperial Guard!" Rogue shouted, and flew to confront Gladiator.

He knocked her out of the sky.

CHAPTER 8

Charles Xavier sat in his private study sipping mint tea. All communications were relayed to him there. Still, he felt detached from both the crisis on Hala, which he could not monitor at all, and the one in Colorado. At the moment, however, the situation in Colorado concerned him the most. Hank ought to have reported in by now, but Xavier had heard nothing. He tried to calm himself, to reassure himself that the X-Men were more than capable of dealing with whatever dangers came their way.

It didn't help. He'd sent them into the field hundreds of times, and still he felt the need to be there with them. Despite his great power, his inability to walk almost always made him a liability in the field. But that knowledge didn't help either. Nothing could keep him from worrying.

A rhythmic buzz began to sound in the study, and Xavier brightened.

"Hello, Lilandra," he said, even as the holographic image of his lover shimmered to life in the center of the study.

"Charles, my love," Lilandra acknowledged.

Though she was galaxies distant, Lilandra's Imperial Insta-Link provided a three dimensional image. The lustre of her skin, her proud stance, and her every curve were perfectly communicated to his senses. It made his yearning for her a truly painful ache.

Charles Xavier had never been very good at relationships. He had, in fact, been accused of having found the perfect lover in Lilandra specifically because of her distance. Their responsibilities kept them apart, his to the X-Men and Earth's mutant population, and hers to the entire Shi'ar Empire. Perhaps it was better that way, in a sense, for they relished whatever little time they did have together. There was, however, a fundamental melancholy to their romance that he found impossible to overcome, for they both feared that distance and destiny would tear them apart.

"I have done all I can, my love," she said in despair. "Deathbird is aware of the X-Men's presence on Hala, and has set the Imperial Guard after them."

"The Guard?" he exclaimed. "But . . ."

"There is nothing I can do, Charles. She is within her rights," Lilandra explained. "Corsair and the others will be executed at midday tomorrow. I only pray that the X-Men do not share their fate."

"I . . . thank you, Lilandra," Xavier said. No other words would come.

"Charles," she said tentatively. "I know that your obligations are as important in their way as are my own . . ."

"But you want to know when I might visit the Imperium again as your Royal Consort, since we both know Shi'ar business won't bring you to Earth any time soon," he finished for her, smiling slightly. "Ah, my love, don't I wish I could simply think of it and be at your side. Or just as nicely, have real time to take a vacation from all of this with the confidence that things wouldn't fall apart in my absence.

"But you know what happened the last time I left Earth for a prolonged period," he continued. "The problem was multiplied geometrically. If the X-Men had been heading to Chandilar instead of to Hala, I would have accompanied them no matter the consequences. As it stands, Lilandra, I just don't know when we'll see one another again."

"I could send a ship at any time, you know," she urged. "Only say the word, and we could be . . ."

"You know it isn't that easy," he said sadly. "Why make it more difficult for both of us?"

"You're correct, of course, Charles. I apologize. I will let you know if I have news," she said, and blinked out of existence, leaving behind a void that began to leech the hope from Charles Xavier's heart.

Little more than a minute had passed before the image of Val Cooper's face, much larger than life, burst onto the vid-screen in the study.

"Cooper to Xavier," she said in a hushed voice. "It's urgent, Charles, where the hell are you?"

He paused a moment before responding, still not recovered from the painful conversation with Lilandra.

"Xavier!" Cooper hissed.

Having eschewed his hover-chair this afternoon for the more conventional steel wheelchair, Xavier used his hands to push himself into view.

"What is it, Valerie?" he asked, though the look on her face filled him with dread as he anticipated her answer.

"It's Gyrich, of course," she said softly. "He's ordered his toy soldiers to capture the X-Men, or terminate them with prejudice. He's going to claim they're responsible for the Colora—"

Cooper's image disappeared from the screen as Xavier disconnected the call. Immediately, he punched in the four digit code that would give him emergency communication with the X-Men. Dead air was the only response. He punched the code in twice more with the same result. The fourth time was the charm. It rang twice, and then connected.

All Xavier could hear was the hiss of static.

* * *

"Bishop, no!" Storm shouted.

Iceman looked over at them just in time to see Bishop take aim at Colonel Tomko with his plasma rifle. He reacted instinctively, raising both hands and simply *willing* the moisture in the air to freeze into a solid block of ice around Bishop's weapon and hands. It didn't stop Bishop from firing, but when he did, the rifle exploded in his hands, throwing him back half a dozen feet. He landed, angry but unhurt, on his butt.

"Are you out of your mind?" Bishop screamed at him. "We've got to get in there, don't you see? The military is probably part of it themselves, you idiot!"

"Not too paranoid, eh Bish?" Iceman mocked, but Bishop's words stung nevertheless. It was the great burden of his life that he was rarely sure of his actions. He didn't know for certain that Bishop was wrong, only that firing first and asking questions later wasn't the way the X-Men did business.

"Good move, kid," Wolverine said in his low, rasping voice. "Though if ya coulda done it without blowin' up Bishop's weapon, I'd be more inclined to applaud."

"It was the sole option, given the circumstances, Wolverine," the Beast said, and Bobby silently thanked Hank for his support. It disturbed him though, that he had to wonder whether that support was genuine, or offered out of friendship.

"Colonel Tomko," Storm shouted, still making no move to approach the soldiers, "we have come as allies, to prevent the Sentinels from being unleashed upon the world. In anyone's hands. You would do well to utilize our skills."

There was a long pause, and they could all see the colonel on some kind of communications rig. They waited, motionless, Storm glaring at Bishop from time to time to keep him in place. The soldiers' weapons never wavered, though the tension must have begun to make their trigger fingers itch. Finally, Tomko dropped the comm rig.

"X-Men, I have my orders," he called through his bullhorn. "You will surrender yourselves to our custody immediately, or you *will* be terminated. You have to the count of five to surrender."

"One," he began.

"You think he can count all the way to five?" Iceman asked with forced amusement, attempting to ignore the nausea that rose in his stomach.

None of the others laughed.

"Two."

"Bishop," Storm said quietly. "They appear to be armed with plasma rather than projectile weapons."

"Don't worry about me," Bishop answered, and Iceman realized what they were talking about. Bishop's mutant ability was to absorb energy and channel it into destructive bursts through his hands. Traditional projectile weapons, which fired bullets of varying types, might harm or kill him. Plasma, or energy, weapons, would only serve to make him more powerful. That Storm had pointed this out could mean only one thing.

"Three."

Iceman had expected nothing less.

"Gentlemen," Storm said. "Please try not to do anyone irreparable damage. Are we ready?"

"Four."

Iceman wasn't ready. They had faced worse odds and come out on top. He had been training for years, honing his skills on this and three other teams over the years, perfecting the use of his powers. Still, he was just "Bobby," the baby of the group though no longer the youngest X-Man. What were his powers compared to Jean's or Rogue's, even Scott's or Storm's? He didn't have Hank's genius, or Bishop's experience as a field leader. Maybe he had a decent sense of humor, but that wasn't much of an asset. In the end, he had his ice powers and he did the best he could with them.

That would have to be enough. But it didn't mean he was ever really ready to face a situation like this.

"Five," Colonel Tomko said, and paused. Bobby supposed he was hoping they would finally give in. They didn't.

"Fire!"

There was a heartbeat when the only thing Iceman could hear was the chirping of crickets in the forest behind them. Then dozens of crackling bursts shredded the very fabric of the air around them and combined to imitate the roar of a catastrophic fire. As the sound of the plasma weapons discharging settled down to a generator drone that reminded Bobby of a dentist's drill, the X-Men were already taking offensive action.

Iceman whipped up an ice wall behind them with his left hand and kept replenishing the wall as the soldiers blasted it away. With his right hand he fired hail, icicles, whatever he could think of to disarm as many soldiers as he could reach. The best he could do was try to see that the others didn't get injured.

Storm whipped up a gale force wind that literally sucked the soldiers from the back of one of the transports and tossed them, none too gently, into the trees beyond. After that, half a dozen bolts of lightning struck the empty transport, which exploded in a blinding flash of heat. Her winds whisked the shrapnel away.

Bobby wanted to remind Storm of her admonition not to injure the soldiers, but thought better of it. Besides, he had more on his mind. A small band of soldiers had seen what he was doing, keeping the rear guard from moving in, and had begun to take aim directly at him. He had to defend himself, which left Hank, Wolverine, and Bishop undefended for the moment.

Which seemed fine by them.

Wolverine grabbed the nearest soldier and used him first as a shield and then as a battering ram as he took out a portion of the ground troops. The Beast dodged dozens of shots aimed at him, leaping over and diving under and finally landing on top of the troop transport. He grabbed Colonel Tomko and disappeared over the side before the colonel's troops knew what was happening.

Bishop, on the other hand, simply walked arrogantly into the midst of the troops and dealt with them hand to hand. He staggered under the impact of their plasma blasts, but he kept moving. Iceman knew that when Bishop absorbed that much energy, his eyes glowed with red rage and power. The man must have been a fearsome sight up close. For a moment, Bobby almost felt sorry for the soldiers.

One of them unholstered a traditional sidearm pistol and pointed it at Bishop's head. Despite the disdain that the man from the future had always shown him, Bobby didn't hesitate a moment. He brought both hands around and froze the pistol to a block of ice in the man's grip. Its weight made him fall to his knees.

Neglected, the ice wall behind him shattered into thousands of fragments, and nearly a dozen soldiers began their assault anew. Before he turned to deal with the threat, Bobby saw Wolverine take a hit, and Storm barely dodged one in the air. He knew Logan would recover, but if Hank or Ororo was hit . . . well, he couldn't let that happen.

"Back off, jarheads!" he shouted. "We're on your side!"

It began as a mental scream, but it built in his chest, adrenaline pumping, until it burst from his mouth like a savage war cry. The air around them became almost unbreathable as the Iceman ripped every ounce of moisture from it. This time his hands guided the waves of cold necessary to freeze the gathered moisture. In seconds, before they had any idea what was happening to them, the entire rear guard, eleven men in total, was buried up to their shoulders in a block of solid ice. They couldn't even move their trigger fingers, and that was how Bobby wanted it.

"Way to go!" Wolverine called from a dozen yards distant. Only the scorched hole in his uniform gave any indication he had been hit. Iceman envied him his healing factor, and not for the first time.

"Attention!" a familiar voice called. "Attention!"

Bobby looked up to see that Hank held the bullhorn in one hand and Colonel Tomko in the other.

"I believe the colonel has something he'd like to say," the Beast announced. Then he handed the bullhorn to the colonel, being certain to keep the commanding officer's body in front of his own.

"Listen closely, troops!" the colonel barked. "None of these muties leave here alive!"

Even from where he stood, fifty yards away, Bobby could see the look of astonishment on Hank's face. He couldn't help but smile. *So much for that idea, old buddy*, he thought. Still, they were winning. It would have gone a lot easier if they weren't so concerned with the health of their opponents, but that was all part of wearing the white hats. As opposed to these guys, who more often than not, wore gray ones.

So it might take a little longer, ten minutes instead of three, but they'd have it all wrapped up in just a . . .

Then the tank rolled up. Bobby had forgotten about the tank, hidden as it had been behind the remaining troop transport. Wolverine kept tearing through soldiers and energy weapons, using remarkable self restraint as far as Iceman was concerned. Storm was blowing a group of foot soldiers back into the woods, and they scurried away once they had lost their weapons. Beast was off-limits because he still had the colonel.

Bobby and Bishop were sitting ducks.

"We're in serious ca-ca," Iceman whispered, but forgot to laugh.

The turret swung around and the tank's big gun pointed right at him. He was moving before he knew it, building an ice slide under his feet, the momentum of its construction carrying him up and away from the battle instantly, even as the tank fired.

Iceman heard the nostalgic zap of a backyard electric bug killer, magnified to a deafening decibel level. His ice slide shattered as the plasma blast struck, and he fell nearly forty feet to the ground amidst a landslide of frozen boulders. Frantic, he looked up to see if the thing was taking aim at him again.

Bobby blinked twice, to be certain he was actually seeing the scene that played itself out before him. Amidst the confusion of the battle, at the center of the crossfire, Bishop walked slowly but determinedly toward the oncoming tank. Its gun turret swiveled until it pointed directly at his chest, but Bishop continued forward. The moment reminded Bobby of the unforgettable confrontation between a tank and a student in China's Tiananmen Square. With one major difference.

This time, the tank fired. Bishop was blasted backward with so much power that Bobby barely had time to erect an ice gutter in mid air that caught him and slid him to the ground as if he'd been running a luge track.

"Bishop, you okay?" Iceman asked as he knelt by his fallen teammate.

Bishop smiled. He stood, eyes blazing with molten crimson fury, and rose to his feet. His clenched fists glowed with barely contained power, and Bobby stood back a few feet, just in case it was too much for him to control.

"I'm better than okay, Iceman," Bishop laughed. "In fact, I'm grateful these morons don't know any better than to provide me with all the power I need to obliterate their armored vehicle from the face of the Earth."

Bishop brought his hands up, about to blast the tank. Above them, swooping toward the spot where they stood, Storm screamed for him to stop. Bobby was too stunned still to react. Luckily, he didn't have to. Just as Bishop let loose with a burst of energy that rocked his body, the Beast slammed into him from the left side, taking him down hard. Bishop's energy blast went wide, nearly vaporizing Storm, and instead decapitated half a dozen tree tops that crashed through lower limbs to the forest floor.

"Are you mad, Beast?" Bishop screamed as he got to his feet. "You could have been killed!"

"That's the point entirely, Bishop," Hank said, and finally Iceman's senses came back and he realized what had happened. Or almost happened.

"You're not supposed to kill anybody, remember, Bishop?" Bobby said.

Then he remembered the tank. He spun on one heel and saw that its turret was swinging around to target them.

"Can't have that," he mumbled to himself.

"Storm!" Iceman shouted. "I could really used some more moisture down here. Let's get this over with, shall we?"

He wasn't certain, at first, if she had heard him. Then she raised her hands and called out a dimly heard command to the sky. In that moment, with her white hair whipping in the wind, and the way she managed to look statuesque despite the fact that she was doing nothing less miraculous than standing on air, Bobby understood why she had once been considered a goddess.

As the big gun leveled itself, trying to lock in on Hank, Bishop, and Iceman, it began to rain. It wasn't a drizzle or even a squall, but a full fledged downpour, the likes of which came perhaps once a decade and brought rivers over their banks in mere hours. It was everything Iceman could have asked for, and more. He wondered, even as he raised his hands, why he and

Ororo had not truly used their powers in conjunction before.

Then he went quiet as he marveled at the effectiveness of the combination. The driving rain seemed to be sucked toward the tank as if it were a black hole, then froze on impact. In seconds, an impenetrable block of ice several yards thick surrounded the entire vehicle, save for the entry hatch on the top.

"Excellent work, Bobby," the Beast said next to him. "The tank is useless, but the soldiers inside will have no trouble getting out."

"That's it, run, ya bozos, before the ol' Canucklehead decides to take off the kid gloves," Wolverine called after the remaining soldiers, who were retreating despite the verbal abuse being heaped upon them by their bullhorn wielding colonel.

"That guy ought to count himself lucky you let him go," Bobby told Hank. "He just doesn't know when to quit."

"If you had to answer to Gyrich back home, you'd think twice about retreating as well, Robert," the Beast replied, prompting a moment of silence in which Iceman almost felt badly for Colonel Tomko. It didn't last long, though. After all, the guy had tried to kill them.

"Nice job, Drake," Wolverine said as he approached, more jovial than Bobby had seen him in quite some time. "We oughta name you MVP o' this little outing."

Bobby was glad to be Iceman at that moment. If he'd been pure flesh and blood, his friends would have seen him blush.

"Well done, Bobby," Hank said.

"You have my thanks, Iceman," Bishop said formally. "It is possible that I owe you my life."

Storm drifted to the ground nearby on winds of her

own creation, and smiled at Bobby as she came toward them.

"We might have been swifter," she said, "but not without doing far more damage than we did. There may be a few broken bones, some burns or shrapnel wounds, and of course, a lot of frostbite . . ."

She motioned behind them, and Iceman cocked his head to see where she was pointing, then laughed out loud. He had almost forgotten the soldiers that he had put on ice earlier.

"They'll thaw," he said.

"My guess is that the hard part is still to come, but all in all," Storm continued, "a job well done, particularly on your part, Iceman."

"Okay, now we're gettin' downright mushy," Logan said. "The kid was good, but let's not get carried away with ourselves. The day ain't over yet."

"Indeed it is not, Wolverine," Storm said. "It is time to turn our attention to the force field surrounding this installation."

Storm went on, but Iceman wasn't listening. He was proud of the part he'd played in the mission so far, and his friends' comments had put an almost painful smile on his face. Somehow, though, it wasn't enough.

Taking on a platoon of G.I. Joes was penny-ante stuff, and he knew it. He'd been all over the place during the battle, instrumental in making it happen, keeping both sides from serious injury. But against a more powerful enemy, Bobby Drake, the Iceman, was strictly a second-string player. Maybe second rate as well. If he was in charge of the group, he'd put his own wisecracking self on the bench until the game was in the bag or he had too many names on the injured reserve.

Normally, he would have shrugged off their praise, and his own insecurity, with bad puns and sarcastic humor. But he just didn't feel funny. Or all that triumphant, now that he thought of it. After all, as self-defeating as his particular neurotic tendencies were, he was convinced that his friends wouldn't have been so complimentary if they didn't expect less from him to begin with. But then, just because you're paranoid doesn't mean they aren't out to get you.

On the other hand, he had stopped Bishop from being shot, maybe killed. There was no doubt about that. And Bishop had no vested interest in coddling Bobby Drake. Quite the opposite. He found every opportunity to point out weaknesses, both in the team and in individuals. That was his way to make the X-Men function better, but it wasn't a really effective way to make friends.

Bishop had thanked him, complimented him. Bishop didn't care about him except in context of his field performance. Hence, Bishop meant what he said. Though he'd known Hank and Storm and Wolverine for a long time, Iceman began to feel a little better about himself because of Bishop's words. Maybe that's what it took, he thought. Someone with no motivation.

Maybe I didn't do too badly after all.

"First thing we do is have Bobby try to freeze the force field, see if we can't stretch a hole in it," Storm said. "If that doesn't work, then . . . well, let's see if that does work."

But Bobby's ice powers, and Ororo's weather manipulation, had no effect on the field. There was little Hank or Logan could do with their bare hands or claws.

"I might be able to rig up a polarity field and cut us

a hole with the *Blackbird*'s communications system," Hank offered. "Not likely, but not necessarily impossible."

Iceman noticed that the soldiers had regrouped, but were keeping a respectful distance. He could only assume that they were waiting to see if the X-Men could get the force field down, maybe do their jobs for them. Once again, he couldn't blame them.

"Before you try that," Storm said thoughtfully, "why don't we let Bishop try to tear a hole in the field by siphoning off some of its energy."

"That just might accomplish our objective," the Beast replied. "Though if we'd been able to generate an ratiocination of the field from the *Blackbird*'s on-board systems, we'd possess a better idea of what we were preparing to confront."

"Bishop, are you willing?" Storm asked.

"As always, I am at your service, Storm," Bishop answered.

Iceman raised an eyebrow. Though he never would have expected it as a kid, or even as a young man joining the X-Men, he considered himself a fairly courageous person. With the X-Men, that was just part of the job description. But that didn't mean that he was never afraid, or that facing danger didn't give him pause. He suspected the same might be true, to varying degrees, of most of his friends and teammates.

It was different with Wolverine and Bishop, though. They didn't just do what needed to be done, they did it without batting an eyelash. Bishop had no idea what effect the force field might have on him. But if it meant the success of the mission, he would try to siphon its energy even if it might fry him on the spot.

"No matter what happens, regardless of what awaits

us inside, we cannot allow the Sentinels to roam the Earth," Bishop said gravely, as if reading Iceman's thoughts. "It would mean the end of your world, and the beginning of mine. Trust me. You don't want that to happen."

Without another word, he jogged to where the crackling energy of the force field met the ground, only inches in that spot from the installation's perimeter fence. Palms up, Bishop slammed his hands against the force field, grunting with obvious pain as sparks flew under his hands.

Then his hands passed through the field. His fingers locked on the fence and he stood rigid, as if electricity coursed through his body. Bobby stood with the rest of them, and he could feel their tension. Each was prepared to pull Bishop away from this contact if he seemed in any danger.

A wondrous thing began to happen. Where his wrists passed through the field, twin holes began to open. They widened quickly, and Bishop stood back from the fence, hands raised above him as the force field's energy flowed into him.

"Hurry," he grunted. "This won't last very long."

They slipped by him, taking great care not to make contact with the edges of the field. Wolverine's claws popped out with their familiar *snikt*, and he slashed them a passage through the perimeter fence.

Once they were all inside, Bishop slipped through and allowed the force field to close behind him. Once again, he was charged to overflowing, power bursting from his eyes and hands. He would have to release it shortly, or it could overwhelm him.

"Welcome, X-Men!" a female voice called. "And farewell."

Iceman recognized them at once, of course. The Acolytes' magenta and crimson uniforms were unmistakable. Voght had spoken, but Bobby saw Senyaka and Unuscione and several others as well.

"Bright lady preserve us," Storm said, just loud enough for the team to hear. "What does Magneto want with the Sentinels?"

"Darlin'," Wolverine growled, "I'd say it's high time we found out."

In seconds, the battle was joined, and Iceman winced at the thundercrack of energy that told him Bishop had found the release he needed. Perhaps he had performed well earlier, as his friends had insisted. But now they'd moved up to the big leagues.

If he struck out now, he was dead.

CHAPTER 9

The marketplace was in chaos. Starbolt and Gladiator flew back and forth above the panicked crowd, and Gambit knew they wouldn't have come alone. Storefronts were quickly shuttered, but merchants with carts were not so lucky. Several were turned over, including one with a cauldron of spicy-smelling stew that splashed onto Gambit's boots.

Run! Try to blend in!

Gambit heard Jean's mental shout as though she were whispering in his ear. His first impulse was to ignore it—Remy LeBeau didn't like to run from a fight. But in his time with the X-Men he'd come to understand their priorities, and to adapt to them. The mission was more important than personal pride. And they couldn't expect help from the Kree rebels, who had long-term concerns. They disappeared, blending into the crowd in an instant.

Gambit saw Cyclops keeping pace with a family. They headed for a side alley and the X-Men's leader helped carry the smallest child, who looked injured. It wouldn't do for all of them to be separated, he realized, and set off after Cyclops through a sea of madness.

A hand clamped on his shoulder, and Gambit reacted instantly. He threw out his hip, grabbed that hand and threw his attacker several feet into a fountain that still bubbled at the market's center. Only when the figure splashed into the water did he realize it was Raza.

"Sorry t' get you wet, *homme*," he said as he helped Raza to his feet. "In de future, you jus' might want to t'ink 'bout saying hello 'fore you put your hands on somebody like dat, eh?"

When Raza looked up, he was not smiling. His face was filled with rage, but his eyes were glazed and seemed to focus on something other than Gambit. But there was no mistaking his intent as he drew his sword and lunged for Remy's gut.

Gambit cursed and dodged to one side. Raza's sword tore a long slice from his ragged Kree jacket, and he shrugged the confining garment off. He slammed his hands down on Raza's back and rammed his knee up into the swordsman's stomach.

"You gettin' slow in your old age, Starjammer," Gambit said. "What does Gambit have to do to show you dis ain't de time for a rematch?"

He and Raza struggled, and the Shi'ar warrior went for his blaster. Before Gambit could stop him, Raza had drawn the weapon and was about to bring it to bear on the Cajun's face. Remy wasn't about to allow that. He let go of Raza's arm and grabbed hold of the blaster instead, instantly charging it was explosive force. He staggered Raza with a southpaw to the temple, then dove out of the way as the blaster exploded in Raza's cyborg hand.

"What de hell was dat all about?" Gambit asked aloud.

"Oracle."

Gambit turned to see that Jean had come up next to him undetected. Her Kree disguise was still working, at least visibly. A young, pink-skinned Kree female slammed into Remy. She looked up at him for a moment, took a fearful glance behind her, then kept running. He looked to see what had frightened her so, and there, towering above the marketplace, was Titan of the Imperial Guard.

He stood nearly forty feet high, perhaps more, though Gambit didn't know if Titan had a limit to how tall he could grow. The shining blue and brown emblazoned across his chest were a startling contrast to the dingy colors of the marketplace. Each step was half a block, and his head turned from side to side as his eyes scanned the crowd.

The thinning crowd. Gambit felt suddenly vulnerable as he noticed how quickly the marketplace was emptying.

"Remy, let's go!" Jean said.

"Wait," he stopped her. "What about Oracle?"

"Well, she's got to be with them or they wouldn't have found us," Jean answered. "I'm scanning for her but she's not only shielded, she's controlling several members of the crowd, and she was controlling Raza. All of that's throwing me off."

"But you're much more powerful den her, right, *chere*?" Gambit said, looking for reassurance.

"Once I find her, sure," she said, pulling him along. "And she can't take over any of the X-Men because of the psychic shields that the Professor has implanted in all of us. It's just a matter of time. If I can't find her, I'll just shield us until . . ."

Jean slammed into a wall and was pushed to one side. Gambit cursed as he saw that the wall was actually the Imperial Guardsmen known as Warstar. The green armored, robotic looking pair were actually mechanoid symbiotes, sentient machines that could not operate separately. C'Cil was the workhorse, stupid but nearly fifteen feet tall and immeasurably strong. B'Nee, the brains of the duo, was the size of an average human, and rode on C'Cil's back. While he was far less powerful, his touch was electrified. Together, they could tear Gambit apart.

If they could get their hands on him.

"We do not wish to harm you, X-Men," B'Nee said from his piggyback position. "We have been instructed to capture you. Surrender and survive."

Remy saw that Jean had already gotten to her feet and was about to attack Warstar. He shook his head, thinking the words *back off* as hard as he could and hoping she would pick them up. She stepped back and looked at him curiously. Warstar must have assumed they'd knocked her out, Gambit realized.

"I don' t'ink you realize who you're dealing with," he said. "But Gambit will be more den pleased to show you."

Even as he spoke, Gambit whipped several playing cards from one of the many pockets inside his long duster jacket. They were charged before they left his hands, and his aim was true. The cards struck B'Nee's shining, android-like eyes. The symbiotes screamed together, feeling one another's pain. C'Cil could still see, and batted an arm out to try to take Gambit down. Rage and pain made Warstar clumsy, however, and Gambit dodged to one side and telescoped his bo staff to maximum length right between C'Cil's legs.

"Get out of here, Jeannie," the Cajun said. "Take Oracle down or we don' got any hope of gettin' out of here."

Jean nodded and ran for cover down the same alley Cyclops had gone down only moments earlier. There was shouting above him, and Gambit looked up to see that Archangel and Rogue were both airborne, battling Gladiator and Starbolt in the sky.

"So much for gettin' away wit'out a fight," he said, and smiled. This was more his style anyway. Something, or someone, crashed through the roof of the building to his left. He didn't have time to see if it was one of the X-Men or the Imperial Guard, however, since Warstar had already regained his feet.

"You move quickly for a Terran, Gambit," B'Nee said in that metallic voice that reminded Remy of crinkling tinfoil. "But in the end you know you are no match for us."

Then Warstar moved, C'Cil's arms flashing forward to grab Gambit by the shoulders. He was stunned at the huge mechanoid's speed, and couldn't dodge in time. In seconds, C'Cil was crushing Gambit between his huge hands. Remy's shoulders and ribs felt like they were ready to snap. No question, the alien was right. He was outmatched.

But Remy LeBeau never gave up. That was a lesson he had learned long before he had ever joined the X-Men.

Gambit swung his legs up, ignoring the popping sound that might well have been his shoulder coming out of its socket. He planted his feet against Warstar's chest and shoved with all his strength. The speed of the movement caught Warstar by surprise and he was able to break C'Cil's grip. But that only lasted for a moment. He was falling toward the ground when C'Cil clamped down on his legs painfully. Once again, he was caught.

But his arms were free. His hands were free. Gambit didn't know, really, what Warstar was made of. The thing might have been nothing more than an artificially intelligent robot, or a sentient, naturally born alien species. He only hoped there was nothing flesh and blood about it, because he had already realized there was only one way to get away from the behemoth.

Remy reached out and grabbed C'Cil's upper thighs with his hands.

"Sorry 'bout this, *mes amis*," he said. "It don' seem like your heart's in dis fight, but dere's no other way."

Explosive energy was funneled through Gambit's hands and into C'Cil's legs, which began to glow. He swung his body up to get his face out of the way, just as the charge released. C'Cil's legs were blown off and Warstar crashed to the ground, the two symbiotic creatures shrieking a duet of agony.

Raza was still unconscious, but Gambit dragged him over to the shattered fountain and splashed water on his face. He sputtered, but when he saw their current situation, he rose in silence and retrieved his sword. Even as they ran to help the others, Gambit heard B'Nee's eerie voice behind him.

"Initiating self repair," B'Nee said.

"Oh, dat's jus' wonderful," Remy said, and they ran even faster.

* * *

In a tiny hovel that a blue-skinned Kree merchant and his family called home, Cyclops helped to set the broken leg of the youngest daughter. She looked at him in terror, and he couldn't blame her. With the insanity raging outside her door, it couldn't have been much of a comfort to be helped by an alien whose eyes were covered by a blood-red visor.

Scott! Jean's voice entered his mind. *We've got to find*

Oracle or we'll never get out of here. I'm showing you my position telepathically. Get here as quickly as you can.

He finished tying the makeshift splint to the girl's leg, and ignored the thanks of her parents as he dashed out to meet Jean. Cyclops had known people with psi talents all of his adult life, and part of his youth. But Professor Xavier and Jean never used their abilities on an individual without consent. Other than in battle, of course. Despite the psionic shields that were in his mind, and the comfort level he had achieved with his constant psi-link with Jean, it disturbed Cyclops deeply to know that Oracle was out there, monitoring their location. Perhaps their thoughts as well.

Jean stood at the corner of a small alley just ahead, and Scott couldn't help being both pleased to see her and anxious for her welfare. He didn't have time to worry further, though. At that moment, Titan stepped into view. Cyclops thought he might dive into the alley and avoid being spotted, but the huge Guardsman clearly knew right where to look.

Jean was right. There was nothing they could do until she found Oracle. Unless . . .

"Jean," he shouted, even as Titan began to reach for him. "Can't you shield us all from Oracle?"

"Of course," she snapped. "But what good will that do unless we're out of sight?"

Foolish question, Scott chided himself. He unleashed a full power optic blast at Titan's chest even as a huge hand was about to close on his chest. The Guardsman was staggered, and stumbled back several steps, which gave Scott and Jean time to disappear down the alley.

It wasn't going to work, though. They were on the next block when Titan called to them.

"Don't try to escape X-Men!" he said. "There's no-where you can run that I can't find you."

Titan had grown even taller, and now simply stepped over the row of low buildings and into their path.

"Quick," Jean said, pulling Scott toward a partially destroyed storefront. "She's this way."

"What about Titan?" Scott asked.

"Oracle's more important . . . Scott, heads up!"

Where Jean was pointing, Oracle had stepped into full view from a darkened doorway. Obviously, she knew that she couldn't keep herself hidden from Jean forever. But what was her plan now? The Royal Elite Corps of the Shi'ar Imperial Guard did not surrender.

Cyclops blasted Titan again as the Guardsman came for him, but this new attack seemed to have less effect.

"She's gotten more powerful," Jean said through clenched teeth, and only then did Scott realize that she and Oracle were locked in a battle of mental will and psionic strength.

Titan was faster than he realized, and before Cyclops could return his attention to their fight, the Guards-man had lifted him off the ground and turned him up-side down. Disoriented and struggling for breath, Cyclops let off a half-hearted optic blast. Titan held him so tight it was almost impossible to breathe, and Scott's vision began to dim.

Jean . . . he thought, but knew that she couldn't take on Titan until Oracle was down. He was in trouble.

* * *

Rogue and Gladiator had been trading blows for minutes, and she knew he was holding back. Her own strength was phenomenal, and her flesh nearly invul-nerable to injury. She could go toe to toe with just about any being she had ever run across, and at least give a good accounting of herself. Gladiator was in another class entirely. His strength was such that any measure she could imagine could not define its limits.

"Pretty clear to me y'all don't wanna be here," she said finally. "Why don't you let us just disappear, sugar? I promise this ol' gal won't tell nobody."

They were more than one hundred feet in the air. Unlike Archangel, who needed his wings to stay aloft, their powers of flight were energy based, generated from their bodies. When they faced one another down, the only reason it couldn't be called a standoff was because they weren't standing.

"As long as I am on Hala, I must do as Deathbird commands," Gladiator said, and struck Rogue a blow that snapped her neck back and shot her more than three hundred yards away.

When she was able to stop herself, she saw Archangel close by, keeping Starbolt busy. The Guardsman was sheathed completely in an undulating wave of energy that was somewhat similar to fire. His red uniform flowed in the same manner, and Rogue thought for a moment that it, too, might be generated from the alien's body.

Archangel was dodging Starbolt, his organic metal wings flashing in the sun. A barrage of silver feathers exploded from his left wing. They were tipped with a chemical that would paralyze any enemy, and Rogue thought Warren had it won there and then. Archangel obviously knew better, for he dodged out of the way of another blast of energy from Starbolt even as his feathers melted to slag before they could ever reach their target.

Rogue wanted to help him, but she had Gladiator to

think of. She massaged her jaw. Invulnerable or not, it was starting to hurt. She was about to go after him, but didn't have to. Gladiator came to her.

"Yer pullin' those punches, Gladiator," she said. "Not that I'm complainin' mind you. But why don't you stop this foolishness? You know Deathbird's a crazy . . ."

Gladiator swung at her again, but Rogue wasn't about to take another one of his punches, whether he was pulling them or not. She feinted left, then simply ducked. The momentum of his punch pulled him forward in the air and Rogue put every ounce of her formidable strength behind an uppercut to Gladiator's jaw. She felt a surge of pride in her chest as he shot up and backward a fair distance. He might be inconceivably strong, but that didn't mean he couldn't be hurt.

"Damn shame," she muttered to herself. "Even with the mohawk and purple skin, he's a fine lookin' man."

She smiled, knowing Gambit would be jealous to hear her say such things. Or at least, she hoped he would.

Even before the smile was off her face, Gladiator was rocketing at her again. Rogue knew that his speed, like his strength, far exceeded her own. Despite her flippant façade, she was an extremely intelligent young woman. She knew, without question, that she was not going to win her battle with Gladiator by using her fists.

Beyond the other abilities she had, which she usually thought of as gifts, was another power. A curse. The bane of her existence. Whenever her bare skin touched that of another being, she absorbed their memories, special skills and abilities and, if they had them, extranormal powers. She knew she would have to risk absorbing Gladiator's powers, and try not to take too much. Once before, she had permanently stolen another person's memories and abilities. She never wanted that to happen again.

Problem was, Gladiator was covered from neck to toe. Only his face was bare. It wasn't going to be easy to get that close. Still, Rogue had to try.

Only seconds after she'd hit him, Gladiator was at her again. Rogue could see that he was angry, that there would be no more punches pulled in this fight, no matter how conflicted he might be about his orders. She tried to dodge and reach for his face, but he was going much too fast.

Gladiator slammed both fists into her at extraordinary speed. Her eyes fluttered as she hurtled backward and she thought she might pass out from the pain and air pressure. Rogue could no longer concentrate on staying aloft, and crashed to the ground like a humanoid meteor. So dazed was she by Gladiator's strike, that she barely felt herself hit the planet's surface.

It took her a precious few seconds to come around, and when she did, the battle had moved directly overhead. Archangel was trying to use both sets of wings to slash at Starbolt, with no success, and Gladiator was moving in on them. Several blocks away, Rogue could see Titan over the rooftops. He had Cyclops in his grip.

All in all, Rogue figured it wasn't going too well. She wondered how Gambit and Raza were faring, and where Jean had gotten off to.

Then she had an idea.

Shooting from the ground at top speed, she reached Archangel and Starbolt just before Gladiator.

"Warren!" she shouted. "Take out the big guy with your wing knives!"

Rogue hauled back her fist and belted Starbolt with only a fraction of her strength, then caught him as he began to fall, barely conscious. She watched as Archangel's wings curled up behind him, reacting to her words seemingly before Warren could consciously command them. Gladiator tried to reach for him, but Archangel's wing knives flashed out by the dozens, slashing through his Shi'ar body armor. Although Gladiator's skin was nearly impenetrable, the feathers were enough to scratch him.

With his strength and speed, Rogue had gambled that Gladiator's metabolism would absorb the paralyzing chemical on Warren's wing knives almost immediately. She was right. The Praetor of the Guard slowed down drastically. He reached for Warren and missed, and then began to drift aimlessly toward the ground under the planet's gravitational influence.

"Way to go, Warren," she cried.

It wouldn't last long, Rogue knew. They had to make the best of it. Pushing away the fear of using her hated power, she pulled off one of her gloves, and reached for Starbolt's face.

"No offense, hon', but I really don't feel like kissin' you, okay?" she said, forcing a smile she didn't feel.

Invulnerable to the flaming energy of his body, Rogue touched Starbolt's cheek. Immediately, she absorbed his powers and part of his psyche. As she pulled her glove back on, she already knew why the Guard had come to Hala and what their responsibilities were to Deathbird. She understood, finally, their hesitation in battle. But there was nothing to be done about it. The X-Men couldn't very well surrender simply because their opponents were half-hearted about their mission.

"Scott's in trouble, Rogue," Archangel called, and

with the fury of battle etched on his face, Rogue
thought Warren looked incredibly sinister.

"What are we waitin' for, sugar?" she asked, and let
go of Starbolt. She hadn't siphoned all his power, and
she knew from his memories that the fall wouldn't do
him too much harm.

Side by side, Archangel and Rogue flew at Titan's
face. She glowed with Starbolt's fiery energy, and
blasted wave after wave of the burning power at the
giant. Simultaneously, Warren shot wing-knives at Titan's upper body. The gargantuan alien began to grow
even larger, trying to counteract their paralyzing effect. Under Rogue and Archangel's combined assault,
Titan was forced to drop Cyclops. As Rogue continued
to keep Titan busy, Warren swooped down to catch
their leader.

She looked down to see Archangel handing a shaky
looking Cyclops over to Gambit and Raza.

When she looked back up, Gladiator's fist was in her
face.

* * *

"*Ma chere, non!*" Gambit yelled as Gladiator pummeled
Rogue, holding her with one hand and landing several
blows with the other.

"'Angel," Remy said, grabbing Warren's arm. "Get
me up dere an' I blow his head off!"

Archangel was already flying. "Sorry, Gambit," he
called back. "You'll only slow me down."

Gambit cursed and chewed his lip as he watched
Archangel streak into the air toward Gladiator and
Rogue. Despite the distance, he could see Rogue trying
weakly to fight back. With her one bare hand, she
reached out for Gladiator's face, and Gambit knew she

meant to absorb his powers. Unfortunately, it appeared that Gladiator knew it too. He struck her one last time, a backhand across the face, but didn't hold on.

"*Mon Dieu*," Gambit whispered in awe and horror as Rogue was thrown by the blow. Gladiator had hit her with such force that by the count of three, she had disappeared from sight.

Archangel flew directly at Gladiator, and Gambit found a new, profound respect for Warren Worthington. Gladiator could destroy him in a heartbeat if he got close enough, but Warren didn't turn away. For Remy LeBeau, who had always been a cynic when it came to the concept of bravery, it was a lesson not soon to be forgotten.

Perhaps afraid that Archangel would use his wing-knives again, Gladiator took the fight to Warren. Just as the two were about to clash, a huge hand shot up from below and simply plucked Warren from the air.

"You're making me angry little bird," Titan said, his voice like intense thunder across the sky, so large had he grown.

Gambit looked back at Gladiator, who was scanning the ground. Their eyes met, and the Cajun's lip began to curl. His hands crackled with explosive energy.

"Come down 'ere, *homme*," he snarled. "Gambit'll show you what we do back in New Orleans to men who hit ladies."

"Gambit!" Cyclops said, shaking him.

Remy was frozen in place a moment longer, then turned to see that Scott seemed to have fully recovered from his bout with Titan.

"Listen to me," he was saying, though Gambit was so stunned by what had happened to Rogue that it took him a moment to hear the words. "Jean is a block behind you. Take Raza and retreat. Warren will be along shortly."

Gambit stared at him. His gaze was drawn to where, past Cyclops' shoulder, Raza was trying to fight off a completely repaired Warstar with only his sword. Gambit had a moment to regret blowing up the Starjammer's blaster, but pushed the thought away.

"You got to be jokin' wit' Gambit, Cyclops," he said. "You t'ink I . . ."

"That's an order, Remy!" Cyclops shouted. "I can't take time to explain myself to you, damn it. Just go!"

He spun on his heel and let off an optic blast of bubbling red energy that cleanly severed C'Cil's left arm. A blast of lower intensity followed and knocked B'Nee from C'Cil's back. Warstar was out of the game for a moment.

"Raza!" Gambit called. "Let's get out of here. De boss man got a plan!"

Raza looked back to where C'Cil had picked up his arm and was holding it to the sparking metal stump. The mechanoid was already knitting itself back together, and B'Nee was advancing on Raza. The Shi'ar warrior lunged toward B'Nee with his sword, then turned and raced after Gambit, catching up to him in mere seconds.

Gambit looked over his shoulder as they ran. Cyclops let loose with a wide beamed blast of red glowing energy that was so powerful it knocked Titan off his feet and forced him to let Archangel go. Remy winced, thinking about the Kree that might be trapped when his enormous body fell on already weakened structures. Archangel flew, somewhat shakily, in the same direction Gambit and Raza were running, and Remy wondered how he had come to know of Cyclops's plan, whatever it might be.

"Gambit! Raza! Come on!" Jean shouted.

Remy looked up to see her in a standoff against Oracle. Oracle was certainly the most attractive member of the guard, he'd always thought. Her ice blue hair and snow white skin were set off by a uniform of pink and lavender. Very feminine but not exactly battle wear. Though, as a telepath, Gambit figured Oracle didn't see much hand-to-hand fighting. As a psi and a physical combatant, Jean was far superior. Gambit didn't understand why she hadn't put Oracle down within minutes of the fight beginning.

"I never imagined the X-Men were cowards," a deep voice boomed behind them, and Gambit risked another glance to see that Gladiator was flying down toward them, ignoring Cyclops, who was busy battling Warstar again.

That was a mistake. Gambit had fought alongside Cyclops long enough to know that, level-headed as he may have been, when his cool, calm leadership tactics were put aside for full-on war, Scott Summers was a dangerous man.

The whipcrack sound of Cyclops' optic blast came simultaneous with the blast itself, which struck Gladiator in the back of the head and sent him somersaulting through the air. Gambit thought he smelled singed mohawk. If there was one thing they all knew about Gladiator, it was that he had a temper. If they hadn't already known it, they would have discovered it now.

The Praetor of the Shi'ar Imperial Guard ignored the other X-Men and shot in the opposite direction, heading for Cyclops. Visible rays of heat and light, like the power of tiny suns, shot from Gladiator's eyes right at the leader of the X-Men, and Cyclops met them with his own optic blasts. Gladiator had seemed to be holding off, wanting to capture the X-Men unharmed. That had changed when his temper finally boiled over. Otherwise he never would have used his eye beams, a power he rarely took advantage of. Gambit wondered if there were limits to that energy.

"Get over here!" Jean yelled, and Gambit turned to face her again.

Jean Grey had seemed to struggle with Oracle, but as Gambit, Raza, and Archangel approached, the look of desperation left her face. She raised her hands in a commanding gesture. Oracle cried out in pain, clutched her head and crumpled to the ground. The Shi'ar woman groaned in pain and moved slowly, trying to rise. Jean ignored her, and turned to face the other X-Men.

"We've got to get to some cover," she said. "I can shield us from Oracle if none of the others can see us."

"You could have taken Oracle out at any time," Archangel said. "What was the point of stalling, Jean? We're in real trouble here."

"Not if we retreat now," she said sharply.

"What of Cyclops?" Raza asked.

"Come on, *chere*," Gambit urged. "You love de man. We can't just leave him behind! And what about Rogue?"

Gambit studied Jean's face. She had seemed colder than he'd ever known her, hardened to the bleak reality of the situation. But if what Archangel said was true about her not fighting full force against Oracle—and Gambit thought it probably was—what was the point of the battle in the first place? As he watched her, Jean's brow furrowed and she bit her lip. It was a look Gambit had seen on the faces of too many people, too many women. It was a look of regret.

"I've already got a mental fix on Rogue," Jean answered. "We'll go to her now. As for Scott, he'll have to fend for himself."

The air was humming with the energy of Scott's optic blasts and Gladiator's super-heated vision. They all turned toward the spot where Cyclops was making a stand against the Imperial Guard, completely alone. Warstar had completed its repairs and was approaching from behind. A newly recovered Starbolt and the infuriated Gladiator were blasting him from the sky. Titan was holding back for the moment, but was just looking for an opportunity to snatch Cyclops up again.

Starbolt fired a solid ball of energy, which Cyclops easily dispersed with his own optic blasts. But the barrage from Starbolt and Gladiator together was too much for him. While he was deflecting another attack from Starbolt, a blast of Gladiator's heat vision knocked him down. In an eyeblink, Gladiator stood on the ground in front of him. The Guardsman hit Cyclops hard enough to leave him unconscious in the dust. The waiting Titan finally scooped their leader off the ground.

"We can't just stand by and watch this," Archangel said.

"An' we ain't gonna," Gambit snarled and started heading back the way he'd come, hoping Raza and Archangel were following him.

Gambit, stop! Jean's thought-command struck him almost like a weapon, and he staggered under its power. Still, it was only communication, not an attempt to manipulate his mind. And his mind had only one goal: to save Cyclops.

"Cyclops gave you an order, Gambit," Jean said. "Follow it now or you'll blow the whole mission."

"You mean all dis is . . . ?" he began to ask, but Jean grabbed his arm and began dragging him away, Raza and Warren with them.

"There's no time for this," Jean said. "We can't allow ourselves to be captured."

Gambit ran alongside the others, but his mind raced even faster, trying to figure out what was going on. They'd been doing fairly well against the Guard, except perhaps for Cyclops and Jean. But maybe that was it. Maybe Cyclops was supposed to be captured.

"If dis was part of a plan," he said quietly to Jean as they ran, "I hope you know what you doin'. Be a shame if Cyclops got killed 'cause we didn't step in for him."

Jean didn't respond. Nor did she look his way. But even in profile, Gambit could see the fear in her eyes.

CHAPTER 10

"**Y**ou are either a spineless coward or a traitor to the Empire!" Deathbird spat in anger as she paced the Great Hall of the Capitol Building.

Her governmental seat, an actual chair in which she sat when making public declarations, was too similar in appearance to a throne as far as Gladiator was concerned. Its ornamentation was a reflection of the ostentatious decoration of the entire room. So regal were her surroundings, that Deathbird's court might be considered insulting and even blasphemous by many on the Shi'ar homeworld of Chandilar.

It was improper. His dislike for the Viceroy had multiplied dramatically over the previous few hours, and yet here he was, putting up with her abuse once more. For one of his station, there could be no retribution, no response at all other than respect and obedience.

"Viceroy, I have attempted to explain," he began patiently and was encouraged when Deathbird merely glared at him rather than launch into another verbal tirade.

"We were on the verge of overall victory and the apprehension of five X-Men and one member of the band of pirates known as Starjammers," Gladiator insisted, and ignored Deathbird's angry muttering about the Starjammers. He himself was bewildered by the actions of the cyborg Raza, who was born of the Shi'ar and yet whose cause was not often the same as the Empire's.

Gladiator gestured toward Cyclops, who knelt on the floor in front of Deathbird's seat of power. His arms and legs were bound, and a clamp had been placed around his eyes. The only other people in the Great Hall were the other four members of the Guard who had accompanied him. Gladiator ignored them, however, and concentrated on Cyclops.

"We had finally felled this one, taking him immediately into captivity," Gladiator announced. "Unfortunately, Oracle had lost her battle with one of the X-Men, and when we searched for the others, they were nowhere to be found."

Deathbird's lip curled and the feathers atop her head and under her arms ruffled with the shiver that passed through her. She strode furiously across the dais to where Cyclops knelt and gave him a savage kick to the head. Gladiator grimaced as the X-Men's leader grunted and fell to the ground, blood spilling down his right cheek.

"They are probably all working with the damned Kree rebels," Deathbird hissed, eyes ablaze with paranoia and hatred.

"None of the Kree came to their aid, Viceroy," Gladiator said. "I doubt that . . ."

"When I want your opinion, Gladiator, I will command it of you," she roared. "If you and your fellow Guards were more than incompetent fools, all of the X-Men would be in this room, awaiting execution."

Gladiator heard hushed cursing behind him and felt the heat of Starbolt's power surging.

"That's enough!" Starbolt growled. "I would dearly have loved to see any of your personal guard last more than a few moments with the X-Men, Viceroy. The Imperial Guard is ever vigilant and loyal to the Majestrix of the Imperium. You would do well not to question . . ."

"Starbolt," Gladiator said coldly, but with an air of command that caused the Guardsman to go silent.

"No, Gladiator," Deathbird said sweetly. "Let your man continue. After all, despite the Imperial Guard's failure and buffoonery, I have yet to question your loyalty. As Starbolt has breached the subject, and seems to hold the X-Men in such high regard, perhaps I was hasty in assuming that your failure was due to cowardice or idiocy. Perhaps I ought to have thought about treachery and treason."

There was absolute silence in the Great Hall, broken only by the occasional groan from the unconscious Cyclops.

Far too often, Gladiator's temper had gotten him in trouble as a youth. As he matured, he had found a way to harness it, to bury it beneath reason, calm, dedication. He was a soldier, and a good one. That meant swallowing his personal pride from time to time and holding the pride of the Imperium above it. It was a hard discipline to learn, and once he had, remaining true to it was his entire life.

And yet . . .

Surely, Starbolt had been out of line. It was possible that Deathbird could attempt to prosecute him for treason and insubordination, and perhaps even succeed. But Gladiator had taken just about all he could stand for from the Viceroy, and he wasn't about to lose one of his best warriors to her rampant paranoia, or worse, in one of her insane games of power and manipulation.

"You are silent, Gladiator," Deathbird said, eyes narrowing. "Could it be my words have struck upon the truth? Shall I have all five of you executed with the rebels, instead of just Starbolt?"

She looked at him with the gaze of a vulture sighting carrion. But Gladiator was no dead thing, unable to fight or even run. In truth, he was most dangerous prey, and not nearly as dull-witted as Deathbird so obviously assumed.

"Starbolt spoke in anger and haste, Viceroy, because you goaded and insulted him," Gladiator declared, stepping onto the dais and stopping mere feet from Deathbird.

"Do not test yourself against me, Praetor," she began, but Gladiator would not be stopped.

"As a member of the Royal Elite of the Imperial Guard, Starbolt will be officially reprimanded for his insolence, and there is the possibility of punitive action," he said. "However, such may only be determined by the Majestrix. And you," Gladiator said in a low, threatening voice, "are not she."

Deathbird's features contorted with rage.

"I do not need a reminder from one such as you!" she shrieked. "For your insolence and insubordination I will have you executed this very day! I will . . ."

"You forget yourself, Viceroy," Gladiator said calmly. "You forget as well that few may claim to know the laws of the Imperium and the responsibilities of its citizens—and that of my post—better than I.

"I am not guilty of insubordination, but if I were, it would be the Majestrix's place to determine my guilt and punishment, just as it is in the case of Starbolt. As you instructed, we found the X-Men. Though we failed to bring them all back, we have captured their leader. You have decided to execute him, and as long as you have cause, that is your prerogative.

"As long as you continue to act on behalf of the Imperium and the Majestrix, and in accordance with her commands, the Imperial Guard is yours to command until the prisoners have been executed or we are recalled by the Majestrix herself. If you think to take some action against the Guard, I urge you to reconsider, at least long enough to consider the repercussions."

Gladiator turned away from the primal fury that warped Deathbird's features. The four Guards who had accompanied him, including the volatile Starbolt, stood well back from the dais, heads lowered and eyes on the stone floor. Cyclops still lay on the ground but, though his eyes were covered, Gladiator thought he seemed alert and awake. He had a moment of uncertainty, knowing that Deathbird was at least partially correct, that they had not fought as hard as they could have against the X-Men. He brushed the thought away. It did not matter to the questions at hand.

Once more on the stone floor, Gladiator turned to face Deathbird once again. She seemed to have regained much of her composure, but still stared at him with hate-filled eyes. She raised her chin and looked down her nose at him with a haughty manner he was long familiar with.

"Take the prisoner to the others," she said finally. "Confine them together, and they may die together at first light. Then take the Guard out again and search for the others. Do not return until you have found them, or the Majestrix herself shall have to come to retrieve you," Deathbird said, smiling cruelly as she gave the order.

Gladiator was tempted not to respond. It would be easy enough to follow the Viceroy's order and allow things to happen as they would. If it were not that he felt some guilt for his reluctance in battle, he might indeed have kept his silence. In the end, he could not.

"I do not question your wisdom, Viceroy," he began. "However, we have battled these X-Men in the past, as have you. You know their loyalty to one another. Don't you think the others will come back for their leader? And if so, should not the Guard be here to prevent them from freeing *all* the prisoners?"

"You slow-witted fool," Deathbird hissed. "They are involved with the rebellion, I have told you. The rebellion will not sacrifice itself for one individual, or four. And even if they were foolhardy enough to storm the Capitol, which they must know would be tantamount to suicide, my own guards would be more than sufficient to repel and capture them."

Gladiator considered her words a moment, fighting the urge to respond. When he had overcome it, he motioned for the other Guards to lift Cyclops and convey him to the prison levels far below them.

Not for the first time, Gladiator wondered if Deathbird was merely an evil, paranoid schemer, or truly insane. He still was unable to make a conclusive judgment, a fact that profoundly disturbed him. One way or another, Deathbird was unpredictable and dangerous. If the answer that his instincts gave was true, and the Viceroy was both evil and insane, then they might all be in grave danger.

* * *

His head throbbed dully where Deathbird had kicked him, and a more traditional ache had spread from behind his eyes to the back of his cranium. Still, Cyclops had lain silent, listening intently to the confrontation between Gladiator and Deathbird. If there had been any doubt in his mind that the Praetor of the Guard was in personal turmoil over the latest conflict with the X-Men, that conversation had erased it.

Unfortunately, Cyclops had encountered Gladiator frequently enough to know that the alien would do nothing to save him. Remorseful though he might be, Gladiator was loyal to the Imperium. Cyclops could not hope for rescue from that avenue. Luckily, that hadn't been part of the plan.

At the very moment the Imperial Guard had attacked the marketplace, Scott and Jean had communicated through the psychic rapport they shared. They had no idea exactly where in the Capitol Building Corsair and the others were being held, except that they were on a lower level. They had to expect that it would not be easy for Jean to telepathically scan for them, that there would be psi-blocks in place even if they had time for a complete scan. With Scott already on the inside, hopefully near or, even better, with the other captives, Jean could pinpoint them instantly through their psychic rapport.

The plan built itself. While seeming to battle in earnest, they had to orchestrate it so the Imperial Guard would capture Cyclops, and only Cyclops. Jean had been concerned that Oracle would catch on, aware as she was how far superior Jean's powers were to her own. Scott had assured his lady love that Shi'ar arrogance would lead Oracle to believe that she had simply grown stronger and more skilled. He had been correct.

Which didn't mean it hadn't hurt when Gladiator's optical heat rays had scorched him, even though his costume kept his flesh from being burnt. And the kick to the head that Deathbird had given him was severe.

Still, he had endured far worse, and the plan had succeeded.

With the other Guards following, Gladiator carried Cyclops over his shoulder. Scott assumed Gladiator knew he was no longer unconscious, but the Praetor said nothing of it. Then again, what did it matter? With his arms bound and his optic blasts reined in, he couldn't have hoped to defeat one of them, never mind all five. Even if he wanted to.

Which he didn't. What he wanted was simply to see his father. From Deathbird's ranting, he knew that Corsair was still alive. But he had no idea what kind of condition the man might be in after a handful of days in the dungeons of Hala. Deathbird was vicious and unstable. Cyclops pushed the thought away and forced himself to look forward to the impending reunion. With the cadence of Gladiator's echoing steps, a wave of memory swept over Scott Summers.

He and his brother Alex had been skinny kids when tragedy had struck their family. Everything had seemed so perfect. Their father, Major Christopher Summers, had just been selected for the space program—the name Corsair had been his pilot's call sign. They were flying home from Scott's grandparents' house in Anchorage, Alaska, their dad at the controls of the vintage DeHavilland *Mosquito* he and Grandpa had lovingly restored.

That's when the UFO had appeared. It fired on their plane, then locked it into a tractor beam that began to tear the wooden ship apart. There was but one parachute on board. Their mom had strapped Scott in and made him promise to hold Alex tight, and not to let him go until they hit the ground. He'd promised, even as tears spilled down his cheeks. The parachute was in flames as they fell, and they'd hit the ground hard, but in one piece.

D'Ken Neramani had been the Shi'ar Emperor then, and though Scott didn't know it, the vessel that attacked them had been Shi'ar. The madman D'Ken had been collecting specimens throughout the galaxy, and Scott and Alex's parents, Christopher and Kate, had been teleported on board the vessel. Dad had fought them too hard. As an object lesson, D'Ken had murdered Kate Summers with his own hands.

Scott's father had been sent to the prison world of Alsibar, where he became known only as Corsair. It was there he had met the Starjammers, there he had become the battle-hardened man who was now imprisoned in the bowels of Kree-Lar. It had been many years later, with Scott now an adult, that he had met and battled alongside Corsair. Even then, it had been some time before the two realized their relation. Only recently had they begun to warm to one another, to forgive fate for the years it had stolen from them.

Whatever it cost, Scott Summers would not allow the Shi'ar to take his father from him again.

The gentle rhythm of Gladiator's stride ceased. There came the loud clacking of cylinders being rolled back. A loud hiss followed, the exhalation of a perfectly sealed room, now open.

"The cell has been prepared for you, Cyclops," Gladiator said, then stepped into the room with Scott still thrown over one shoulder.

"Scott?" another voice said, his father's voice. "Oh, no, Scott. I don't think I can . . ."

"Silence, Starjammer!" a guard barked, and Cyclops was sure it wasn't one of the Imperial Guard. Of course, Deathbird would have posted some of her best soldiers as sentries around Corsair's cell. The sentry's voice had come from close by, just to Scott's right. His head throbbed from Deathbird's kick, and hanging over Gladiator's shoulder had caused the blood to rush there, making it even worse. It was hard to think, now. But he knew the plan, and he had to stick to it.

"You shouldn't have come, Scott," Corsair said calmly.

"Silence!" the sentry yelled, and his command was followed by a loud buzz and a cry of pain from Corsair.

"Don't touch him!" Scott screamed, and swung the restraints clamped around his hands with all his might toward the point where he thought the sentry stood.

The heavy metal connected with a satisfying thud, but Scott's momentum threw him off Gladiator's shoulder. He landed on the floor of the cell, jarring his head wound. As he struggled to rise, he became entangled with the guard he'd struck. Cyclops was pleased to note the man was both down and, apparently, out.

Gladiator sighed heavily, then grabbed Cyclops just below his left wrist and lifted him as easily as if he were an infant. The feeling, the recognition of the power in Gladiator's limbs, was disorienting. Cyclops felt incredibly vulnerable. He paid little attention as Gladiator held him by one arm and removed the hand restraints, only to replace them with individual clamps. He did the same for Scott's feet, and in a moment the X-Men's leader was spread-eagled quite uncomfortably.

"Get him out of here," Gladiator's deep voice rumbled.

"Yes, Praetor," another Guard answered. Cyclops thought it was Titan. There came a rustling noise that he imagined was the sentry being removed from the cell.

Cyclops tried to get used to his predicament. Though his legs were spread enough that it couldn't really be called standing, he was able to put his weight on the foot restraints that held him. Unfortunately, he knew that wouldn't last long, and then all his weight would be on his arms and wrists where they were clamped tightly above him.

He let himself relax, testing those restraints, getting a feel for what it might be like when his legs couldn't hold him anymore. He sagged backward and unexpectedly hit a cold wall. Gladiator must have seen the surprise on his face. Though he'd been standing there in silence, he finally addressed Cyclops.

"Though I doubt you'd call it comfortable, you'll find that leaning against that wall makes your restraints bearable," Gladiator said. "In a moment, I will take off your optical restraint. You are quite familiar, I know, with Shi'ar technology. This room is equipped with an inhibition system which will drain all non-essential energies, effectively preventing you from using your optic blasts."

Cyclops said nothing as he felt Gladiator's arms snake past his cheeks and unsnap the restraint that had been clamped around his head. As he did so, he whispered more quietly than Scott would have imagined possible of him.

"There is little evidence against you," Gladiator said in that hushed voice. "The others will still die, but if the Majestrix comes to Hala, she may find a diplomatic way to save you. If not, you will be executed in the morning. I will try to see that it is as swift as possible."

Gladiator backed away, taking the restraint with

him, and did not look back at Cyclops. Scott was surprised that his visor had not been taken from him, in light of the cell's inhibition system. Perhaps Gladiator hoped they would find a way to escape, or perhaps it just had not occurred to him. In any case, Cyclops was glad. He hoped it wouldn't be very long before he would need his visor again.

The Imperial Guard filed out, leaving four sentries in the hall outside the cell. Oracle stood in the doorway a moment, looking quizzically at Cyclops, obviously trying to get into his head. But Professor Xavier had spent years teaching him how to erect psychic barriers in his mind, and Oracle was not adept enough to overcome them. Finally, she left. The door was closed and bolted, the process requiring two of the sentries, and Scott noted the process, filing it away.

"I'm going to kill Ch'od and Raza when we get out of here," Corsair growled, and Scott finally turned to see his father hanging in a restraint system not unlike his own. Hepzibah and a woman Cyclops assumed was Candide were there as well, but his first instinct was to be sure his father was okay.

"Nice to see you too, Dad," Scott said, making the words a jibe.

It was the truth, though. Despite the circumstances, it was reassuring to see his father in the flesh. And a relief to observe that, though bruised in several places, he appeared none the worse for his ordeal. Corsair was roughly the same height as his son, but Scott outweighed him by a good twenty pounds. Father was also far more liberal than son. Cyclops had never been able to completely equate the gravely serious pilot and warrior he knew as his father with the roguish leader of the Starjammers. Corsair had a moustache and wore an earring, neither of which his son would ever have even considered.

Then there was Hepzibah.

Kate Summers had been a good mother to her boys, a good wife to her husband. Cyclops knew that his mother had died nearly two decades earlier. The world had moved on. The universe had opened itself up and swallowed father and son. They had both evolved. Perhaps it was as much of a shock for Corsair to meet his eldest son, now grown and a powerful leader in his right. But as long as Scott lived, he would not believe it was as big a shock as finding his father alive, and in the arms of a feline alien warrior.

In some ways, it was easy to separate the two. The past was so unlike the present, it seemed almost a sweet, idyllic dream. In other ways, however, the spectre of the past, of his mother's death, of the perfect family life that ended so tragically, all cast a gloomy pallor over his current relationship with Corsair. Especially in light of his father's love for Hepzibah.

She was a valiant warrior, and it was clear that she loved Corsair fiercely. In his years with the X-Men, Scott had seen many things and opened his mind enough to see why his father had been attracted to Hepzibah at first. With her cat's eyes, her perfect grace, and her slim, supple form, she was unquestionably beautiful. The fact that she wasn't human never entered into Scott's appraisal of her.

Maybe he just didn't like cats. Maybe it was the spectre of his childhood, the memory of his mother. Whatever it was, Cyclops and Hepzibah had never been able to really connect.

On this day, though, his heart went out to her.

"Hello, Scott," she purred, wincing at the pain those simple words caused her.

Hepzibah was injured far worse than Corsair. Her fur was singed black in several places and matted with blood. He knew without question that the wounds weren't merely from capture. Deathbird's Inquisitors had been there, trying to elicit some kind of information about the rebellion, no doubt.

"Mademoiselle," Scott said in greeting, and nodded as best he could. His father had used that form of address for Hepzibah so long, as a gesture of respect for her grace and beauty, it had nearly become part of her name. His use of it clearly touched her, and she closed her eyes and nodded in return.

They hung next to one another: Cyclops, Corsair, Hepzibah and Candide. When his eyes fell on the latter woman, a Kree half-breed, Corsair made the necessary introduction.

"Scott, this is Candide," he said. "I'm sure you've heard a lot about her from the other Starjammers. Perhaps from the Kree themselves."

Candide's eyes narrowed at this last comment, clearly not pleased at Corsair's implication that she was, indeed, part of the Kree rebellion on Hala.

"Candide, old friend, this is my son, Scott Summers, also known as Cyclops," Corsair finished.

Candide's eyes widened.

"You never told me you had a son," she said, her attractive blue features drawn into an expression of incredulity.

Corsair laughed. It wasn't the full-throated, good-natured bellow he'd come to associate with Corsair, but the quiet chuckle of his father. It brought a wave of sentimentality that Cyclops was unprepared for. He breathed long and deep, letting it pass.

"When you and I were working the trade passages together, I thought my whole family was dead," Corsair said. "Obviously, I've learned otherwise. It's a real blow to the ego to be forced to acknowledge your age, but it's worth it when your son has become such an honorable, formidable man."

Scott was thrilled. Though he and Corsair had formed a bond as comrades in arms and father and son, he had never heard his father speak of him with such pride. As a rule, he tended to internalize his own emotions. Yet he could not let Corsair's comments pass unanswered. At the same time, their relationship called for a less than intimate response.

"Gee thanks, Dad," he said with a genuine smile. "But you know, I'd be more flattered if you said such nice things about me when we weren't about to be killed."

There was a moment of silence in the room, a sober pause wherein they all recognized the truth of Scott's words. Then, one by one, they began to grin, even to laugh.

"When we get out of here, I really am going to knock some sense into Raza and Ch'od for bringing the X-Men into this," Corsair said good-naturedly. "Scott, I hate for you to be put in jeopardy on my account."

"You or I would have done the same," Hepzibah purred. "As would any of the X-Men."

"That's not the point," Corsair mumbled, though it was clear he knew Hepzibah was right.

"I appreciate the concern, but I can take care of myself, thank you," Cyclops said.

"As we can all see by how well you managed to get

yourself captured," Candide observed with a sarcastic chuckle. "And so quickly, too. I imagine it's some kind of record."

Hepzibah laughed and Corsair shot her an admonishing look.

"Hey, Candy, don't worry," he said. "Scotty's the tactician of the family. I'm sure he's got a plan to get us all out of here."

The three of them looked at him gravely, then, not a trace of their former smiles in evidence. Candide's eyes were narrowed in skepticism. Hepzibah's ears pricked up, her eyebrows rose in an open, hopeful expression. Corsair raised an eyebrow and gave Cyclops a sidelong, conspiratorial glance.

"You do have a plan, don't you Scott?" Corsair asked.

CHAPTER 11

The media was in a frenzy. A fiasco like the one in Colorado could not be kept quiet for long. Once the troops were sent, a leak, perhaps several, was inevitable. The Secretary, who was also the Director of Operation: Wideawake, had known that, and had prepared for it. Of course, he couldn't speak to the press himself. And Gyrich—well, over the years, the media had come to hate Gyrich as much as Val Cooper had, starting with his days as the somewhat volatile National Security Council liaison to the Avengers. And telegenic was one word that would never describe Henry Peter Gyrich.

That left her.

The Secretary had met with the President, and they had all agreed that, due to her public relationship with X-Factor, Val was the most logical choice to make a statement. She only hoped that they didn't shoot the messenger. Val was escorted through narrow passageways in the White House that were not available to the public. Secret service agents so cold they reminded her of the T-1000 robot in the second *Terminator* movie flanked her on either side. She was used to the type, but they never failed to unnerve her.

The corridor opened into a large hall with French doors overlooking the south lawn, but the view was mostly obscured by bodies. Noisy bodies. As she entered, there was a roar of shouted questions that began with "Ms. Cooper" but then degenerated into gibberish. Val scanned the crowd and recognized some of the faces. Some of them were celebrities in their own right, and yet in here they devolved into a mob mentality, sharks fighting for the last scrap. She wondered if it would have been wise to wear riot gear.

And this was just the press. How would the average American citizen react? The question sent a shiver coursing through her, even as a hush fell over the room. Though the media would have no idea that he, himself, was the Director of Wideawake, the Secretary welcomed them and introduced her. When Val looked at the sea of faces, cameras and microphones again, they seemed to melt into one another.

"I'll read a brief statement, and then answer whatever questions I can," she said formally.

"At approximately nine a.m., eastern standard time, an unknown terrorist group attacked and seized control of a federal research facility in the Rocky Mountains of Colorado," she read. "The identity of this group is unknown, and it is not known whether there were any casualties. Federal troops were immediately dispatched to the site. They have surrounded the facility, but due to the likelihood that the facility's staff may be hostages, they have as yet made no offensive move. We expect to receive demands from the terrorists within the hour."

Val tried not to grimace while reading the last part, which was a bald-faced lie. Still, it would be what the media expected, unless they were able to figure out what was really going on.

"Questions?" she said, and began to randomly choose hands. She concentrated on just answering the questions, wanting to be away from there as soon as possible.

"Exactly what is the purpose of this research facility?"

They don't waste any time, Val thought, but was pleased that, to this question at least, she could provide an honest answer.

"I'm sorry," she said, "but that information is classified. I am permitted to tell you that this situation does not present any danger to the public, however."

Okay, so her answer was only partially honest. It was better than they'd be getting for the rest of the session.

"What of the reports that a Syrian splinter group threatened to take precisely this action only days ago?"

"Fabrication," Val answered, pointing to another hand.

"Are the terrorists mutants, Miss Cooper?"

"We are not eliminating any possibilities right now."

"I've heard reports that the X-Men were involved, and that they've already engaged our troops."

"That's an unsubstantiated rumor," Val snapped, sweating a little now. "I can say unequivocally that the X-Men are not involved with whomever has taken the facility."

She was pleased with her answer, knowing how it would infuriate Gyrich. He was pissed off enough when Tomko reported that the X-Men had forced his troops to retreat. Val's public declaration would enrage him even further. She both dreaded and greatly anticipated their next meeting.

"But you haven't denied that the X-Men are somehow involved."

"At this point, we don't have enough information to answer that question."

"Miss Cooper, Miss Cooper! Martha Powers, CNN. My producer has just informed me that an anonymous federal source claims that the terrorists are being led by Magneto. . . . . "

Silence. For the length of time it took the entire room to draw a surprised breath, the press was silenced by the awesome dread the mere name evoked. Magneto.

Then all hell broke loose. Decorum flew out the window. Journalists shouted questions, jockeying for position. Some of them ignored her and began calling in on cellular phones. The worst part of it all was that Val didn't know the answer. Most of the other leaks had been accurate, which led her to believe this one probably was as well. And if it were . . . God, she didn't even want to think about it.

Anti-mutant hysteria was bad enough as it is. Magneto attacking the U.S. government would bring it to epidemic proportions. And that was with a public who didn't know what Val Cooper knew, didn't know that the facility contained a fleet of Sentinels. She couldn't even begin to fathom what he might want with the damned robots, and she hoped she would never find out.

"I'm afraid that's all we have at the moment," she said, trying to retain her composure.

The Secret Service hustled her back into the private hall that ran the length of the White House, and Val knew she had to find Gyrich immediately. The word crisis had taken on an entirely new meaning.

*　*　*

"Can I get you anything, Professor?" a polite, neatly dressed young woman asked. "Soda? Juice? Water?"

"No thank you," Xavier responded, smiling kindly, and falsely.

Xavier could not have produced a genuine smile at

that moment if the fate of the world hung in the balance. In some ways, he could not escape the ominous feeling that it did. He was filled with concern for all of the X-Men, both Cyclops's team on far-off Hala, and Storm's team in Colorado.

When he'd been unable to raised Storm or the Beast on their commlink, and Val Cooper had not returned his calls, Charles had turned on CNN to see whether the crisis had become public. Indeed it had. Rumors were flying about a standoff in Colorado between mutant terrorists and the U.S. Army. There was supposed to be a press conference within the hour, and CNN had already scheduled interviews with Senator Robert Kelly, whom Xavier knew to be notoriously mutaphobic, and with Graydon Creed, the leader of a radical anti-mutant group called the Friends of Humanity.

The question had been a simple one. Stay at the Xavier Institute and hope that he was able to contact the X-Men, or get to the CNN studio in Manhattan as quickly as possible for some damage control. No contest, really. The X-Men knew how to take care of themselves. He could hardly hope to help them in the field. But as Professor Charles Xavier, world-renowned expert on mutants and mutant affairs, he could try to curtail Kelly's fear and Creed's anti-mutant propaganda.

He'd already been in the studio, a makeup assistant dusting his head with powder so his bald pate wouldn't reflect the megawatt lights, when Val Cooper made her speech. When it was over, Xavier knew that coming down to Manhattan had been the wisest thing he could ever have done. Kelly and Creed were going to have a field day, and anti-mutant sentiment would become mania if someone did not take on the role of the voice of reason.

It was a role Charles had played before. Disturbingly, where he had often hoped he would never need to do so again, now he only prayed that, after today, there would be an opportunity to do so.

"Ignore the crew and the cameras, Professor," an assistant producer told him. "Just keep your eyes on the monitor and speak as if you were talking directly to the TV set, okay?"

Xavier nodded and studied the monitor. The host was a CNN political reporter he recognized but could not name. She was tall and thin, imperfectly attractive, and much too serious about her work to have gotten a job with any of the broadcast networks. Creed and Kelly were to her left. The three of them, in CNN's Washington studio, would have a monitor which showed Professor Xavier back in New York, while viewers at home would see Xavier in a split screen whenever the conversation turned to him. It paled beside the technology the X-Men had access to, but it was all the mainstream world could handle for the moment.

"This is Annelise Dwyer for CNN," the host began. "In the wake of that White House press conference, and in light of what we heard and, perhaps more importantly, did not hear, CNN has gathered three of the nation's most outspoken figures on the mutant issue."

"To my immediate left, author of the Mutant Registration Act, Senator Robert Kelly," she said, and welcomed Kelly. Xavier could see that the man was anxious, likely unnerved by Val's press conference. The kind of fear that filled Senator Kelly's eyes could be very dangerous.

"To his left, one of America's most popular captains of industry, and author of the controversial new book, *Being Human*, Graydon Creed. Welcome, Mr. Creed."

"Thank you, Annelise," Creed replied, though the woman had clearly not meant for him to do so. "In a time of crisis such as this, when the world's attention is turned to the mutant problem here in the U.S., I feel it is my duty to stand up and issue a call to arms, to urge all Americans to make a stand, to protect their country from the vile plague that has befallen all of humanity."

"Yes, thank you, Mr. Creed," Dwyer said without conviction. "We'll get to that in a moment. Finally, my third guest, joining us live from our studio in New York City, is Professor Charles Xavier, world renowned expert on mutants and founder of the Xavier Institute. Thank you for being with us on such short notice, Professor."

"My pleasure, Annelise," Xavier said respectfully. "And, if Mr. Creed's words are any indication, I'm here to fulfill *my* duty to the people of the world as well."

"Really?" Dwyer asked, her eyebrows raised. "How so?"

"Mr. Creed is peerless in the field of business," Xavier said quickly, taking advantage of the opening he had succeeded in creating with his opening statement. "Yet that doesn't mean his political views, or his intolerant, bigoted opinions have any purpose but to drive the public into a frenzy with misinformation and hate-language."

"Now, Professor," Senator Kelly said swiftly, "don't you think you're carrying this a bit far? Your views on this subject are well known, but you cannot deny that, if it is indeed Magneto leading this band of terrorist mutant rabble—and for that matter, whoever it is—such a direct strike at the federal government could signal a wave of mutant-generated terrorist activity toward the government, and the American public?"

Before Xavier could respond, or Dwyer interject, Creed jumped in.

"Your suspicions are leaning in the right direction, Senator, and your fears certainly well founded," Creed began, emphasizing the words *suspicions* and *fears*. "Unfortunately, you are too naive to see the big picture. This is a government project so secret that, even now, with it under attack and possibly already in the hands of mutant terrorists, the President still won't tell us what it is.

"Don't you see what that means?" Creed asked, playing to the camera now, ignoring the other guests. "That means that the muties have people already inside the government, infiltrating and corrupting our country, stealing our secrets. Not to sell them, no sir. As we're seeing at this very moment, they are going to use our technology, our tried and true American know-how against us!

"This nation will be lucky if it isn't already too late to rise up and save ourselves from this insidious menace!" Creed said, feigning despair. "And if Magneto is truly behind it all, if the most powerful, most evil enemy the world has ever faced has come back to wage mutant war on mankind, well then . . ."

Creed hung his head and let out a theatrical sigh.

"May God help us all," he said softly.

Xavier only wished he was stunned by Creed's performance, but he'd become all too familiar with the man's manipulation tactics over the past couple of years. The whole thing was ugly and getting uglier by the moment. If he was fortunate, and skilled, he might be able to at least balance the scales. It was too late to tip them in his favor, in favor of sanity.

"Mr. Creed, we are all familiar with your tirades," Xavier began. "Out of fear, you might bring people over to your way of thinking. Even now, the senator and much of our audience might be terrified into submission by your performance . . ."

"I resent that . . ." Kelly began to say, but Xavier would not relent.

"Sadly, historians are all too familiar with your kind of speechifying. We saw it in Berlin in the thirties, in the American South just before the Civil War, and in Washington every day from the mouths of lobbyists. Unfortunately, too often it succeeds. But I believe that people are basically good and decent. I believe that prejudice is a primal human reaction to fear, we hate what makes us afraid. Bigots are generally cowards, sir, but you are something else entirely. Fear creates prejudice, and that fear can be manipulated into great power. That is what we have seen from you here today.

"As far as your insinuations about the government being unsound are concerned, I should think, as a member of the U.S. Congress, that Senator Kelly would take offense," Xavier continued, on less solid footing but hoping this final gamble would pay off. "You may be able to tell the American people that they're too foolish not to see this enormous mutant conspiracy you claim exists, and not have them rebel against you because they just aren't that sure of themselves anymore. But I don't see how the senator can sit here and let you imply that the U.S. government is compiled of morons and imbeciles who wouldn't see such a threat if it actually existed."

Professor Xavier took a breath, but he didn't have to wait long. He'd played both Creed and Kelly expertly. Especially Kelly. The senator didn't believe in a conspiracy. He was merely frightened at the power mutants held and the thought that they might not be able to control it. That some might turn those powers against the government, as had already happened numerous times. Of course, the X-Men had been there to prevent things from getting out of control.

No, Kelly wasn't an evil man. Just scared. And Xavier had used that fear, as well as the senator's pride, to create what was quickly becoming a battle royale between him and Creed. Charles was not used to that kind of politics. He generally tried to be as diplomatic as he could, as genuine as he could, and still get his point across.

Difficult times called for difficult measures.

Kelly had to defend the government, even though Creed hadn't really indicted the government directly. And after Xavier's words, he was forced to make a public stand against racism, sexism, ageism, homophobia, anti-Semitism and intolerance in general, and define his stance against mutants solely in relation to the danger of their abilities. He likened it to passing laws curtailing public smoking for the good of smokers and non-smokers alike.

In saying these things, Senator Kelly was effectively attacking Creed, who was forced to respond ardently. Argument ensued. The end result was that Creed's opinions had been soundly trounced by a well-respected government official who didn't completely disagree with him. Though Creed's message had gotten out, and many people would have taken it to heart due mainly to their already instilled terror of mutants, the general population would not collapse in a frenzy.

At least not yet.

When the camera and monitor were finally turned off, he looked up to see the makeup assistant who'd powdered his skull standing just beyond the harsh lights. The man offered him a huge smile along with a double thumps-up. Charles returned the smile. He felt dirty after engaging in such manipulation—that was the other side's way. But as the makeup man turned and walked off into the darkened studio, Xavier realized that he also felt proud.

His dream of harmony between mutants and humans had lost ground today, there was no question of that. But not nearly as much as it might have, had he not confronted Creed and Kelly. In a sense, he'd beaten Graydon Creed at his own game.

As he wheeled his chair down the hall toward the elevator, his anxiety over the safety of the X-Men began to return. Despite his fears, however, Charles Xavier felt good. Very, very good.

* * *

Magneto was terribly impatient with substandard technology. Compared to the near-sentient computer systems on Avalon, the operations of Wideawake and the entire Sentinel program were ancient. And, more importantly, interminably slow. It was ludicrous. All that power at their control, the ultimate weapon—the Sentinels—in their hands, and it was still necessary to wait minutes for the computers to process even the tiniest bit of new information.

But he was getting close.

Magneto glanced out the control center's window at the fleet of Sentinels. They were dark and silent, motionless in the silo. They gathered dust and attracted nests of spiders and whatever other insects and vermin might breed in the cold dark underground facility. But it would not be long until they roared through the blue American skies at Magneto's command. And America was just the beginning.

In the Sentinels, Operation: Wideawake had the most powerful non-explosive weapon ever created. They were sheathed in an armor made of nearly impenetrable alloy, and armed with an array of lasers, tasers, explosives, and crowd-control modes including smoke and tear gas. Their near-sentient minds were able to learn and adapt.

Originally, the Sentinels had been programmed with the identities and abilities of all known mutants. Should they ever be needed to fulfill their purpose, they would have enough knowledge to neutralize whatever mutants they happened upon—or so the covert pitch went. They were humanity's final option if the world's mutant tensions raged out of control.

How deliciously ironic, Magneto thought, that the ultimate anti-mutant weapon would now be used to implement an agenda that would have given the Sentinels' creator, Bolivar Trask, a heart attack. It almost made him wish Trask were still alive, just so Magneto could see the horror on the man's face. Almost. But in truth he was glad Trask was dead. At least a portion of the current anti-mutant hysteria was due to Trask's obsession.

If not for Trask, Xavier's dream might have had a chance of becoming reality. Paradoxically, if not for Trask, Magneto would not have the means of making his own Empire Agenda real. A man who can leave that kind of legacy behind is a dangerous man indeed. Yes, Magneto was glad Trask was dead.

The control center's door hissed open and Voght strode in.

"The X-Men have made short work of the military, as you predicted," she said, carefully avoiding calling him Lord the way the others did. It was prideful, yet endearing.

"Once they begin battering my magnetic force field in earnest, I won't be able to keep it intact and reprogram the Sentinels simultaneously," he replied. It was a truth he would never have admitted to any of the others. "Gather the Acolytes, Amelia, leaving only Milan behind to guard the prisoners. Go to the surface and, when the X-Men have breached the field, engage them. Drive them off or capture them, one or the other. I will not sanction their termination just yet. It is still possible they may be of use to me in the future."

Voght raised her eyebrows but did not argue Magneto's decision. Beauty and wisdom were so rarely given to the same individual, he thought fleetingly. Amelia Voght was a formidable woman. She mumbled her acknowledgment of his orders and backed from the room. He could hear her swift footfalls in the hall, as she rushed to gather her comrades.

Magneto turned his attention back to the computer. He was almost through with the reprogramming, but the computers were taking far too long to process the new directives. With the work that Shaw had already done, it was only a matter of using the appropriate commands to force the Alpha Sentinel to rewrite its programming. The others would follow its lead, the same way that drones followed queens in the insect world.

SIEGE

The computer screen offered a new prompt, and Magneto entered the appropriate command. So close. For the first time in recent memory, Eric Magnus Lehnsherr was filled with an anxiety it took him half a minute to recognize as excitement. The means to fulfill his dream and destiny were about to be delivered into his hands.

Magneto knew he was arrogant, and that self-awareness was what prevented him from becoming psychotic. His arrogance was not a matter of dreams of self-importance or grandiosity, but a certainty that he was one of the most powerful beings on the planet. Creating the magnetic force field around the base had required concentration. Sustaining it, however, was effortless, nearly involuntary.

Until the X-Men attacked.

The sudden conflict caused a massive adrenaline rush, and every muscle in Magneto's body tensed. It was as if he'd been driving a car at high speeds and been forced to slam on the brakes to avoid an accident, without being certain that he could.

After the initial attack, which he held back easily, he relaxed again. He might have kept them out indefinitely were it not that he needed to concentrate on the Sentinels.

"Alpha Sentinel online," the computer told him, and slowly, Magneto smiled. Perhaps he could hold the X-Men off after all.

As he began to focus on his force field once more, he was startled to sense a sudden tear in the fabric of the field. He concentrated on the location of the hole, but as much energy as he poured into it, Magneto could not stop the breach.

Then it was gone as quickly as it had appeared. And

Magneto knew what it meant. The X-Men were on the grounds. Any moment, Voght would take the Acolytes out to greet them, and the battle would begin.

None of which mattered to Magneto in the slightest.

For in the darkened silo, twenty pair of dead red eyes glowed brightly. Running lights popped into life on each of the Sentinels, and they began to power up. The hum of their generators filled the silo and the command center with a wall of vibratory sound.

"Preparing to accept password and sound sample for voice command mode," the computer voice said. *"Please speak clearly. Announce password now."*

"Empire," Magneto said. The password had simply been the latest "door" the first time. This was different. At the final stage, if the word or voice patterns didn't match, the Sentinels first order of business would have been to expediently destroy whomever was in the control center. Magneto listened as the computer cycled his voice through analysis after analysis, matching it to previous samples and locking onto his vocal patterns so there could be no mistaking his commands.

It wouldn't be long now.

Chapter 12

The sun still burned bright over Hala, but in the cold, moist darkness of the tunnels, lit only by flickering torches, Jean Grey found it hard to remember, even to imagine, the sun shining high in the sky. They were in a cavern, apparently just one of the many safe houses used by the Kree rebels. As long as they were able to keep the Shi'ar from discovering the tunnels and caverns that existed beneath Kree-Lar and its suburbs, the cavern would be safe.

Which was, sadly, the subject of some controversy at the moment.

"I have given the Terrans my word!" Kam-Lorr shouted, his face flushed with the heat of argument. It was impossible not to hear the discussion, as no attempt was made to keep quiet. Obviously, Kam-Lorr's fellow rebel leaders did not care one whit about whether the X-Men heard their disparaging remarks or not.

"You may have given your word, Kam-Lorr, but we have not!" a slim, pink-skinned Kree woman said evenly. "These Terrans may be noble, as you say. They may have the best of intentions, but we cannot jeopardize the entire rebellion for the sake of a few lives."

Jean stopped listening. Not because she was offended or disgusted, but because, despite the prejudice the Kree had for Terrans, she knew that their arguments were sound. Kam-Lorr was a man of honor. But honor could be a dangerous thing. What was the saying? "Pride goeth before a fall." There was something to that.

Yes, Jean understood the arguments against the rebels helping her and the other X-Men to rescue Scott and the others. But when it came right down to it, she didn't care. She was selfish and she knew it. If it were anyone else, maybe she would have felt different. But it wasn't anyone else. It was Scott Summers, the only man she had ever loved. And if it meant risking the entire rebellion, if it meant risking war between the Shi'ar Empire and Earth . . . well, none of it mattered.

Scott mattered. That was all.

Jean had been a self-conscious teenager, made even more so by the appearance of her psi powers. She'd been luckier than most, though. Her parents were loving, intelligent people, who'd sought help for their daughter and themselves. That help had come in the form of Charles Xavier. Xavier had promised to give Jean the best education she could hope to receive, while simultaneously teaching her to deal with her mutant abilities and to be proud of who and what she was.

In retrospect, it was wonderful. At the time, however, the day she arrived at the Xavier School for Gifted Youngsters—as it had then been called—was the most terrifying day of her life. A new life at a new school, a boarding school for that matter, with none of her family or old friends around; no wonder she'd been scared.

But her fear had not lasted long. Professor Xavier had intimidated her at first, but he was so kind that she warmed to him quickly. And the other students, well, that was even easier. There had been only four other kids there, and they were all boys. Jean wasn't conceited enough to consider herself beautiful, though it had been said of her frequently. It didn't matter at Xavier's School though. She was the only girl in class, and so of course she was the most beautiful girl in the school. Hank, Bobby, and especially Warren, fell all over themselves to make her feel welcome.

Not Scott Summers, though. Sure, he was nice enough. But Jean had never met a boy as handsome and as shy as Scott. That first semester was the happiest, most innocent time she could remember. Though Warren had pursued her, all Jean could think about was Scott. She'd had dreams about him, about kissing him. As often as she could, she would ask him to study with her just so she could breathe the same air as Scott.

It was silly. It was romantic. It was love. It had seemed like forever to her as she waited for Scott to show some sign that he cared for her in return. But even at that age, though she'd been terrified he did not care for her as she did for her, Jean had sensed that he loved her in return. She would never have used her psi powers to steal the truth from his mind, but there was something between them already, a precursor to the mental rapport they now shared, that told her she need only be patient. That Scott would come around.

Years had passed. They had weathered crisis after crisis together, and apart. In that time, their love had only grown. They had become more than partners, more than lovers. Scott Summers and Jean Grey were two people with one soul.

Jean smiled. The concept sounded corny, even as it echoed through her mind. But it was true nevertheless. She could not survive without Scott, any more than she could survive without a soul.

So, in the end, whatever the Kree rebels decided did not matter. She would rescue Scott from Deathbird's dungeon or die trying. Though she didn't think it would come to that. Jean fully expected that even if the other rebel leaders didn't support him, Kam-Lorr would at the very least help them into the Capitol Building. She and Scott had counted on that when they had hatched their plan.

The part of her psi powers that was instinctive, almost involuntary, sensed a familiar thought pattern nearby.

"Hello, Warren," she whispered without turning. It was an ability that had often spooked those who hadn't known her for long. But she and Warren went back to the very beginning, when he had been simply called the Angel, and Jean had embraced the embarrassing codename of Marvel Girl. Even then, though, Warren had never spooked easily.

"Jean, we need to talk," he said in a hushed voice.

He dropped lightly down beside her to sit comfortably, legs crossed. She gazed on his pretty-boy handsome features, so strangely altered since he had become Archangel. He had always been every girl's dream: young, fabulously wealthy, sweet, funny, and drop-dead gorgeous.

Warren had the kind of body that women not only admired, but envied. At six feet tall, and as muscular as he was, he should have weighed at least two hundred pounds. Yet, even with the organic metal wings that lay flat and heavy in their contracted state on his back, Archangel barely tipped the scales to one hundred and fifty. At puberty, his body had begun to mutate, but the wings he had grown were only part of it. His entire structure was adapted for flight. His bones were hollow, and he had less body fat than Sylvester Stallone on his best day.

His skin was blue now, the sky blue of his eyes, but there was no hiding it. Sure enough, Warren was without a doubt what Jean would call a babe. But, despite what Warren may have once felt for her, and despite the fact that she was and always had been attracted to him, there was only one man for Jean Grey. In fact, Jean believed that Warren, Hank, and Bobby, the other original X-Men, loved Scott—in their own way—almost as much as she did.

The X-Men were a family, new and old. They were loyal to Professor Xavier, to the dream, and to each other. But Jean, Archangel, Beast, and Iceman were also loyal to Scott Summers. Hank and Bobby were back on Earth, but Jean knew that Warren would follow Scott's lead, no matter the cost.

"Jean?" Warren asked, and she realized she had been staring at him, at those ice-blue, Paul Newman eyes.

"We'll be going in a moment, Warren," she said. "Kam-Lorr's not going to let us go alone, but we've got to be careful. We can't have him sacrificing himself or his people for us, and the rebellion won't back his action, not for us anyway."

"If I didn't know better, I'd say you were a precog as well as a telepath and telekinetic," Warren mused. "So what now? I mean, as long as Kam-Lorr can deliver on his promises, as long as he gives us blueprints for the Capitol Building, why can't we just go in ourselves?"

Jean smiled. Typical Warren.

"We can if we have to," she answered. "But with the Guard on Hala, I'd like a little diversion, and some cover for our escape."

Warren nodded.

"What did you want to talk about?" she asked, eyes wandering from his handsome face to the ghostly flickering on the cool cavern walls. It occurred to her that it had been fortunate Storm was not able to come along on this mission. With her claustrophobia, the tunnels would have driven her mad. As it was, Jean felt cramped and skittish.

"Raza will do whatever it takes to save Corsair and Hepzibah," Warren said. "He'll follow our lead. But with Scott captured, I wonder if we can count on Gambit and Rogue in a pinch. I know you said that you and Scott planned for him to be taken captive, and the way the Imperial Guard was holding back, I can't imagine them taking Cyclops unless he let them, but I'm afraid I still don't understand the point of it."

"And if you don't," Jean sighed, "it's a safe bet Gambit and Rogue won't either."

Warren raised his eyebrows, blond slashes of hair that looked out of place on his blue skin. He tilted his head, the expression on his face one that was familiar to Jean from their years of friendship. *You said it, not me.*

"Despite the mental barriers all of the X-Men are trained to erect, I've been cautious because I don't want Oracle picking up the plan," she said, then smiled sadly. "Unfortunately, Warren, there isn't much of one. You know that Scott and I share a mental rapport. In close enough range, it should be undetectable, even by a psi as adept as Oracle."

"I'm an idiot," Warren said, chuckling softly. "You and Scott arranged for him to be captured so your rapport would lead you right to him, and hopefully, Corsair and the others as well. That answers that question. But I have another one for you. What happens after that?"

"That's the key," Jean replied. "You're not an idiot,

Warren. I'm sure you were just looking for a more complex plan, otherwise you would have figured it out immediately. Unfortunately, the rest of the plan is simple. Once we've found them, we free them and retreat."

"Sneak in and fight our way out?" Warren asked, eyes widening momentarily. "Oh, that's a beautiful plan."

"It was the best we could do on the spur of the moment," Jean said, looking away self-consciously. "We didn't expect the Imperial Guard to be here. They've complicated matters tremendously."

She stared at the stone floor of the cavern, at her crossed ankles, at her hands clasped in front of her. Warren's right hand came into view, and he clutched both of hers in reassurance. Jean looked up slowly. Warren's face was intense.

"Don't worry, Jean," he said confidently. "We're all getting out of here, all of us. The X-Men don't leave anybody behind. Not Scott, not his dad, not even that cantankerous girlfriend of Corsair's."

"Thank you, Warren," Jean whispered. "You know, after you lost your wings, when you pushed us all away in your despair, I felt terrible for you. Then, when Apocalypse changed you, gave you those wings, when you came back to the X-Men as Archangel . . . well, you were so different that I felt terrible for myself because I thought I had lost one of my best friends. You have no idea how happy it makes me to know I was wrong."

Warren smiled, and this time it was his turn to look away.

"Come on," he said then. "The hell with the rebels. Let's go get our friends and get off this godforsaken planet."

Together, Jean and Warren stood and dusted themselves off. She saw that the conversation between Kam-Lorr and the others had broken up, and Kam-Lorr was walking toward the alcove where they stood. His face was grim with distress and determination, and the dull orange glimmer of torch light made him almost frightening to see.

"They have made their decision," Kam-Lorr said through gritted teeth. "They will not help."

Jean laid a hand on the Kree man's broad chest, and met his surprised look with one of understanding and compassion.

"It is what we expected, Kam-Lorr," she said. "But we are honored that you would try, that you would speak on behalf of Terrans at all."

Kam-Lorr opened his mouth and took a breath, about to respond, then blinked and let the breath out slowly. He nodded several times, almost imperceptibly.

"Come with me," the Kree said.

* * *

Kam-Lorr was as good as his word. He had shown the X-Men blueprints of the Capitol and its ancient lower levels. From there, it was not difficult to hatch a plan. The tunnel system they had been hiding themselves in led to an underground sewage network that was a part of the original building's foundations. Before that, however, it ran directly beneath the Great Hall of the Capitol Building.

The perfect place for a diversion.

They crept through the tunnel system for what seemed like miles but was probably not much more than half of one. Raza was at point with Kam-Lorr, and the Starjammer's cyborg parts shone dully in the torch light. Sword in one hand and new blaster in the other,

Raza seemed to Jean to be extremely on edge. He was suspicious by nature. All the Starjammers were, even Scott's father, and Jean wondered if it was part of being a pirate and mercenary. Raza obviously suspected treachery, though he never spoke a word of it.

Jean and Warren were at the middle of the group of Kree rebels Kam-Lorr had gathered to aid them. There were perhaps eighteen, surely no more than that, and Jean recognized some of them from the meeting at the marketplace. She assumed that seeing the X-Men fight, seeing Cyclops captured, had made the Kree feel a certain kinship for the outworlders. Maybe it had been enough for them to realize that Candide, Corsair, Hepzibah, and now Cyclops, should not have to die for the sake of the rebellion.

Or maybe, and Jean could not discount this possibility, they simply wanted to rescue the prisoners before Deathbird tortured them enough to make them talk.

Either way, though, they were well armed and on the side of the X-Men. Their motivations were secondary.

At the rear of the pack, Gambit and Rogue had cleanup detail. They hung back to be certain the infiltrating group was not followed, and could not be flanked by enemies waiting in hiding. Jean didn't think Deathbird or her minions would have any idea how they would come. But if Hala's Shi'ar Viceroy wasn't completely insane, if she had learned anything from her previous confrontations with the X-Men, she was certain to know that they *would* be coming.

The tunnel began to narrow considerably, and the flickering light became even more haunting in such close confines. They were forced to walk single file, with jagged slate striated walls on either side and a floor that sloped slowly down. They were completely vulnerable, sitting ducks. If the Shi'ar knew the route they would be coming, now would have been the time for an ambush.

Jean searched the tunnel ahead and behind for hostile thoughts that weren't directed at the Shi'ar. She did not want to invade the privacy of the Kree soldiers who had offered their help, but she could take no chances. While she would not dare delve deeply into another's mind without permission, a light psi-scan of the unit revealed nothing. She had expected, at the very least, to find someone with hostility toward Kam-Lorr. Soldiers were always looking for promotions. But even that was absent. They were all focused on the mission, and that alone.

The ceiling lowered sharply as they walked, and soon all but the shortest of them was forced to move in a crouch. Jean heard water running. Fortunately, the tunnel had widened enough for two people to walk abreast, and she moved up through the unit until she was at Kam-Lorr's side.

"If that's the sewage network, haven't we gone too far?" she asked quietly, not wanting to spook him by using her telepathy.

"It isn't the sewage," he answered. "I've no idea what it is."

They moved forward even more cautiously after that. Fifty yards later, Raza rounded a corner, and swore as his feet splashed into water. Kam-Lorr knelt at his side with a torch, and Jean could see that the water was running fast and clear from a spring in the wall of the tunnel. As the tunnel continued to slope down, the water had flooded the area ahead of them.

"Ground water," Kam-Lorr whispered. "No way to tell how deep."

"I canst not swim well," Raza hissed. "But I wouldst prefer to drown than turn back."

"We've got to go on," Jean agreed. "A little water never hurt anyone."

They waded in, two by two, and though Kam-Lorr had said it was cold, Jean had no idea how cold. In moments, she was chilled to the bone, and her legs were numb to the spot on her upper thighs where the water reached, despite the double layer of her uniform.

Several moments later, when the water had reached her waist, she heard Gambit curse in French, somewhere in the flickering gloom behind her. Jean Grey smiled, but only for a moment.

The water had reached the middle of her belly when the ground beneath her feet radically changed direction. It had been sloping down for several hundred yards, the last seventy or so filled with water. Suddenly the slope reversed, and the upward incline was steep enough that Jean had to reach out with her hands in an attempt to find purchase. A large hand found her wrist, and she looked up to see Kam-Lorr, smiling. It was a welcome change of demeanor on the Kree man. Jean smiled back as Kam-Lorr hauled her out of the water, which rushed away into an unseen lower level through a natural slice in the stone.

"The floor of this tunnel has sunk since last I was in it," Kam-Lorr said softly. "But we are back on the old track now. And almost under the Great Hall."

Jean nodded, and helped pull a pink-skinned Kree soldier out of the water. The man did not thank her, but Jean did not expect thanks. This was a war. Soldiers watched each other's backs, or died. There was no other way.

Kam-Lorr took point, examining the tunnel as he walked. Several minutes later, he stopped and ran his fingers over some markings etched into the wall above his head.

"We are here," he whispered to Jean. "The Great Hall is above us. I will have my soldiers blast the ceiling, but it will take time to climb up the rubble. We will be at a disadvantage."

"It's taken care of," Jean said.

Cyclops and Storm were co-leaders of the X-Men. But that did not mean that other members of the group were not capable of leadership. They had learned more than math, science, English and history at Xavier's school, and as members of the X-Men. Some of them had learned military history, strategy, and creative thinking.

X-Men, to me! Jean thought, and in moments, Gambit, Rogue, and Archangel were working their way up the tunnel to where she stood with Kam-Lorr and Raza.

"Canst thou tell, Jean Grey, if the Imperial Guard be in yon chamber above?" Raza asked.

"I can't telepathically scan the room, Raza," Jean admitted. "If Oracle is there, she would sense it immediately. It's all I have been able to do to shield us from detection until now."

Raza nodded grimly. "What is thy plan?" he asked.

"As long as it means we're getting outta here, I'll be a happy camper," Rogue said, shivering. "I don't like it down here one bit, girl."

"You be okay, *chere*," Gambit said, pulling her close. "Ol' Remy, he here to protect you."

"Time for that, later, Gambit. Let's just get Scott and the others out of here, okay?" Warren said, and Jean silently thanked him.

"If the Guard is up there, we're in for a hell of a fight," she began. "But we better be prepared for it, because you know we're not getting off planet without going up against them again. If they're not there, on the other hand, this should all go pretty smoothly.

"Gambit, Rogue will lift you to where you can touch the ceiling. I need you to give it the biggest charge you've got . . ."

"Jean," Gambit said, shaking his head. "You know I do whatever you say, but a charge like dat gonna drain me good. Be five, ten minutes fore I can fire up again."

"Whatever it takes, Remy," Jean said sincerely. "Rogue, you and Warren take the fight to the Shi'ar immediately. I don't want a second wasted. If the Imperial Guard aren't there, it'll just be Deathbird's personal sentries. Between the two of you, I don't expect we'll hit much resistance. If so, we'll be right behind you."

"Jean," Kam-Lorr interrupted, using her name for the first time. "If these two meet more than mild resistance, we'll be easy targets trying to climb up into the room."

"You won't have to climb, Kam-Lorr," Jean said.

The Kree rebel began to speak again, but Jean held up a hand.

"You'll just have to trust me. We don't have time for this," she said. "It's been dark outside for hours now. At dawn, they die. We can't allow that. Everyone back down the tunnel ten feet, except for Gambit and Rogue."

Rogue bent and Gambit stepped into her clasped

hands. She boosted him to the ceiling and he laid both palms on the jagged stone. As many times as Jean saw mutants work their magic, use their special abilities, it never ceased to amaze her. First Gambit's hands, and then the stone above them, began to glow with an orange light. That glow spread along the rock, ten feet on either side, to just in front of where Jean stood.

She had a moment to marvel at the trust Remy had placed in her. Rogue would not be badly hurt even if the entire building collapse on her. But other than his power and his fighting prowess, Remy LeBeau was just a man. The fragments of the Great Hall's floor would crush him to death. If Jean let that happen. Though he had always been tough to read, the trust Gambit placed in her spoke volumes for Jean about his place in the X-Men. He was one of them, now. No question.

"Dat's it!" Gambit hissed, and Rogue pulled him down and lay on top of him, protecting him with her body. Jean didn't take it as an insult, but as a gesture of Rogue's love for Remy.

It wasn't necessary, however. The ceiling exploded, blasting the Great Hall's floor up into the room, and showering tons of stone down into the tunnel. Almost all of which Jean caught in a telekinetic net. She felt the weight in a nearly physical sense, and the strain was painful but far from the worst she had felt. With an enormously powerful psychic shove, Jean used her mind to push all of the debris to one side, making a graded ramp of crushed stone that the Kree rebels could use to enter the Great Hall.

Rogue and Archangel flew up through the hole the instant the debris was clear, and the rest of them followed on foot. Jean, Raza, and Kam-Lorr entered the Great Hall simultaneously, nearly twenty Kree rebels at their backs, and the room was already in chaos.

In the light of chandeliers powered by Shi'ar technology, Jean could see the grand balconies and stained glass windows of the Hall, which reminded her of nothing so much as the Catholic cathedrals she had seen on Earth. Deathbird's throne sat on a dais on the uppermost balcony, so that no one in the room would be higher than she. Jean realized that the woman had been holding court. The Great Hall was filled with Shi'ar citizens and dozens of soldiers. Screams and shouts echoed throughout the room, and the citizens made for the exits.

Though she assumed that they were not far—not when an ego the size of Deathbird's was holding court—Jean was extraordinarily relieved to see that Gladiator and the other Guard members were conspicuously absent. Archangel flashed through the upper reaches of the Hall, wing knives flashing out and taking down soldier and citizen alike. Jean felt a stab of sadness for Warren, knowing that he was not intentionally paralyzing the innocent citizens in the room. Archangel simply did not have enough control over his wings.

Rogue plowed through a small corps of soldiers who stood no chance against her. Kree rebels met Shi'ar soldiers in open combat, hand to hand where necessary. It was an incredible diversion, exactly what they needed. She did not want to chance using her powers in case Oracle was very close by, and she had to hope that she would be able to contact Scott using very little power, relying on their rapport.

Though the Shi'ar numbers were increasing, the Kree rebels seemed to be winning. They might even be able to hold the Great Hall if they could defeat those

Shi'ar soldiers already in the room. There was only one problem.

Deathbird. She had stood, gape-mouthed, at the foot of her throne, stunned into inaction by the audacity of their attack. Jean had hoped the X-Men and Raza could sneak away, rescue Scott and the others and be back in time for the Kree rebels to retreat, which they would inevitably have to do.

That wasn't going to happen.

Deathbird had seen them.

From her high seat, she looked down at Jean with hate in her eyes. She sputtered furiously, and Jean reveled in the tyrant's surprise. She smiled up at Death-bird, and basked in the venom that dripped from her voice as Deathbird screamed, "You!"

"Kill her if you can!" Kam-Lorr shouted to his fellow rebels.

That's our cue, X-Men, Jean thought, sending the message to Raza, Warren, Remy and Rogue. She no longer cared if Oracle sensed her presence. With Deathbird already aware of them, the Imperial Guard would be along any moment.

She led the others to a back stairwell that Kam-Lorr had shown them on the Capitol Building's blueprints. It led down to the prison levels, which were a labyrinth of hallways and cells. But she knew that Cyclops was down there somewhere, with Corsair, Hepzibah, and Candide.

Scott, my love, Jean thought, putting all her strength and emotion into the telepathic message, *where are you?*

CHAPTER 13

Late afternoon in the Colorado Rockies. Breezy, peaceful, birds chittering in the forest as the shadows grew long. Any other day, it might have been all those things. On this day, however, it was nothing short of chaos, and closing in on disaster.

The moment the X-Men had passed through the force field surrounding Operation: Wideawake's mountain base, the Acolytes had appeared from within the low, simple building which served to mask the complex beneath. When the Acolytes appeared, the force field surrounding the base evaporated. And they all knew, then, what the field had been. Knew who was behind the takeover of the facility, and the Sentinels inside.

"Magneto," Wolverine growled, though he could not see the Acolytes' master anywhere.

"Oh shit," Iceman whispered beside him.

Time seemed to halt a moment, as the X-Men and Acolytes faced each other down over fifty yards of wind-bent grass. For Wolverine, it called to mind that high noon in Tombstone, when the Earps faced down the Clantons. It was almost as if he could hear the melee, see the violence shimmering in the air, smell the bloodshed, all in that moment.

The Acolytes were more dangerous, more vicious, more disturbing than most of the enemies the X-Men had faced over the years, for one reason. To them, it was *jihad*, Holy War. To die for Magneto would be the greatest honor they could imagine. Wolverine knew what it was like to lose all sense of self-preservation. He knew how dangerous he became when the fervor of a berserker rage came over him. It was similar, in its way, to their devotion to Magneto. It was blind rage.

The X-Men had always been noble and benevolent. It had been, in large part, due to his involvement with them that Wolverine had been able to keep the savage beast inside of him at bay. But there were times, as the Acolytes had proven to them in the past, where nobility was secondary to victory. It had been a hard realization for all of them. All but him. Wolverine had been saddened to realize it was a lesson he had never had to learn.

If savagery was what it took, that was all right with him. For Wolverine, it was like the intimate, knowing kiss of an old love: bittersweet, unwelcome, exhilarating.

All of which occurred to him in that moment when time stood still, when Iceman still stood jaw agape at his side and Storm locked eyes with Amelia Voght across the field. Voght was no madwoman like the others, but her face showed the fierce resolution with which she followed Magneto. Wolverine watched her mouth form the words, the command that broke the silence, shattered frozen time, sent birds flapping from the trees.

"Acolytes!" she commanded. "Destroy them!"

The seven Acolytes surged forward, the Kleinstock brothers merging into one. The X-Men responded in kind. Wolverine saw Storm call lightning down on the merged Kleinstocks, who took flight themselves to battle her. Iceman blasted Cargil with a hail of knife-sharp icicles. Out of the corner of his eye, Wolverine saw

Bishop flattened by Unuscione's exoskeleton.

Two of them rushed to attack Wolverine: the hulking Javitz, whose ruined left eye was obscured by a red bandanna tied across it, and the hooded Senyaka, whose psionic whip even now flashed toward him. Logan barely tensed, and his adamantium claws burst once more through the flesh between his knuckles, already streaked with his own blood.

"Only the strong will survive the Mutant Empire!" Senyaka snarled as his whip whisked toward Wolverine's face.

"Guess you're out o' luck, then, bub," Logan said, sidestepping the whip and slicing through its psionic length.

Senyaka cried out and staggered back, but Wolverine knew from experience that he would be off-balance only for a moment. But a moment would be all he needed.

"True mutants follow the lord Magneto!" Javitz bellowed, his voice a rumbling bass.

The big mutant moved much faster than Wolverine had expected, and his first swing connected with Wolverine's left cheek. His teeth clacked together and he allowed himself to stumble into a backward somersault, then came up to face Javitz again. Logan spit blood, the wounds in his mouth already healing, and dove for his prey.

"Time for the ol' Canucklehead to give you a right eye to match the left," he growled. "When I'm done with ya, you'll have to read your comic books in Braille."

Javitz grabbed for Wolverine's extended left arm, which was precisely what he wanted the huge Acolyte to do. It was a feint that had worked many times before. No matter how hard Javitz squeezed, he could never break Logan's adamantium bones. All the fool had done was give him an opening to slash.

His claws sliced the wind, and then the taut muscle and tendon of the shoulder and arm that were holding Wolverine aloft. Javitz screamed, loud and long, but miraculously, he didn't let go. In a flash, he had Wolverine's other arm, and was holding those flashing claws, glinting in the sunshine, away from him.

With his enhanced senses, Wolverine scented Senyaka on the cool breeze, heard the low crackling of his whip, even before the mutant was within range. Such was Javitz' strength, however, that he was unable to get out of the way. The psionic whip coiled around his neck, and Wolverine roared in pain. Where it touched his skin, the whip burned. His flesh blackened and Logan smelled it cooking. His limbs began to slow, reacting belatedly to the whip's paralyzing effect.

He looked up into Javitz' smiling face, and just completely lost it. The berserker rage was on him, now. There was no holding back anymore. With all of his strength, he thrust his forehead up into Javitz' face, the head butt smashing the Acolyte's nose. Blood spurted and Javitz lost his grip. Wolverine hit the ground, adrenaline and healing factor surging together to overcome the paralyzing whip. He reached behind his head and twined his arms in the burning touch of Senyaka's mind.

And yanked.

Senyaka flew, but in his rage and pain, Logan paid no attention to where the hooded Acolyte might land. Javitz, furious and bleeding from face, neck and shoulder, came at Logan again. This time, Wolverine was ready for him, operating on fevered primal energy. He ducked Javitz's swing, and raked his claws across the tall mutant's rib cage, spilling fresh blood onto the grass.

Javitz fell, and did not get up again.

Logan looked around, his feral senses testing the air. Nearby, the Beast had Amelia Voght in his grasp. Hank held the woman aloft, trying in vain to talk sense into her. Wolverine tensed to rush them, to show the Beast how to deal with these psychotic mutant terrorists.

But Hank and Amelia disappeared.

"Amelia! No!" he heard the Beast shout above him.

Above him.

Wolverine looked up, just in time to see Voght and the Beast falling, perhaps a hundred twenty yards in the air. Then Voght teleported away, and Hank McCoy was falling to his death. In a moment, the rage had gone, and Wolverine was in motion. In his peripheral vision, he saw Amelia pop up next to the unconscious Javitz, then both of them disappeared.

Still, the Beast fell. Wolverine's healing factor had kicked in, but the burns on his neck were still there, still hurt, and the charred skin cracked and tore as he moved. His legs pumped hard and he looked up to see that Hank was almost to the ground.

Hank McCoy had eight inches on him, and at least one hundred and fifty pounds. Logan knew he could cushion the Beast's fall, that he wouldn't die, that his adamantium skeleton would not give way. That was something, at least.

"This is gonna . . ." he started to say, and then he was under the Beast, and his arms were up. McCoy's blue furred body slammed into his arms and chest and drove him to the ground. Logan lay there, wind knocked out of him, his entire body beginning to bruise even as his neck healed.

Hank rolled off of him and groaned.

"We're accomplishing nothing," the Beast said. "Time for some tag team action."

"We're getting somewhere," Logan replied. "They're down to four, or five, depending how you count the Kleinstocks."

* * *

"Lord Magneto!" Amelia Voght cried as she appeared in the comman center.

Magneto started in his chair, stunned by her sudden appearance. Voght knelt on the floor next to Javitz, who was bleeding profusely from wounds on his neck and chest. The slash marks told their own story, and a sudden fury filled Magneto.

"Wolverine!" he hissed through gritted teeth. "I have always hoped the X-Men would see the light, would see the flaws in Xavier's dream. But that man has tried my patience once too often. There will come a time, I can see, where his potential usefulness does not balance the pain and damage I have suffered because of him. I wonder if he knows the harm I could do him. I wonder if he cares."

Voght only looked at him, wide-eyed, then back down to Javitz. Magneto knew she was right, that indulging his anger was foolish. Javitz was not the most intelligent of his Acolytes, but even in his ignorance, the one-eyed giant had been one of Magneto's most loyal followers. To him, Magneto might as well have been God. Magneto knew that faith had to be repaid.

"I will try," he said simply.

While raw power had always been his strength, over

the past few years, Magneto had attempted to learn precision as well. And precision was certainly necessary here. By manipulating the iron content of Javitz' blood, he forced the mutant's life fluids to coagulate. While the wounds were still grievous, they were covered in a crust of dried blood in mere moments.

Voght stood quickly, but Magneto stopped her.

"Where are you going?" he asked.

"I am field leader," she answered. "I must return to the battle."

"No need," Magneto said. "The Sentinels will be ready in a moment. Stay and care for Javitz, then we will leave together."

* * *

The tide had turned. Storm had been handily beating the merged Kleinstock brothers, easily matching their plasma bursts with the lightning that was hers to command. They flew, and joined, their strength was far greater than her own. But Ororo Munroe controlled the wind itself, and so there was no chance that the Kleinstocks would get near her if she did not wish it.

And she most certainly did not wish it.

Storm blasted the merged brothers with gale force winds that shot them out over the forest where they crashed into the treetops. Before moving to help her teammates, Ororo wanted to be certain the Kleinstocks were down for the count. Gathering the winds around her, glorious aloft, weightless in the sky, she glided high over the trees. There was movement in the branches below, and she squinted in the dimming sunlight of near dusk to see what had happened to her enemy.

SIEGE

A plasma blast jetted from the cover of the treetops, burning branches away as it shot toward her. Storm's control over the weather was as fundamental to her as breathing, as speaking. She moved without thinking, but still the blast hit her thigh, singing her badly. Stunned, she fell toward the trees, but recovered quickly.

As she regained her equilibrium, she saw the merged Kleinstocks flying at her from the forest, blasting her again. This time, she dodged easily, and lightning flashed from the sky at her nearly subconscious call. It struck, and only then did she realize that the Kleinstocks had shrunk. A heartbeat later, she knew what that meant.

They had separated.

Storm spun in the air and saw the other of the twins rushing toward her, yards away, clearly hoping for a surprise attack that would likely have ended her life. She evaded his plasma blast, but his brother had already recovered and was rising into the air on the other side. Storm called icy sleet down from the skies on either side of her, slicing at her enemies.

Then she flew back toward the others, hoping for reinforcements. At the edge of the field, Iceman was attempting to keep Cargil, whom they had once known as Frenzy, at bay. But the woman was far too powerful, and continued to shatter whatever Bobby threw at her. Storm wanted to help, but she had to deal with her own problems first.

Then she saw them. Hank and Logan, far below, waving at her with beckoning arms. It took her a moment before she realized their intent. The Kleinstocks would be right behind her, in hot pursuit. Wolverine and the Beast were not engaged in combat, at that particular moment. Storm was happy to provide them with playmates.

Turning toward the Kleinstocks, she summoned all the strength of the winds, raised her arms and brought them down swiftly. Hurricane gusts threw the mutant twins at the ground with devastating force. If that did not take them out of the battle, and Storm doubted that it would, then Logan and Hank most certainly would.

Now, she thought, *to aid Iceman*.

* * *

"You are a fool, Bishop!" Unuscione cried. "Don't you see you are hopelessly outmatched?"

The woman was right, Bishop had no doubt about that. But he did not relent. She had stripped him of his weapon in seconds. Now it was all he could do to simply survive the onslaught of her psionic exoskeleton. It surrounded her, enveloped her in a green glow, its edges shining brightly and showing the outline. It was constantly changing, its shape molded by her mind second by second. She was deadly.

Bishop tried to duck as Unuscione's exoskeleton morphed into the shape of a huge warhammer, and descended toward him. Try as he might, he could not escape. She pummeled him to the ground. Were it not that his mutant abilities absorbed some of the energies of the blow and the exoskeleton itself, it might have killed him where he lay.

He struggled to his knees and let loose with a blast of energy, siphoned from her own powers. It dispersed harmlessly against the exoskeleton, might even have been absorbed back into it. Bishop wondered whether he might absorb enough of the exoskeleton, without returning it through energy blasts, that Unuscione might be drained dry of power.

Then she hit him again, and he had to shake his head to clear his thoughts. Disoriented, he had neither the time nor the mental cohesion to consider a move against her. He'd been put almost completely on the defensive. He still had his wits, though, his experience and his fear. That he could share with her, and hope.

"You are the greater fool, Acolyte!" he cried. "No matter whether the Sentinels are slave to your master, or another. Eventually, they must employ their prime directive, which is the subjugation of all mutants on Earth."

For once, he was able to avoid her attack, and Bishop thought she might actually be listening. And if she would listen, he might actually have a chance.

"You know who I am," he called to her. "You know I come from the future. The Sentinels will not only subjugate us, they will attempt genocide! Unuscione, the Sentinels must be destroyed if my future is not to come about. If they are set upon the world, you and the rest of the Acolytes will be destroyed."

"Liar!" Unuscione screamed, and slammed Bishop to the ground again, a loud crack telling him that this time, he had not been so lucky. When he moved, there was a stabbing pain in his side.

"It's history to me, don't you see?" he shouted at her, clutching his side.

But clearly she didn't. In her eyes, Bishop saw only madness. Her exoskeleton flared and he let off what saved energy he had in one blast at her head. It barely made her blink. He knew then that Unuscione was going to kill him.

* * *

Iceman had fought Joanna Cargil before, back when she'd gone by the name Frenzy. He hadn't had much better luck then. She was an Amazon, or at least, that's the way Bobby thought of her. He figured her to be about seven feet tall, with the muscles to match. None of that counted, though. It was her sheer strength that made her a threat. Raw, unadulterated physical power.

Cargil had a constant scowl on her face. Otherwise, Bobby thought, her African features would have been strikingly attractive. Her black hair had white streaks on the sides, but he thought they were dyed rather than natural.

"Great," he mumbled. "Here I am playing hairdresser while she's trying to kill me. You need a date, Drake."

Bobby often talked to himself during a battle. Particularly when none of his teammates was close enough to hear, or to help.

"Time to say goodbye, Frosty," Cargil sneered, and shattered the block of ice he had imprisoned her in. "I'm getting a little numb, but otherwise, you're only slowing me down."

He encased her again, and poured on the ice, hoping it would hold her a bit. But he built her cage too slow, and she shattered it again. There was only so long he could keep her away from him. When she caught him, he worried that she might shatter him as easily as she did the ice that he whipped up around her.

Unconsciously, he began to build an ice platform beneath him, and he moved away from her on it without taking a step.

"That's right, human lover, you run away," Cargil

laughed. "But don't run far. I'll have to kill you eventually."

With a half-hearted punch, she smashed his platform to bits and brought him crashing to the ground amidst hundreds of pounds of ice chunks and shards. Cargil stomped toward him, and Bobby glared at her.

Bobby Drake had never liked to fight. His parents had instilled that in him at a young age. He was going to grow up, get married, have two point five kids, own a house, be an accountant. American dream. The word *mutant* had never entered the equation. In truth, he didn't think he'd ever heard the word before his first day at Xavier's School. He'd never really been in a fight in his life.

Until the X-Men first went up against Magneto. He held his own in battle, did fine as the Iceman, learned to use his powers. But he never, ever, wanted to fight. For a long time he secretly worried that he might be a coward, but as he'd matured he realized he was just smart. That nobody in their right mind wanted to fight. So he held his own.

But the X-Men quickly learned that, despite the way he belittled himself, if they were really in trouble, Iceman would rise to the occasion. Many times he had surprised even himself. If his friends were in trouble, he became a whole different class of warrior. If his friends were in trouble . . . or, if he was really pissed off.

And Joanna Cargil had really pissed him off.

"Enough, you lunatic!" he snapped.

Bobby Drake was never entirely sure what happened when he became Iceman. Was he flesh still, under the ice, or did his entire body transform? Sometimes, he was certain the latter was true. When he was fed up enough to strike out in true anger, Bobby had a sub-zero heart. His eyes crackled with breaking ice as he moved and his breath turned to mist as it hit the air.

The power built in his head and chest, it thrummed down his arms and into his fingers. It felt . . . huge, within him, bursting from his body in a torrent. Wave after wave of cold emanated from him. Unlike Wolverine's berserker rage, Bobby was not blinded by his fury. Rather, it focused him in a way that was unfortunately rare.

By the count of two, Cargil was frozen in a block of ice more than twenty feet high and nearly as wide. Her head poked from the top of the block, and she screamed in fury as she tried to escape. She couldn't move a muscle.

"Bishop! No!" Storm screamed above him, and Iceman spun to see that Unuscione was about to crush Bishop with her exoskeleton. He looked injured already, and maybe even a little scared, as hard as that was for Bobby to believe.

Still with the surge of power that had come from fighting Cargil, Iceman acted without thinking. He had gone against Unuscione before, to no avail. Her exoskeleton was impenetrable. Or at least, it was in some respects. But just because Bobby couldn't blast a torrent of ice at her did not mean that he could not freeze the air between her body and the exoskeleton.

Which is precisely what he did.

Unuscione stood, frozen in an instant, at the center of a bizarre caricature of the human form. Part of the ice shattered as she fell to the ground and Bobby ran to her side to make sure she didn't get up again. Inside the clear ice, he could see her eyes.

And then he realized his mistake.

"Oh my God," he said, stunned. "She's suffocating. I'm killing her!"

Bobby's eyes locked with Unuscione's, and he saw the fear and horror there though she could not even blink.

"Somebody help!" he cried finally, and turned to see that the chaos was not over yet.

Bishop was rushing to his side, and Storm was drifting down to where he stood in a panic. Suddenly, beyond Bishop, Bobby saw Senyaka running toward them, roaring in anger. The Acolyte brandished his psionic whip, and Bishop turned to face him.

The whip lashed out, and Bobby was startled when Bishop didn't even try to move. Instead, he lifted his hands to be sure the whip caught him around the wrists rather than the neck. There was a moment when the two froze in place, perhaps both paralyzed by the psionic power of the whip, and then the backlash hit Senyaka, who dropped unconscious to the ground, the whip disappearing.

"Stand aside, Robert!" Bishop said, and unleashed Senyaka's energy at the ice that encased Unuscione.

It shattered into pieces, but the woman was already unconscious. Maybe even . . . but no, he wouldn't let himself think that. No matter how terrible the enemy, the X-Men would not knowingly kill. Perhaps Gambit, or Wolverine had made exceptions in the past. But not Iceman. Not Bobby Drake.

A thin layer of ice was still covering Unuscione's face, like a shroud. She wasn't breathing. Bobby knelt to wipe it away, even as Storm stepped up behind him. Without a thought to his own safety, he transformed into flesh and blood once more, and began giving the Acolyte mouth to mouth resuscitation. In seconds, she was breathing again, and Bobby sighed with relief.

He looked around to see that Hank and Logan were still trading blows with the Kleinstocks. Otherwise, they seemed to have won.

"It looks like the fight is almost over," he said.

Both Storm and Bishop looked down at him.

"Despite their greater number, the Acolytes have fallen," Bishop agreed.

"I fear that their defeat does not mean we have won, however," Storm added somberly. "For I am forced to wonder, while we have been busy fighting his followers, what terrible plot has Magneto been hatching. Why has he not emerged to rescue the Acolytes?"

"Maybe he just isn't here," Bobby suggested, but even as he said the words, he didn't believe them.

* * *

Magneto stood alone in the silo. The floor under his feet leaped with the thundering power of the Sentinels.

"Alpha Sentinel, do you know me?" he asked, tilting his head slightly as he watched the monstrous robot, waiting for its response.

"*I do,*" it said after a moment. "*You are the mutant known as Magneto.*"

Now was the moment of truth.

"And do you have programming regarding this particular mutant?" he asked, prepared to defend himself if necessary.

"*I do.*"

"And that is?"

"*To obey your every command.*"

Magneto smiled.

Chapter 14

Lamps burned with false light in the courtyard between the two extended wings of the Capitol Building and the main structure. Starlight danced in ethereal hues off the crystalline spire that housed Deathbird's aerie. Citizens strolled arm in arm, talked quietly together on benches, stood in a circle around the stout Rigolletian piper whose music filled the night.

Hushed whispers carried across the courtyard and the populace stiffened slightly. Children craned their necks to get a good look and one small girl said, "Look, Mama!" in her high, sweet voice.

The Royal Elite of the Imperial Guard was passing by. They were not royalty, merely soldiers. But this moment might be as physically close as any of Hala's Shi'ar citizens would ever come to their Majestrix. They would tell their grandchildren about it.

And about the chaos that followed.

* * *

Gladiator was filled with doubt and self-recrimination for his earlier behavior. He knew his duty. In truth, he had carried out more grievous tasks under both Deathbird and D'Ken. A small voice inside him suggested he might be maturing, or growing a conscience, but that was the kind of psychobabble he had always despised. Finally, he was forced to assume that age had begun to make him volatile. It was something he would have to watch for in the future.

On the other hand, Deathbird was not helping. She had sent them on this fool's errand, to hunt the X-Men in places they would have to be imbeciles to hide. Now she had failed to notify them that she would be holding court, and so they were significantly late. Of course, the Viceroy would show no mercy in denouncing them for the insult of their tardiness. Very typical.

What was worse, they had not had time to dress in proper court regalia. Instead, they wore their Guard uniforms as always. Titan and Starbolt whispered conspiratorially together, lagging behind the others. Gladiator sometimes envied them their friendship. The two symbiotes that made up Warstar were socially self-sufficient. They needed no one. And Oracle, lovely Oracle. She walked beside Gladiator in silence, not even favoring him with a glance. With all of the voices in her mind, she could never be truly alone.

Though he allowed no outward sign, Gladiator became frustrated with himself again. His was a soldier's life. There wasn't room in his perspective or his existence for such nonsense. And yet it seemed to come to him all too often of late, thoughts that he considered foolish and pointless.

What was it about the X-Men? The Guard had fought them before, several times. Certainly, the Majestrix had an interest in keeping them safe, though she dared not order them protected. Gladiator had to keep her concerns in mind. But without her direct order, he must follow Deathbird's commands. He didn't know why that should concern him so. Yet he knew the others were reluctant as well.

Perhaps, it occurred to him, it wasn't solely that they

had been sent against the X-Men. Perhaps there was something more. Though the Kree were the most hated enemy of the Shi'ar Empire, Gladiator had been deeply disturbed to see firsthand how their homeworld had been reduced to little more than rubble, how their once-proud people, a warrior race not terribly different from his own, had been driven to an almost primitive lifestyle.

None of which mattered in regard to his duty or his loyalty. Even so, he hoped that he and the rest of the Guard would be off Hala as quickly as possible.

At the first scream, he looked up, frowning. The doors to the Capitol Building burst open, and Hala's tainted Shi'ar nobility came streaming out in a frenzied rush. Some were screaming, even crying. Gladiator knew that the game of political cat and mouse Deathbird had been playing with the Guard had backfired.

"Oracle," he commanded. "Scan them."

The nobles flew past them, barely noting the presence of the Guard. Several seemed to make an attempt to regain their composure, but they didn't slow down in order to do so. Anywhere else in the Imperium, simple courtesy would have forced Gladiator to ascertain their condition, to see them all to safety. But they were of Deathbird's court. On Hala, Gladiator would fulfill his duties to the letter, but no further.

"Oracle," Gladiator snapped. "Report."

Her eyes closed as she scanned the frantic minds around them, but his harsh tone was enough to snap her back to reality.

"Kree warriors, Praetor," she said, a grim set to her white features. "I imagine it's the rabble Deathbird has been prattling about, the so-called rebellion."

"The Kree may be there, but I'd gladly wager we'll find the X-Men inside as well," Gladiator declared.

"No sign of them in the scan," Oracle replied, "but I'll continue to scan the Capitol as we enter."

When Gladiator didn't reply, Oracle frowned and cast a sidelong glance in his direction.

"We are going in, aren't we, Praetor?" she asked.

"Hmm?" he mumbled, then gave her his full attention. "Oh, yes of course we are. We will do our duty. I will personally reprimand any of you who do not fully execute Deathbird's orders, unless and until the Majestrix countermands them."

A sly smile crept over Gladiator's face.

"But that doesn't mean we have to like it. Nor does it mean we have to hurry," he said.

Gladiator was a stern leader, rarely given to humor or warmth among his charges. The Guards respected him, but he doubted very much that they liked him. Oracle smiled with mischief at his words, and both Titan and Starbolt laughed aloud. It felt good. Yet he wanted to be certain they did not misunderstand him.

"We will capture the X-Men," Gladiator announced. "With every bit of power and cunning at our disposal, we will follow our orders. Most especially, we will see that the three prisoners scheduled to be executed in the morning do not escape Hala alive."

Gladiator knew they would hear his unspoken words, implicit in his earlier humor. He hoped the X-Men would make good their escape before the Imperial Guard arrived. And if not, he hoped that they at least caused great agitation for Hala's Viceroy. Deathbird deserved that, and much more.

"Now, attack!" he commanded, and the Guard obeyed.

The pair of huge double doors that opened onto the high-ceilinged entry hall of the Capitol Building were of the finest, heaviest wood in the Imperium. Warstar stomped through one, and Gladiator streaked, fists first, through the other, splinters flying around his head.

Starbolt followed quickly, in position to torch anything or anyone who stood against them. Gladiator had worked out this attack strategy years earlier, and it never failed. No matter what Guard members were involved, Gladiator had the appropriate attack scenario in his head. This time, Oracle brought up the rear, scanning the building, with Titan as rear guard. The ceilings were high enough that he had already grown to at least sixteen feet. In the Great Hall, he would have almost unlimited room to grow and maneuver.

Ahead, sounds of blaster fire erupted from beyond the colossal doors to the hall.

"Starbolt! Your turn for the doors!" Gladiator shouted, and despite his reservations, felt the adrenal surge of battle as Starbolt vaporized the doors with one enormous blast.

Then they were inside the Great Hall. Deathbird's sentries had not lasted very long against the Kree rebels, but a squad of Shi'ar foot soldiers had also been at court. It was they who were holding the rebels at bay, even as Deathbird swooped down from the balconies above, picking off the Kree rabble one by one.

Still, neither side seemed assured of victory. And there were no X-Men in sight.

"Gladiator!" Deathbird shrieked. "The X-Men are after the prisoners. Stop them, or you will die in their stead!"

Though he knew the Majestrix would not allow such an irrational waste of his talents, that did not allow him to ignore the order. Still, he could not simply abandon the madwoman to the Kree. Though he would dearly have loved to do so.

"Oracle, Starbolt, with me!" he shouted to be heard over the din, and squinted against the flash of blaster fire. A laser struck him in the chest, forcing him backward. It singed his uniform, and he wrinkled his nose at the smell.

"Titan, Warstar, stay here and protect the Viceroy," Gladiator ordered, then set off down into the prison levels at a run.

* * *

The first time Rogue had met the X-Men was in battle against them. She had been raised by one of their greatest enemies, a shapechanger named Mystique. Though she'd loved her foster mother for the home she'd provided, Rogue had never seen the world in the same way. When her powers went awry, she had reached out to Charles Xavier for help. Not only because she believed he could help her, but because the X-Men represented something she desperately wanted. A simple thing, really. To be good, to be confident in her actions, in the cause she was fighting for.

What she got was so much more than that. Though Mystique would always be Rogue's mother, with the X-Men, she had a family. Together with honor, they were the only things worth fighting for, worth dying for if it came to that.

They had just turned a corner, and were rushing

down a gleaming metal hallway. Archangel was airborne, his wingspan limited in the hall. From time to time the organic metal would strike the wall, and sparks would fly, but Warren didn't even slow down.

Beside Rogue, Jean Grey ran hard. Though her mind was an extraordinary weapon, her body was that of a normal, human woman. With her own enhanced physiology, Rogue tended to forget what kind of exertion a normal body could take. Running next to Jean, she was both reminded of this, and astounded by the degree to which Jean surpassed it.

The footfalls echoed on the metal floor.

"Might as well have a herd of elephants comin' through here, Jean," Rogue said. "No way we're gonna get the drop on these folks."

"No time for subtleties," Jean said between breaths. "I've even stopped trying to block our location from Oracle's probes. They know we're here. They've got to also know where we'd be headed."

"Okay, then," Rogue said, determined. "We'll hit 'em fast and hard and get out of here."

"Thanks for backing my play, Rogue," Jean said.

"Any time, sugar."

They came to a junction, and Jean called ahead to Warren that he should go left. Rogue marveled at the precision with which Archangel made the maneuver. At that flight speed, she figured she probably would have hit the wall. Course, hitting the wall wouldn't hurt her near as much as it would Warren.

Rogue heard slapping footsteps resounding off the floor even as she and Jean turned the corner at the junction. Blaster fire followed, but far back in the hall where they had come from. She heard Gambit and Raza cursing, then the crackle of energy as they returned fire. Remy and the Starjammer were covering their rear, keeping the Shi'ar soldiers who had pursued them at bay.

She heard them running again, but didn't dare look back. Their only priority was getting to Cyclops and the others and getting out. Remy knew what he was doing. This type of running battle might not be his style—he was more at home with intrigue and one-on-one confrontations—but Gambit knew what the job was, and how to get it done. And after all, Raza was there as well. Rogue figured the Starjammers had been so despised as pirates that they were probably bored by close-quarters armed conflict.

We're close, now. Turn right at the next junction, and I think it'll be at the end of the hall, Jean's voice was in her head, but Rogue thought the words were for Archangel, and perhaps for Cyclops as well.

They were close, though, that was good. Soon they could get off this devastated, poverty-stricken world, and back to their own. She smiled grimly at her own cynicism. Then she realized that, after seeing Hala, Earth seemed to be in pretty good shape. Rogue didn't know whether to be cheered or depressed by the thought.

There was more blaster fire behind them. She heard Gambit and Raza cursing again—bonding under fire, she thought. Then the entire hallway lit up orange with an explosion that knocked Rogue forward off her feet. Jean was on the ground as well, but only for a moment. They were back up in the time it took for Rogue to scream "Remy!"

"Keep goin' *petite*," Gambit called from the debris strewn hall behind them. He and Raza were up and dusting off, seemingly unhurt other than a bloody scratch on Remy's forehead. "It gonna be a while before de Shi'ar blast dere way through de little road-block we just left behind."

"Let's go," Jean said, tugging her arm.

Rogue looked at Remy one last time. Even at the other end of the hallway, she could see him wink at her, that mischievous smile on his face. With Raza moving backward, keeping his blaster trained on the pile of debris that blocked off the junction, they started toward where Rogue and Jean stood. Gambit was limping.

"Don' worry, Gambit's comin'," he said. "Jus' twist my ankle, is all. You get going, we be along pretty quick."

"Rogue," Jean urged.

Then they were running again. Archangel had stopped before the junction up ahead to wait for them. Now, he took two steps and lifted off once more. At the junction, he arced wide and started down the final hallway.

Suddenly, he whipped his wings out in front of him and dropped his legs down to stand. Blaster fire sparked off his wings and several of his wing knives shot out down the hall in response. Then he had ducked back down toward Rogue and Jean.

"Six of them with blasters," Warren said as they reached his side. "Two more cranking up something else. Something big. Looks a little like a plasma cannon, but the nozzle has some kind of dish on it. I have no idea what it is."

" 'Tis a neural disruptor," Raza said as he and Gambit caught up with the others. "Thou wilt find it far more effective than a mere blaster. Whilst a blaster may wound thy body, this weapon shall cause all of thy nerve endings to fire at once."

"Try dat again in English, *homme*," Gambit said, shrugging his shoulders.

"It hurts," Jean said simply. "And my guess is that even Rogue might not be able to stay conscious if she was hit by it."

"So what now?" Rogue asked.

"We take it away from them," Jean said grimly. "This has already been too long a delay as far as I'm concerned. Gambit, Raza, be ready with blasters. Warren, when the weapon is out of their hands, take them all down with your wing knives."

"Jean, you know I don't like to . . ." Warren began, but then let it go.

Rogue knew what he was going to say, that he didn't like to use his wing knives because he could not truly control them. Her ability to steal skills, memories, powers bothered her in much the same way. She understood. But she also knew that Jean's plan was the most expedient. And time was of the essence. Warren obviously knew that as well.

"Rogue . . ." Jean began, but she was way ahead of their leader-by-proxy.

"I'll shield you, of course," she said quickly. She could see that Jean was about to protest, to offer her an out, to warn her of the possible danger. There wasn't time for any of that.

"Let's go," Rogue said.

With Jean behind her, Rogue stepped out into the hallway into a barrage of ineffective blaster fire. It was impossible to see the force, the psionic "hands" that Jean's telekinetic power used to manipulate objects. But that didn't mean she couldn't see its effects.

Even as the Neural Disruptor erupted, the dish around its muzzle focusing its energies on her—even as Rogue screamed with pain, her brain overloading with signals from every point in her nervous system—she saw the weapon explode into dozens of pieces. At least it seemed to. In reality, Jean had reached out for the thing with her telekinesis and torn it apart, flattening the two soldiers who had wielded it.

Rogue couldn't appreciate the drama, however. She had collapsed in the hall. Jean was at her side immediately. Rogue felt her teammate probing her mind for damage, felt Jean's relief, and shared it, as she found none. In a moment, she was sitting up. Gambit sat by her, holding her right hand, stroking it gently, unconsciously. He didn't say a word, but his grin when she got to her feet was communication enough.

"I guess I missed the exciting part," Rogue said as she surveyed the hallway, where the Shi'ar soldiers lay, paralyzed by Archangel's wing-knives.

They all stood there looking at her, even Jean, whose lover was still captive only yards away. Even Raza, who had no reason to care for her. Their concern was just another reminder of what she was fighting for. This was her family. For better or worse, they were the only family she had ever really had, or was ever really likely to have.

"What are y'all gawking at?" she asked. "Let's get the hell outta here."

* * *

Cyclops sagged against his restraints in despair, hoping desperately that Jean and the other X-Men would arrive soon. He was not in any extraordinary pain, nor did he have any real doubt or anxiety about their ability to come to the rescue. Put simply, he couldn't stand being in the same room with his fellow inmates.

"Guilty she is!" Hepzibah snarled, then hissed at Candide, who glared back at her. "Fool you, Corsair. Cannot believe you, I. Death sentence, we have, all because still love her, you!"

"I don't still love her," Corsair insisted, and his exasperated tone matched Scott's own waning patience.

"Oh, thank you so much," Candide said, honey sweet voice filled with sarcasm.

"Don't you start," Corsair snapped, and the Kree/Shi'ar halfbreed only smiled. "I figured you for a mercenary to the core. If I'd had any idea you knew what you were getting into, that you were actually smuggling arms to the Kree rebellion, I never would have risked my life and the lives of my crew to come and get you."

"So, what you're saying is, because you thought I was a heartless bitch whose only concerns were financial, you felt like you needed to save my life?" Candide asked with a knowing smirk.

"Still love her, you do," Hepzibah growled. "Admit it, can you not?"

"Enough!" Corsair shouted, then continued through clenched teeth. "Hepzibah, you know that I love you. Only you. I'll admit I had a little crush on Candide back in our early freebooting days. But that was a long time ago, and nothing ever happened between us. Did it, Candide?"

The smuggler was silent.

"Candide?" Corsair asked again, the warning clear in his tone.

"Not for lack of my trying," she answered finally, and everybody seemed to relax. Scott himself breathed a sigh of relief, though none of the conversation pertained to him.

"Okay, maybe I was stupid to come after her," Corsair went on, speaking only to his lover, Hepzibah, now. "Maybe I've still got an old-fashioned damsel-in-distress program running in my head. The Starjammers wouldn't be in trouble now, and I wouldn't have dragged my son and his friends in after us. But it's too late for recriminations now. We've been in tighter spots than this and gotten out. Scott's already told us all we have to do is just sit back and wait for the cavalry to arrive."

There was a moment of silence when all three of them looked at Cyclops, who smiled sheepishly at the attention.

"Believe you, maybe I do," Hepzibah said. "Love you, that you know. Doubt your handsome son, not at all do I. But what if never come, the cavalry? Then what do we?"

"An excellent question, Mademoiselle Hepzibah," Candide agreed.

"Scott?" Corsair said, and looked at his son with inquiring eyes.

"They'll come," Cyclops said confidently. "And if they don't, we'll figure a way out of here. Or we'll die. Pretty simple, really."

Silence descended upon the cell once more. Moments later, it was broken by the screech of tearing metal, a distorted underwater-style echo that made Cyclops wince and close his eyes. There was a series of loud, staccato popping sounds, then the door seemed to burst outward, sparks flying as the cell's techno-security shorted out.

Rogue stood just outside the cell, holding the crumpled door in her hands. She threw it aside with ease and it landed in the hall with a resounding crash.

"The cavalry," Scott said simply, as Rogue rushed into the cell with Jean Grey at her side.

"Jean!" Corsair boomed. "It's a pleasure to see you, as always. My son offer to make an honest woman out of you yet?"

Cyclops blushed, but Jean merely laughed.

"Not yet," she said with a wink, then her demeanor became far more serious. "We're all present and accounted for, Scott, but the Imperial Guard will probably be along any second. We've really got to get out of here."

"You can start by getting us down from here," Candide snapped, and Cyclops saw Jean's eyes narrow in annoyance and contempt.

"Candide, I presume?" Jean asked.

"Is not her strong point, charm," Hepzibah sneered, and it took Scott a moment to decipher the insult. Jean, apparently, had no such difficulty.

"That's fairly obvious," she said. "A lot of people have risked their lives to get you out of here. A little gratitude might be in order."

"You didn't come here for me, Terran," Candide observed. "But you get me out of here alive, and you can be sure I'll be grateful."

"The cell is offline," Corsair said, ignoring the exchange. "It shouldn't take much to shake us loose from these restraints.

He was right. After a few moments, and several well placed optic blasts from Cyclops, they were able to free themselves with relative ease. In the time it took to do so, Archangel, Gambit and Raza had all joined them in the cell.

"Beautiful," Warren sighed, "now we're all in prison."

"Not for long," Cyclops replied, then turned to Corsair. "Dad, why don't you signal Ch'od to teleport us out of here, and we can all go home?"

Blaster fire shook the hall outside the cell.

"And perhaps thou ought to make haste, my captain," Raza added.

Corsair pressed the comm-badge on his chest and was greeted with the hiss of static.

"Interference," he said confidently. "Ch'od, this is Corsair, do you read me? Come in, Ch'od."

Static, crackling, popping, then finally: "Ch'od here, Captain. Good to hear your voice."

"You too, old friend. But we're in a bit of a hurry here. Prepare to teleport nine aboard the *Starjammer*," Corsair ordered.

More hissing, then: "There's nothing I would enjoy more, Corsair, but I'm afraid it's impossible. Teleporter's still down. It will take days to fix it."

"Damn," Corsair said under his breath.

Cyclops felt the dread overtake him in an instant. For once, nobody had a wisecrack to make. They all simply stood, in silence, glancing around at one another to see what the next move would be. Corsair looked at Hepzibah, and though they did not have the psychic rapport that he shared with Jean, Scott could see that some unspoken communication passed between them.

"Only chance, it is," Hepzibah said, and laid a comforting hand on Corsair's shoulder.

"Not to rush you," Cyclops said to his father, "but the blaster fire sounds closer, and the Guard's probably . . ."

"Probably nothing!" Jean said, holding one hand to

her head as she often did while making a psionic scan. "They'll be here in seconds!"

Corsair slapped his comm-badge once more, making his decision in that instant.

"Ch'od! Planetfall!" he barked. "Come and get us!"

Before he could ask another question, Corsair put his hands on Scott's shoulders and looked into his eyes. "We've got to go up," he said, "as far as we can."

Then he looked around the cell at the others gathered there, Starjammers and X-Men, and one lone half-breed smuggler.

"If we don't make it to the dome, we're going to die in this hellhole."

CHAPTER 15

The Acolytes were still putting up something of a fight, but the tide had clearly turned. It would be mere moments before the last of them, the Kleinstock Brothers, were contained. The X-Men had defeated the Acolytes in open combat.

That in mind, Hank McCoy could not figure out what was causing the anxiety that was rising to a fever pitch in his mind. Just as the X-Men were not at full force, neither had the Acolytes had their entire roster present for the confrontation. It was possible there were more still inside, but Hank had to assume the others would have come to the aid of their comrades when the battle turned against them.

The same was true for Magneto. If he was inside the facility, why had he not emerged to protect his flock in their time of need?

"What is it, Hank?" Storm asked, and he explained.

"What might he conceivably expect to accomplish, other than the demolition of the Sentinels?" the Beast asked. "And if that is Magneto's design, the ultimate strike against Operation: Wideawake, I'm not unconditionally confident I would be predisposed to thwart him."

"Nor I," Storm agreed.

"That isn't it, though," Hank continued, more to himself than to Ororo. "If it was, Magnus would anticipate that the X-Men would have conflicting emotions. He would not have directed the Acolytes against us."

As they were speaking, Bishop had absorbed what energies the Kleinstocks had still had, and they had fallen unconscious to the grass. Wolverine stood by Storm as Hank spoke, and the Canadian's response was typical.

"We can stand out here and jaw about this 'til mornin', folks," Wolverine said, brandishing his claws. "But the only way we're gonna find out anything is by goin' up there and knockin' on Magneto's door. Believe me, if he's in there, he'll answer."

The Beast looked at Storm. She was the field leader, but due to his experience, not just with this team, but with the Avengers and Defenders, she often looked to him for guidance. There was a question in her eyes, which was uncommon. Hank had found that, more often than not, Ororo knew what to do merely by instinct. He suspected that was one of the reasons Charles had made her the team's second-in-command, after Cyclops. This time, however, she seemed unsure.

He understood her trepidation. They had already encountered federal troops. Though they had defeated the Acolytes, if Magneto was not inside they would be breaking into a top-secret U.S. military base. That would be bad. On the other hand, if Magneto were actually inside, one reason for him not to have emerged during the battle was if the entire thing was an claborate ruse. Some kind of trap.

"We can't take any chances," Hank said, and Storm nodded.

"Bishop and Iceman take point," she said. "Iceman, give us an ice slide down. Wolverine, watch for more Acolytes once we're in. If Magneto is down there, we'll have to take him out quick if we're going to take him out at all."

The X-Men moved swiftly toward the unassuming brick building that masked the huge military base and silo that existed under they ground they were crossing. The Beast knew it was unwise to leave the Acolytes simply laying about the field, that any moment one or more of them might revive and attack once again, but there was nothing to be done about it.

Bobby and Bishop were in the lead, perhaps twenty yards from the two-story structure, when it exploded, blasting them across the field to slam hard against the chain-link fence that surrounded it. Hank didn't see what happened to Storm and Wolverine, but in a moment he found himself lying on his back, staring up at the darkening sky. The Beast blocked his eyes from the glare of the sun. It took him a moment to realize that what he was seeing was not the sun at all.

Magneto hung suspended in the air above the field, a sizzling, green ball of magnetic energy around him and three of his Acolytes: Voght, Javitz, and another that the Beast recognized as the techno-linguist, Milan. Javitz seemed to have recovered quite well from the wounds Wolverine had inflicted upon him, Hank noticed.

The Beast picked himself up off the ground, not worried about whether or not his actions appeared threatening. They had skirmished often enough that they both knew Hank posed no danger to Magneto from the ground.

"Hear me, X-Men!" Magneto declared. "For the duration of this conflict, you have lived by my sufferance alone. From this day forward, the same will be true."

Hank was stunned to see that, though she was usually the least fervent of Magneto's followers, Amelia Voght was gazing at her lord and master with a look he could only perceive as awe. Javitz still seemed disoriented, but Milan stood rigid by Magneto, his face beaming with serenity. In that moment, the Beast grasped the profound nature of the Acolytes' worship of their master. Not the basis for it, but its depth.

The blue fur stood up on his back and neck, and Hank McCoy gnawed his lip, deeply disturbed.

"They're moving!" Wolverine shouted behind him, and Hank turned quickly to see that, indeed, the Acolytes were rising from the field. One Kleinstock twin—Hank could not tell which—carried his still unconscious brother, and Frenzy had Senyaka over her shoulder. But the Acolytes had become a threat once again, now that their master had arrived.

Beyond them, across the field, Hank saw Bishop carrying Bobby toward them, slung over his shoulder in a bizarre imitation of Frenzy and Senyaka. He knew that Bishop's powers would have allowed him to absorb the brunt of the explosion Magneto had caused. Iceman had not been so lucky. Either the force of the explosion itself or his impact with the fence had knocked Bobby unconscious.

Hank wanted to go to him. They had been friends for a long time, and it was hard not to put his friends first. But there were far more pressing matters at hand.

"Though I fear I know your answer, I make you this offer now," Magneto continued. "Mutants *must* conquer humanity. There is no other option which will guarantee the survival of our race. I open my arms to you all. There will be sanctuary for our kind, I will see to it. And there is a place for you in the hierarchy of that sanctuary, should you choose to seek it."

Silence followed this pronouncement. The Acolytes they had so recently battled glared at them as they passed, but in a moment they were lifted, one by one, to hover in the ever-expanding bubble their master had created and was sustaining with only a portion of his power. Hank, Logan, and Bishop—with the unconscious Iceman—gathered close around Storm.

"What's the plan, 'Roro?" Logan asked, but Storm held up her hand.

"As you say, Magneto," she called to him. "You know our response all too well. Whatever your current plot is, we stand against you as always. There is nothing noble in conquest. You are sadly deluded if you believe the world will ever bow to you as its emperor."

"Not deluded, my dear Ororo," Magneto said pleasantly. "Merely practical."

"That's it!" Wolverine snarled. Hank tried to hold him back, but Logan ran ahead until he was almost directly beneath the shimmering ball of magnetic energy that held Magneto and his followers aloft. In the descending darkness, the green glow bathed the X-Men's faces in a sickly aura.

"We're all a little sick o' your delusions o' grandeur, bub," Logan called up to him, brandishing his claws. "Why don't you come on down and we can discuss this like the savages we are?"

Magneto shook his head. His sigh was audible, even from the field.

"One of these days, Wolverine . . ." Magneto began, and it was almost enough to get Hank to smile when Logan interrupted.

"Yeah, yeah, I've heard it before. To the moon, Alice," Wolverine sneered. "Now you gonna get down and dirty, or not?"

"I think not," Magneto replied.

The mutant master of magnetism lifted one hand

and a blast of the same green energy flashed around his fist, then arced high above the field and into the forest beyond.

Hank was the first to realize what Magneto's target had been.

"The *Blackbird*," he said aloud.

"Indeed, McCoy," Magneto confirmed. "You will not, however, have to walk from here to the Xavier Institute. Rather than tear your vessel apart, I generated a focused electro-magnetic pulse that should make it inoperable for several hours. At the very least, that will keep you from inconveniencing me while I put my plans into action."

"How benevolent," Hank said, rolling his eyes.

"You forget yourself, Magnus!" Storm yelled suddenly.

She raised her arms above her head, and immediately, the rain began to fall hard upon the X-Men. The wind came up strong enough to force Hank back a step. Lightning flashed from the sky and struck Magneto's levitating force field, and some of the Acolytes cursed and ducked, shielding their faces. They need not have worried, however, as the lightning was immediately absorbed into the ball, which glowed yellow for a moment before returning to its green hue.

"You forget that one among us has the power of flight!" Storm called, above the roar of the wind which began to lift her off the ground.

"Ororo, no!" Hank shouted. He reached for her legs, trying to keep her from facing Magneto and the Acolytes alone. But he was too late. In the blink of an eye she was airborne, calling down the lightning to strike repeated at their enemies.

"I have no wish to hurt you, Storm," Magneto said.

"One day you, all of you, will come to me in supplication. Until then, I bid you adieu."

Magneto turned to Voght and nodded. The green energy field flared brightly. Hank squinted, shielded his eyes with one hand, but still he could not see beyond the glaring light. Then as suddenly as it began, the flare ended.

With total darkness.

Only the moon and stars gave them light. Magneto and the Acolytes were gone. Amelia Voght had teleported them away, and the X-Men had no way to track them, or to even begin to understand what Magneto's purpose might have been. All in all, Hank thought sullenly, it had been a very unproductive day.

"Whoa! Hello? Bishop, put me down, man," Bobby said weakly, finally conscious again.

Hank watched his old friend steady himself as Bishop lowered him to the ground. Iceman looked around, obviously confused.

"Okay, let's see," Bobby said, the usual jesting tone in his voice. "Dark out, nobody here but us chickens. We won, right?"

"Sadly, no, Robert," Storm answered.

"Didn't even get the chance, kid," Wolverine added.

"We are here, however," Storm reasoned. "Before the military is able to erase this event and this base from history, we must determine the extent of Operation: Wideawake's capacity here, and the amount of damage Magneto has done."

"Once more into the breach, my friends," the Beast added with a laugh.

They had not taken a dozen paces toward the rubble that had once been a building when the ground began to shake violently. Its vibration threw Bishop and Iceman to the ground and Storm lifted off with the wind beneath her. Hank and Wolverine were able to keep their footing, but only barely.

"An earthquake?" Bobby asked. "What else could go wrong today?"

"I've got a real bad feeling about this," Wolverine said in his gravely voice.

Hank was filled with dread once again. There could only be one explanation for the way the ground was pitching and rolling beneath them. A moment later, Bishop confirmed his worst fears.

"Not an earthquake," the future-born mutant shouted over the rumble of the Earth. "I know the sound all too well. It's the Sentinels preparing for deployment."

"Goddess, no!" Storm cried. "X-Men, fall back! Fall back!"

They all moved to follow her orders, streaking toward the metal fence and the forest beyond. Storm whipped the wind up into such a hurricane-like frenzy that it tore the fence away, leaving only the dense forest beyond.

As they ran, the ground shook beneath them. Then it buckled. Behind them, a huge hole began to open as two massive plates of Earth lifted like a drawbridge. The X-Men pitched forward into a yawning chasm where the ground rushed down to fill the space opening beneath it.

"It's a modified missile silo!" Hank yelled. "Everyone get clear!"

His words were too late to warn them. But these were the X-Men. They didn't need to be told. Storm grabbed Wolverine beneath his arms and held tightly as the winds she controlled rocketed them both to safety. Bobby whipped up an ice slide and Bishop held onto his back as he propelled himself along by constantly adding to it. The ground on which the slide was built was crumbling by the second, the ice cracking, shattering along with it. But by that time, they were close enough to stable ground for Bobby to instantly create a ramp of ice down which they slid to safety.

Which only left Hank. They had fought beside the Beast for years. Obviously, they were counting on his strength and agility for him to be able to save himself. It was the only thing they could have done, the wisest course of action. Hank knew they were right to leave him behind. Just as he knew they were right that, with one or two enormous leaps, he could get himself to safety.

If he could find one foot of solid ground from which to leap.

It didn't look promising. The Beast raced toward the churning ground ahead as the huge door he now knew he stood upon opened beneath him. He had to continue that forward momentum, though it brought him closer to certain death with each step. If he slowed, he would most certainly lose his footing, and if he lost his footing, this avalanche of soil would trap him and crush him to death.

Hank didn't look up. He couldn't afford to. In any case, he knew it would be too dangerous for Storm to try to save him. Each time one of his feet touched ground, his primal instincts tested the ground for stability. He was rapidly losing hope of finding any, and he was certain there would not be a long enough patch of solid ground for him to make a decent jump.

He had to count on Bobby Drake to know what to do. Iceman couldn't come after him without the real probability that he would sacrifice his own life and not be able to save Hank. But if he was thinking, if Bobby was paying attention, he could catch Hank in the air with a slide or a ramp or something.

If Hank could just get in the air. If he could find something solid from which to propel himself. His feet slid in the dirt and with each step he had to pull them out before he tore or twisted something vital, something that would end it all.

The genetic x-factor that had made Henry McCoy a mutant had given him senses that matched his savage appearance. Otherwise he never would have seen the enormous tree stump that slid along atop the crumbling Earth ahead, only a handful of yards from where the opening door had pulled away from solid ground, allowing millions of tons of soil to pour off the edge of the world.

Hank assumed that the stump had been too large to remove when the facility was built, and so the laborers had simply buried it. He praised them, then pushed the thought from his mind as he increased his speed. He had to get to the stump before it went over into the maelstrom of dirt.

Then it was there, under his feet. The Beast crouched and used all of his considerable strength, and the momentum he had accumulated to leap up and forward. Only when he was in the air did he look to see if he would make it to the edge of solid ground where the earth had been cut away to build the silo. He found it, and knew instantly that it was too far.

Then the X-Men were there, in his line of sight, and Iceman was furiously fashioning an ice slide that seemed to burst from the ground and shoot toward the spot in the air where Hank was already beginning to fall short of his goal. The slide was coming fast, as Bobby poured everything he had into it, and Hank suddenly realized that Bobby had miscalculated, hadn't taken his fall into account.

But it wasn't going to miss. Oh, no, that would be too simple.

It was going to hit him.

"Oh, my stars and . . ." Hank began to say, but he didn't have time to finish the phrase. The slide shot toward him, fast enough and thin enough that he was afraid it might slice him in half.

With every muscle straining, using all of the agility that had kept him alive this long, the Beast flipped himself into a somersault, pulling his legs up into the air above his head. It didn't slow his descent, but it changed his position enough that the ice flew past underneath him, solidifying so fast that when he hit it, on his back, the wind was knocked out of him.

It was freezing cold against his back, but it felt good. In a few moments, Hank had slid to the bottom of the ramp, and his team mates had crowded around him. Storm and Wolverine helped him up, as Bishop brushed ice particles off his fur with a wide grin.

Then Bobby was in front of him.

"You about skewered me that time, Mr. Drake," Hank said.

"You'd make some tasty barbecue, Dr. McCoy," Bobby replied.

Hank threw his arms around his best friend and lifted him off the ground, shaking his head in amazement.

The rumbling continued, though the silo doors were open all the way now, gleaming metal standing vertical from the ground. Dust still rose from the slowly settling pile of dirt that was nearly Hank McCoy's grave. They heard the sudden firing burn of a jet engine.

"Here they come," Bishop said quietly.

Two by two, the Sentinels emerged. Twenty in all. Their eyes, chest plates, and running lights glowed an eerie red against the sky. All of the X-Men were stunned when the colossal robots did not stop to attack them, or even seem to notice them.

The X-Men were silent as the Sentinels grew smaller in the sky, until all that could be seen of them were distant red lights.

"They're headin' east," Wolverine quietly observed.

"They ignored us," Storm said. "I don't think I want to know what Magneto's next move is going to be."

Then they were silent again. A moment later, Hank heard a tiny sniff to his right, and looked over at Bishop in the darkness. The night was black, but with his enhanced senses, the Beast thought there were tears in the time-lost X-Man's eyes. Bishop had often spoken of the terror the Sentinels had wrought over the world when he was a boy, and even a young man. The newest member of the team, Bishop was also one of the bravest, most fearless warriors they had ever known.

Tears. Not of fear; not from Bishop. No, Hank imagined that these were tears of sorrow. Sorrow for all he had lost in that far future time. And all he stood to lose now. Today.

Suddenly, Hank McCoy realized that he was deeply, deeply frightened of what was to come.

* * *

Valerie Cooper was in the White House for the second time in a single day, a personal record. While most anybody she knew would likely be impressed by this fact, Val was singularly unnerved. When she was called to the White House, it was never good news. And considering what had already happened that day, it could only be a catastrophe.

Her heels clicked on the marble floor as she followed the two Secret Service agents who were to guide her to the meeting. She knew the topic of the meeting, certainly. Mutants. Otherwise, why invite her? But she shuddered to think what the specifics of it would be.

The only thing that made the trek down that hall bearable was the thought that at least she would find out what had transpired in Colorado. At least she would learn the truth.

The two broad-shouldered agents, looking for all the world like mindless clones, stood to either side of a heavy oaken door. The one on the left, whom she had come to think of as Tweedle-Dee, reached his right hand around and rapped lightly on the door. There was a buzz and then the loud triple click of bolts sliding back on the door. A voice inside called out, "Enter!" and the other, Tweedle-Dum, twisted the door knob and pulled it open.

Val Cooper walked inside and the door shut behind her. The buzz came again, followed by the snap-snap-snap of the locking mechanism.

"Please, Ms. Cooper," the President said warmly, "come in and take a seat."

For a moment, Val could only stand there. Other than herself and the President, there were only two other people in the room: the Director of Operation: Wideawake, and its guard dog, Henry Peter Gyrich. Her heart sank. With Gyrich in the room, she'd be more likely to get the truth from the devil himself.

Finally, after what seemed to her an uncomfortably long pause, she took a seat in the one empty chair at the small table. This was not a traditional meeting room for the White House, or anywhere. It was a room that was soundproof, bug-proof, bulletproof. There were no windows, and only the one door. It was a room where conversations never happened, where plots were never hatched, where coverups never took place.

It was a room that didn't exist.

"Valerie," the President began, "as you know, we've had our share of mutant problems today. With X-Factor unavailable, we've had to deal with it ourselves, and I'm afraid we didn't do a very good job of it."

"If Colonel Tomko had obeyed orders, Mr. President, we wouldn't be in this . . ." Gyrich began, but the President cut him off.

"The colonel isn't here to defend himself, Henry. Why don't we give him that opportunity when he reports back to Washington?" the President suggested. Though his tone was noncommittal, Val sensed that the man didn't like Gyrich very much. Her opinion of the President rose considerably.

"I've asked you here so that you could offer your opinion on what to do next," he continued. "Mr. Gyrich has made some suggestions, several of which the Director has endorsed, but I wanted to see what you have to say. I don't think there's anyone in the administration with more experience when it comes to mutants."

"Thank you, sir," Val answered. "I'm at your service."

"Mr. Gyrich," the President said, "why don't you outline the events of today so Ms. Cooper is fully caught up?"

"Sorry to interrupt, sir, but if Mr. Gyrich had not specifically ignored the Director's instructions, I would already be caught up," Val said, feigning a benevolence that did not reflect her mood or her words. "I just wanted to point that out."

"Your point is well taken, Val," the Director said, speaking finally. "Why don't we put that aside for now. The President's time is precious."

"Yes, sir," Val replied, not even bothering to glance in Gyrich's direction.

"As Ms. Cooper is well aware," Gyrich began, "Operation: Wideawake was occupied by terrorists this morning. Our on-site troops encountered the X-Men at the Wideawake base. Those well-known mutant terrorists immediately set upon our troops . . ."

"How dare you?" Val snapped.

Both the Director and the President looked at her as if she were mad.

"Would you care to explain yourself, Valerie?" the Director asked, his tone warning her to tread carefully.

"I'm not sure if Colonel Tomko is too terrified of Mr. Gyrich to file a true report, but if he is, it will show that the X-Men arrived at the scene after our troops," she said evenly. "It will also show that they made no hostile move toward our troops. Only when Colonel Tomko and his men attacked did the X-Men act to defend themselves."

"How do you know these things, Ms. Cooper?" the President asked, the suspicion evident in his voice.

"She's obviously involved with the X-Men," Gyrich sneered.

They all looked at him, and Val had to keep from smiling. Gyrich had reacted to the President's words too quickly, trying to implicate her rather than defend his own claims. He'd definitely put his foot in it.

"Mr. Gyrich told me as much in my office earlier today, just before he ordered Colonel Tomko to capture the X-Men, and to shoot to kill if they resisted," Val responded.

"Henry?" the Director asked, no longer confident in Gyrich.

"I had reason to believe that the X-Men were there to meet their teammates, who I supposed were already inside the base," he said, glaring at Cooper now.

"And that reason would be?" Val asked, enjoying this now.

"Look, none of this changes the basic facts. Magneto and his Acolytes took over Operation: Wideawake. After defeating our troops, the X-Men attacked Magneto and his people, and seemed to be winning when the terrorists fled. Not long after, the Sentinels were launched, but we have yet to determine whether it was Magneto or the X-Men who caused that launch, and who now controls the Sentinels," Gyrich said, his words one long eruption, diverting attention from his negligence.

"Oh my God," Val gasped. "Magneto stole the Sentinels?"

"So it would appear," the President nodded, concern furrowing his brow.

"But the X-Men . . ." Gyrich protested.

"Enough about the X-Men, Henry," the Director said. "We will address your handling of this situation later. We will also assume that the X-Men's part in today's events was a good faith effort to stop Magneto, an effort that they have made several times in the past. Despite whatever else they may have done to become outlaws, which may, in the end, be nothing more than having been born mutants, for the moment at least, the X-Men are not the enemy."

Gyrich slumped back in his chair, fuming. Val had a momentary image of his chair melting out from under him with the heat he was generating, and had to suppress a smile. She had warned him that she would put her claws into him deep, and now it looked as though she might actually be able to fulfill that promise.

"Whatever Mr. Gyrich's motives, Valerie," the President said—and Val noted with smug satisfaction that he had stopped calling the weasel by his first name, "he has made a few suggestions that bear close attention.

"Clearly, we must apprehend Magneto and his followers as quickly as possible, and get the Sentinels back. Or destroy them if that becomes necessary," the President went on.

"The Acolytes or the Sentinels?" she asked.

"Perhaps both," the President said gravely, the look in his eyes leaving no room for jest.

"Since we are unaware of the identities of these so-called Acolytes, or even how many there are, Mr. Gyrich has suggested a national curfew on all known mutants," the President continued. "Actually, that was the least radical of the suggestions."

"I think I see where this is going, Mr. President," Val said, shaking her head and sitting up straight in her seat. "Before you continue, if you don't mind, I have a few suggestions of my own."

The President raised his eyebrows at her interruption, but lifted his hand to urge her on. "By all means," he said.

"Impose a curfew if you like, sir, if you feel it might have some effect," she began. "But I don't think any mutant aligned with Magneto would pay any attention to your instructions. They see him as their lord and master, their only authority.

"I do have a number of suggestions regarding the tracking and capture of Magneto, the Acolytes, and the missing Sentinels," she said, "but there is one suggestion that eclipses them all."

"And that is?" the Director asked.

"Don't let Gyrich give the orders."

Chapter 16

The hallway was close quarters for battle, but the X-Men and the Starjammers made do. Rogue had point, with Cyclops and Corsair right behind her. Cyclops was pumped, exhilarated in a way he had not experienced for quite some time. They were in grave danger, that could not be denied, particularly with the risky escape they had been forced to attempt. But Scott was confident they would make it.

As he ran, shoulder to shoulder with his father, he sensed an electric charge between them. They moved as one, Christopher Summers and his son, Scott. They were a force to be reckoned with. Despite the gravity of their situation, Cyclops savored the moment. In his life, there had been far too few of them.

The sentries responsible for security on the prison level, and the soldiers who had come down from upper floors, had not presented much of a challenge—it had taken less than a half a minute to overcome their resistance outside the cell where he and his father had been kept captive. Deathbird's personal guard and most of her soldiers were involved in repelling the Kree uprising that was being staged in the Great Hall.

"Looks like smooth sailing from here," Corsair grinned at his side.

"Dreams are for dreamers, Dad," Cyclops replied. "We've still got to face the Imperial Guard."

"You're far too serious, Scott," his father said, shaking his head. "You told us already that the Guard wasn't fighting full strength when they came after the X-Men."

"That was before we raised the stakes," Cyclops answered. "Gladiator and the others know the X-Men only showed up here to bail you out. But as far as they're concerned, you, Hepzibah, and Candide belong in here. They're not going to just let us go."

"Not need to *let* us go, they," Hepzibah hissed behind them. "When to leave, Starjammers want, hold us back nothing can!"

"I wish I felt your confidence, Hepzibah," Rogue said from the point position. "But the Guard knows little Miss Candide is really a black marketeer working with the Kree rebels. That makes her a legitimate political prisoner."

"I'd choose your words more carefully, girl," Corsair grunted. "Nothing about what the Shi'ar have done here on Hala is legitimate, especially putting Deathbird in the driver's seat!"

Rogue cast a glance back at Cyclops and Corsair, then continued ahead without another word. Scott was glad she didn't respond. Rogue had dealt with more volatile personalities than Corsair's many times, and knew better than to let such bitterness offend her. Still, Scott felt something needed to be said.

"You knew she didn't mean it like that," he told his father. "Why were you so harsh with her?"

Corsair raised his head, his jaw thrust out in a contemplative look that Cyclops recognized from his own, personal repertoire.

"This godforsaken planet is getting to me, Scott," the leader of the Starjammers said, finally. "We backed Lilandra's play many times, been part of the Shi'ar's galactic games when, just maybe, we should have been paying closer attention. I've got to wonder, after all that's happened, if we were really on the side of the angels all those times, or just helping to make hell a little hotter for a bunch of other grunts like us."

"Intergalactic war and diplomacy are a lot bigger than we are, Dad," Cyclops replied. "If things haven't worked out the way we expected, it's because not everyone defines nobility and honor the same way, or even cares to define it to begin with. You've always been on the side of the angels."

Corsair cast a sidelong glance at Cyclops, then slowly shook his head.

"That's a good son talking about his old man, Scott," he said. "Doesn't mean it's true. But I hope to hell it is."

"Cyclops!" Rogue shouted.

Scott looked up to see that she was flying back down the hall toward them, an urgent expression on her face. Past her, he saw that the hallway ended in a T-junction, with only left or right as options.

"More'a Deathbird's shock troops up ahead!" she said. "We can go through them, but we ain't makin' any upward progress."

"God help Ch'od if he gets to the dome of the building before we do," Corsair said, echoing Rogue's concern. There was a sort of apology in his tone, and Rogue nodded, almost imperceptibly, in acknowledgment and acceptance of this.

"We go through them," Cyclops answered. "But we've got to find stairs, or an outer wall, and I mean now!"

"Scott, wait!" Jean said, coming up past Gambit and Hepzibah.

"These new troops aren't alone," she said. "The

Guard is with them. Not all of them, but at the very least Oracle and Gladiator, maybe Starbolt as well, though it's hard to read him from here."

Cyclops glanced quickly back to the T-junction ahead.

"It's not a problem, Scott," Corsair said. "Only three of them against nine of us. No contest."

It had taken Scott a long time to resolve his conflicted feelings about his father. For a long time, he was angry that Corsair had never tried to find him and his brother Alex, though he knew that was irrational given the distance to Earth and the fact that their father had thought them dead. Then he had struggled with the seemingly free-spirited life Corsair led as an interstellar pirate. But he'd gotten over all of that. Now he was merely happy that his father still lived. And he hoped that Chris Summers was proud of his oldest boy.

That boy that lived inside him screamed in terror at the decision that Cyclops was in the process of making. He had to fight, and valiantly, so that his father would be proud of his skill and courage. But Scott had not been made leader of the X-Men without reason. There wasn't a warrior among them who was cooler under fire. And as far as he was concerned, there was only one logical course of action. No matter what his father thought.

"In these close quarters, anything can happen," he said. "And if we slip up, even a little, and if he wanted to, Gladiator could kill us all without help from anyone."

Cyclops turned to face his extended crew.

"All of you, listen up," he snapped. "We're in full retreat. Forget the Guard. From this moment on, we concentrate on avoiding confrontation, and making it to the roof with our lives. Fan out and find us an egress from this hotspot. Now!"

They moved instantly, even Candide and the Starjammers. Even his father. The Starjammers had a tendency to fly by the seat of their pants. Cyclops believed that the others saw his Dad's willingness to defer to him in such dire straits, and acted in kind. There was no room for maverick decision-making in this scenario, he knew. It was obvious to him that they all did.

They ran, full steam, back the way they had come. All of them pounded on the walls to the left or right as they ran, hoping to find some kind of passageway they might have missed. It seemed useless. Any moment, the Imperial Guard would arrive, and they would never make it to the dome before Ch'od arrived. Cyclops wasn't willing to accept that fate.

"Stop!" he screamed. "We've only got one option now! Up!"

He tilted back his head and let loose with a full power blast of destructive force. His optic beams vaporized the ceiling above them. Rogue followed his lead, shattering a huge section next to the hole he had made. Metal and marble tumbled down into the hall.

"Go, go, go!" he ordered, even as Warren, Jean, and Rogue helped the rest of the group through the hole in the ceiling.

In seconds, they stood in a darkened foyer of marble and wood. Dim light emanated from an archway to one side, which appeared to be the entrance to a wide stairwell.

"Dis look maybe like its Deathbird's private passage," Gambit observed. "Maybe de lady like to sneak down an' look at her prisoners in de middle of de night?"

"Who cares what it is?" Candide snapped. "It leads up."

"Mine heart doth cringe at the call to retreat," Raza said. "Yet whither go the Starjammers, so there must I also go. Lead on, Cyclops."

Scott was way ahead of them all. In seconds, they were pounding up the wide, winding, marble staircase. The dim light they had seen was filtering in through heavy glass windows set deep in the wall at intervals each time they circled round to the outer wall. Though it was night outside, the city and the stars shone brightly enough so that they could see the steps at least. The red glow of Scott's ruby quartz visor led the way like a torch.

There was shouting far below, and Cyclops knew Gladiator and the Imperial Guard were on to them. They would already be in pursuit. He could only hope that, though Oracle could signal the other Guards wherever they might be, she would have no idea what the winding stairway was or where it might lead.

Then the sounds from below were joined by the sounds of battle from above. The Great Hall was close by, though Scott knew they had to be approaching it from the end opposite where Jean and the others had first infiltrated the building. The stairs wound around twice more, and there it was, stretched out before them behind a gossamer curtain of some unknown substance which allowed them to view the entire scene. Cyclops assumed that, from the other side, the curtain or gate must be opaque.

It was an ugly scene. With reinforcements and Titan and Warstar, Deathbird's forces were routing the Kree rebels. It was going badly for them. Even as they watched, Warstar cut down a pair of blue-skinned Kree soldiers, one male and one female, who lay together in death the way they ought to have lain together in life.

The Kree had been one of the most feared, war-mongering races in the universe before the Shi'ar defeated them. They were proud and vicious, but this time, their rebellion was going to fail. It was horrific. It was war. But as much as he wished the X-Men could right the wrongs, erase the atrocities, that had taken place and were still taking place, there on Hala, Cyclops knew the X-Men could not win a war with the Shi'ar Empire. Nor was it their place to do so. But no matter the logic, it was one of the hardest commands he had ever given.

"Keep moving," he said, and turned back to the stairs.

"No!" Candide shouted. She leveled her stolen blaster at the panoramic curtain, and obliterated it.

"There!" Deathbird screeched from somewhere above. "The prisoners have escaped. Destroy them all!"

"X-Men!" Gladiator shouted from the stairwell beneath them. "Surrender or we will be forced to attack!"

"So much for dat whole retreat business, eh?" Gambit said with a wry grin.

All eyes were on Cyclops as he looked around, finally locking on Archangel's blue-tinted features. Warren raised his right eyebrow, his whole face dedicated to the question, "What now?" that he had asked so many times without ever speaking the words.

"Let's cover the Kree for their evac," he decided.

"Good," Warren said, and shook his head in disbelief before taking to the air in the Great Hall.

He headed straight for Deathbird.

SIEGE

* * *

His rows of razor sharp teeth clamped tightly together, Ch'od piloted the cloaked *Starjammer* through the maze of Shi'ar battle cruisers and vessels co-opted from other planetary governments within the Shi'ar empire. It was more than a challenge, more than simply running a gauntlet. It was foolhardy, near suicidal.

Each ship in the Shi'ar armada that hung in orbit around Hala was equipped with the most advanced technology in the galaxy. It was a miracle the sensitive equipment had not picked up the *Starjammer*'s cloaking signal yet. Even worse, if Ch'od piloted too close to one of the ship's, he would set off proximity sensors that no cloaking system, no matter how advanced, could deceive.

A slick sheen of moisture began to build up on his scaly flesh. Not because of the spatial labyrinth he was currently flying, but because of what was to come. So far, he'd had it easy. Once he entered Hala's atmosphere, things would be different. The moment the *Starjammer* burned through the planet's cloud cover, he'd be visible to every sensor on the surface of the planet. De-cloaked. Or, as Corsair would have put it, screwed.

The *Starjammer* might as well be a brightly painted target. Any sane pilot, any sane pirate, would turn tail and run. But the Starjammers were the only family Ch'od had. There was no way he was leaving Hala without them.

On the other hand, he really didn't relish the thought of dying. He had a plan, of course. He was too good a pilot not to have a plan. It was dangerous, almost ridiculously so. If anyone had suggested to him even days earlier that he might attempt such a feat, he would have laughed heartily and honestly. But he would rather take his chances with his own skills, take his life into his own hands, than offer himself up as target practice for ground-to-air gunners and armada captains all bucking for a promotion.

Even as Ch'od considered again the lunacy of his plan, the *Starjammer* slipped between two battle cruisers and into open space just shy of the high, thin layer of clouds that marked Hala's outer atmosphere.

"It really ought to work," Ch'od said aloud.

There was a loud chittering noise behind him, and he allowed himself a moment to turn and face his long-time companion, Cr+eeee. The small, mammalian creature had his long tail straight up in distress. His head turned slightly, and he brought one foot up to itch the gentle curve of his proboscis. Cr+eeee stared at him, still chittering in his own, unintelligible language. There was no mistaking his message. Cr+eeee thought that his old friend had gone entirely mad.

"I'm sorry, my friend," Ch'od responded, though he really could not understand Cr+eeee's words. "I wish you were not with me now. In that way, I could make this decision only for myself, and not endanger you as well. Sadly, there is no other choice for me. I hope you understand."

Cr+eeee's eyes closed and he nodded, slowly, in resignation.

Ch'od turned back to the view of Hala that presented itself before him.

"It really ought to work," he said again, and he knew it was true. He had calculated to the most radical decimal the location of the Capitol Building. The hyper drive was burning hot, but the warp engines were offline. By firing the hyperburners, he ought to be able to both draw and divert attention. Planetary sensors would pick him up immediately, but they would see the trace energies of the hyperdrive kicked up to full thrust, and automatically assume the ship was gone.

That should give him at least one full minute before they realized the *Starjammer* was still within the planet's atmosphere. Their disbelief would carry him for several more minutes, and even after that, it would take a few minutes to actually find him.

It should work. With the warp engines down, he'd be on hyperburn, but never make the jump. The trick was going to be pulling the *Starjammer* out of hyperburn before it hit the surface of the planet, with gravity working against him. If he couldn't do that, and he wasn't at all sure that he could, then the *Starjammer* would be obliterated, and he along with it. But if he didn't go in after them, the others were as good as dead. Ch'od preferred death to the knowledge that he had abandoned his friends, his family.

The fins on his head and forearms folded back against his scales, an instinctive reaction to danger. He had not prayed since he was a child, but he said a silent prayer to the gods of Timor, his home planet. The fingers of his right hand found the control panel and he snapped a glowing yellow switch, the safety on the hyperdrive, which now lit up red. Beneath it was a green button that would kick the *Starjammer* into hyperburn.

Ch'od checked his coordinates one, final time.

"It should work," he told himself again.

Then he hit the button.

* * *

Above the massive doors to the Great Hall was a huge octagonal window in a swirling spider web of frame. Deathbird rose above the melee, holding one of the two-and-a-half-foot javelin-quills that she was so expert at wielding. Her wings were attached to her wrists, forcing her to use her arms in flight. Yet she had so mastered the art of it that she was able to hurl the javelin, spin into a dive and then glide back to her previous height. And her weapon found its mark.

A Kree warrior let loose her final battle cry, and Archangel winced at the keening wail that followed.

Deathbird wore twin armbands which housed eight-inch quills that, once removed, telescoped to four times that length. Her talons could score steel, and Warren didn't want to even think about what they might do to human flesh. In strength and endurance, she was his superior by far. But Archangel didn't think she was much faster than he was.

It didn't matter, though. None of it. If they were going to get off Hala, somebody had to take Deathbird down. With Rogue and Gladiator a natural match-up, that left Deathbird for him.

Archangel was terrified. Not of Deathbird, despite her savagery and greater power. No, Warren Worthington was afraid of himself. When his natural, mutant wings had been destroyed, and Apocalypse had given him bio-organic replacements, had significantly *changed* him, it was not the act of a Samaritan. Apocalypse had been creating an engine of death, a killing machine. Warren had struggled for a long time to be certain he would never become what Apocalypse had envisioned.

But sometimes he felt that bloodlust surge to the surface of his mind. More often than not, he felt the phantom twitch of muscles he no longer had, muscles that were now bio-organic steel. That twitch sent paralyzing wing-knives flying at the merest whim, even at a subconscious order. Controlling them took an intense concentration that he had not dared reveal to the other X-Men.

Though they would have accepted him no matter how he had changed, what Archangel had been through affected him so deeply that he could barely accept it himself. There was a new distance between himself and his old friends, and it was almost entirely his doing. He was healing, he knew. But he had been violated, and it would take some time to get over that.

At that moment, however, Warren felt more freedom than he had at any time since he had stopped being simply the Angel, and had become Archangel forevermore. Deathbird's cruelty freed him. No matter what the nobility of purpose behind a war, its results were always heinous. Deathbird reveled in atrocity. She thrived on the vile, obscene thing that the Kree homeworld had become, on the wretched lives of the people barely surviving there.

And now that they had dared to attack her, dared to act against her depravity, she butchered them, delighted by the carnage. Archangel believed that Deathbird was truly evil. Others might have called her insane, but in the time he had spent as a mental slave to Apocalypse, he came to know evil intimately. Insanity and evil, he believed, were inherently the same. One did not excuse the other.

Deathbird's perversity gave Archangel the freedom to explode. If she was the victor, the X-Men would die. Warren wasn't about to let that happen. No matter what it took, he was going to win.

She rose again, silhouetted against the artificial light streaming through the octagonal window from the square outside. Archangel could fly at, or at least very near, the speed of sound. There was no time for any of her sycophantic bootlicks to even call out a warning.

At top speed, he drove his right shoulder into Deathbird's belly, and together they shattered the spider web pattern of the window. Broken glass cascaded down into the square beneath them.

"You're sorely outmatched, X-Man," Deathbird snarled as she shook loose from Warren's grip, her strength outstripping his just as his speed eclipsed hers. That was his edge. And he had another. Her wings were attached, while his arms were free. He had to use those advantages, and his fury, or he would die.

They might all die.

* * *

There were a lot of things about his son that Corsair arrogantly assumed Scott had inherited from him. On the other hand, Scott was an optimist, and that was something Corsair had never been.

They burst into the Great Hall on a wave of vengeful fury. The Kree rebels shouted an uncommon welcome, testament to how badly they were losing the battle. Archangel exploded into the air and slammed into Deathbird, shattering a huge window and carrying both of them outside.

It felt good. But Corsair knew it wouldn't last. It couldn't. No matter how good a leader his son was, or how courageously they all fought, they were, very simply outmatched. Not by the Shi'ar troops, but by the Imperial Guard.

Yet, that was the story of Corsair's life. He was always a pragmatist, perhaps even a pessimist. He'd gotten himself, and the Starjammers, into no-win situations dozens of times, and they were all still alive to tell of it. There was a reckless ferocity that overcame Christopher Summers when he expected to die. In a way, he thought that lady luck admired that in him, that she protected him when he abandoned all hope of survival, all concern for his own safety.

Either that, or he'd used up all his luck, and his number was definitely up.

"If we can keep the Guard busy, the Kree will have no problem with the Shi'ar shock troops that are left," Scott said, running beside him.

"Good plan, son," Corsair laughed. "Then who's going to cover our asses on the way out?"

Cyclops said nothing, but Corsair noticed a grim set to his jaw that was unsettling. In anyone else, he would have assumed the look and the silence meant he didn't expect to be able to get out. In Scott, Corsair figured it was just single-minded determination to save the Kree and everyone else as well. Corsair knew the Kree could not be saved. They had lost a war, and their conquerors were making their lives hell. They could fight back and fight back, but as long as they remained a conquered people, nothing the X-Men or Starjammers did would help.

But hey, Corsair wasn't about to burst his son's bubble. If they lived to see the sunrise, it would probably be because Cyclops never considered losing as an option.

"Starjammers!" he shouted. "Titan is ours, now! Concentrate fire!"

Out of the corner of his eye, Corsair saw Candide wade into the Kree rebels and begin to whip them into a frenzy with her battle cries. He'd never seen her as a warrior, and now he realized he never really knew her at all. He only hoped that her hatred for the Shi'ar did not prevent her from leading the Kree into a strategic retreat.

Corsair was firing his blaster in a seemingly erratic pattern, creating an arc of cover fire in front of him. Two Shi'ar soldiers ran toward him, firing wildly as they attempted to duck within the arc of his fire.

Suddenly, he stopped firing. He took a moment, their weapon fire singing his hair. He lined up his shot, and took them down with two concentrated bursts from his sidearm. His erratic fire had been a lure, one he'd used many times before to instill false confidence in his enemies.

"C'mon guys," he said as he jumped over their fallen forms. "Would I have lived this long if I was really that bad a shot?"

"Die, faithless cur!" a voice shouted behind him.

Before Corsair could turn, he heard the pulse of blaster fire and the crackle of its impact. The Shi'ar soldier was already hitting the ground by the time he'd completed his turn, and Hepzibah stood over him, her weapon smoking.

"Learn to take cover, you must, if continue to live you wish," Hepzibah said.

"What fun would that be?" Corsair laughed, even as they turned to defend against other attackers. "You'd hate not having to worry about me, and not being able to rub it in that I need your backup. And I wouldn't have to pay you back with my own, personal services, later on."

Even as her sword flashed for a bloody close-quarters conflict, Hepzibah was laughing. She shared her lover's hopeless abandon in this struggle, as she had so often in the past. As she had that first time they met on the prison planet of Alsibar.

"Didst thou not issue a call to attack yon ogre, Titan?" Raza said as he joined his companions.

"We've been a little busy," Corsair responded.

"The Kree hath rendered aid unto us," Raza explained.

Corsair saw that he was right. Though Candide did seem to be leading the Kree in retreat, they were also drawing the concentrated response of the Shi'ar soldiers. The battle was splitting into two parts, the real war, and the elite one. One would affect the outcome of this battle, but the real war would go on.

He took a glance around, and was disheartened by what he saw. Cyclops and Rogue were double teaming Gladiator, but even with Rogue's strength and endurance, and Scott's optic beams, it was only a matter of time before Gladiator overwhelmed them. Gambit was dancing around Warstar, trying to keep out of range of C'Cil's hands and B'Nee's electrical charge. The Cajun was launching explosively charged debris at them every chance he had, but was not having much luck.

Then there was Jean. In many ways, Corsair considered her the most powerful member of the team. She was a superior psi-talent. Somehow, though, Oracle had gotten the drop on her. With Oracle on one side of her and Titan on the other, Jean spun wildly, lashing out at phantom sparring partners. Even as the Starjammers approached, Titan was reaching for Jean with one massive hand.

It didn't look good. But that was when the Starjammers were at their best. With Raza and Hepzibah at his side, Corsair opened fire on Titan.

"Starjammers attack!" he shouted.

Their three blasters on full, the Starjammers did not let up their assault. Titan slammed back against the balconies, which crumbled under his weight. He fell to the ground, flailing his arms in an attempt to fend off their blasts. Beaten, he began to shrink, but the Starjammers poured it on. Moments later, Corsair stood triumphantly above Titan, the point of his sword just nicking the flesh of the Guardsman's neck.

"Feel free to grow once more," Corsair said. "Though I would advise against it."

Hepzibah and Raza hefted the Guardsman to his feet, Corsair's sword still dangerously close. Then Hepzibah swung a roundhouse kick at Titan's temple, and the Guardsman went down, unconscious.

Corsair grinned. He didn't know how she'd been taken off guard, but Jean Grey would have no trouble with Oracle now that the distraction had been taken care of. The tide was turning.

"No!" he heard a male voice scream.

Corsair turned to see that nearly all of the Kree had retreated through the hole in the floor from which they had invaded. The Shi'ar soldiers were down to a mere half dozen or so. But the remaining Kree had no chance. It was one, lone Kree rebel, and he was not even defending himself. Instead, he was kneeling by the bloodied corpse of a fallen comrade.

"God, no," Corsair whispered to himself. "Candide!"

CHAPTER 17

ven combining their skills and powers, Cyclops and Rogue were only barely keeping Gladiator at bay. The Imperial Guard's Praetor would slam Rogue to the floor, or batter her against one of the crumbling balconies, and Cyclops would let loose with an optic blast that would, at best, disorient Gladiator. At worst, it simply focused his attention on Cyclops.

Scott dove out of the way of Gladiator's energy blast and scrambled for cover. Thankfully, Rogue recovered quickly. Before Gladiator could get to Cyclops, Rogue had grabbed Praetor by both legs and swung him, with every ounce of her strength, into the marble face of the second level balcony. It shattered on impact, and Scott had to dodge the falling debris. But for the moment, Gladiator was dazed.

But Starbolt was moving in.

"No more games, X-Men!" Cyclops shouted. "We've got to go, now. The only way to do that is to take the Guard down. Hard!"

Even as he shouted, Gladiator was rising to his feet in the second balcony. Rogue shot across his line of fire toward Starbolt, who blanketed her in his stellar energy. Rogue was not deterred. Once, she had stolen his power, and Cyclops knew she hated that aspect of her abilities. But the time for strategy was over. He'd said it, and apparently Rogue had taken it to heart.

In the center of the ruined Great Hall, high above the debris-strewn, cracked marble floor, Rogue and

Starbolt clashed. More accurately, she jerked to a sudden stop just before barreling into him, and pummeled him in the face with one flashing fist. Starbolt's left cheek seemed to explode, not with blood, but with uncontrollable energy that strafed Rogue, and the barely recovered Gladiator. And then Starbolt fell to the floor of the Great Hall and lay still.

"Sharra and Ky'thri!" Gladiator cried, dazed once more by Starbolt's powers. "On my honor, X-Men, if Starbolt is dead, then so are you all!"

"None of this would be happening, Gladiator, if you would just sit down and shut up!" Cyclops shouted, and put all his will behind a massive optic blast which nailed Gladiator in the chest and sent him crashing through the rear wall of the room.

He did not immediately emerge, and Cyclops had a moment to regret his words. If Starbolt was dead, the X-Men were not to blame. But they would grieve nonetheless, for Starbolt, for the Imperial Guard, and for themselves. They had all once been allies, and the X-Men did not kill even their greatest enemies.

For the moment, perhaps not more than that, Gladiator was down. But he knew it wouldn't last. It couldn't. Eventually, Gladiator would beat them. Unless they had help.

Jean! Scott thought, mentally pushing her name out of his head. *We could use a little help over here!*

Even as he completed the thought, Cyclops turned to see Jean and Oracle facing off again. Corsair and the other Starjammers were pressing an attack against Titan, who looked very near beaten. Scott realized they were doing better than he'd thought. Still, though, there was Gladiator. And why had Jean not taken Oracle out of the fight already?

I'm on it, lover, her mental voice whispered in his brain. With her thoughts, his brain was filled with her feelings, her recent experiences, as if they were downloaded directly into his own memory and passion. Oracle had gotten the drop on Jean while Titan momentarily distracted her. It turned out the Guard's resident psi had indeed gotten more powerful. Oracle had been able to mentally manipulate Jean into seeing many multiples of herself and Titan, and though she knew most of them weren't real, she had had to guard against them just the same.

She would have broken out of it, given a few more moments. But those moments might have been costly. Fortunately, the Starjammers intervened. With Titan out of the picture, she had focused her psi abilities, pinpointed Oracle, and now . . .

The two women stared at one another across a space of several yards. They were locked in a silent mental combat, but now that Jean had her focus back, it was no contest. She'd even been able to communicate with Scott during their clash. Oracle was sweating, her white face pinched with concentration, perhaps even pain. Indeed, the more he watched her, the more Cyclops realized that the Shi'ar woman was in severe pain.

Scott could have ended it there. One, quick, optic blast would have taken Oracle down and ended the fight. For several reasons, he chose not to do that. His energy was depleted, and he needed to conserve what he had left. It would be over in a moment regardless. And, most importantly, Jean would not take kindly to him interfering in her fights. She hated the thought that he ever needed to protect her. Which amused Scott, because more often than not, it was he who needed her help, their current situation a case in point.

As Cyclops watched, Jean gave an exasperated sigh, walked the few paces that separated her from Oracle, and simply decked the other woman. When she looked up at Scott, she was smiling. But her smile quickly faded as she looked past him.

Turning instantly, Scott saw that Gambit was having trouble against Warstar once more. The symbiotic mechanoids were going to be a problem. Their regenerative powers meant that the only way to stop them was to kill them. If they could be killed. Scott was happy to realize that they didn't need to stop Warstar, only buy themselves some time.

Scott let loose with a weak optic blast that yet managed to free Gambit, for the moment, from Warstar's clutches.

"That's about all I've got, Remy!" he called. "Make it count."

"C'Cil's mind is almost too dense for me to manipulate," Jean said as she jogged to his side. "But I might be able to confuse B'Nee for a few moments."

She focused on Warstar, and B'Nee, the smaller biomechanoid who rode C'Cil's back, shrieked with panic and begin to look wildly around.

"Rogue!" Scott called, pointing to where Gambit was still trying to get close enough to the flailing Warstar to do some damage. Rogue swooped low toward Remy and Warstar, but Gambit didn't see her coming. He dodged a blow from C'Cil, popped up behind Warstar, and reached out for B'Nee's back, both hands already glowing with an explosive charge.

"Gambit, no!" Cyclops yelled, but neither his warning nor Rogue's aid arrived in time.

Remy's hands landed on B'Nee's back, and he was

immediately electrocuted. His entire body was stiff, every muscle taut, and he shook from head to toe as electricity coursed through him. The charge passed from his hands to B'Nee's body, and B'Nee shrieked once more as he began to glow.

"Remy!" Rogue cried as she pulled him away from Warstar, still jittering with the electricity induced seizure.

In a shadowy corner of the Great Hall, B'Nee exploded, throwing C'Cil forward onto the marble floor. Warstar had been separated. B'Nee's head rolled toward Scott and Jean. As he stared at it in horror, Scott realized that where the head lay, debris and marble were being absorbed and subtly changed. Already, B'Nee was reconstructing himself. It was an extraordinary example of alien life unlike anything he had seen before. And C'Cil was already rising, prepared to help his other half with repairs.

It was only a matter of time.

"Surrender, X-Men, or you will die! You have done enough damage this day!" Gladiator shouted from the shattered balcony above.

"What does it take to put this guy down?" Jean asked next to him.

Scott was about to reply that he didn't think Gladiator *could* be put down. But another voice, crying out with pain, anger, and hatred, interrupted him. It was the voice of his father.

"Murderer!" Corsair screamed. "How dare you, Gladiator? How dare you?"

Scott turned to see Corsair, Raza, Hepzibah, and the Kree rebel Kam-Lorr, coming toward them. Corsair was carrying someone in his arms, but it took Scott a moment to realize that it was Candide. And what had

Corsair said. Murderer? Which would mean that Candide was dead.

Scott Summers had never truly understood war. In his mind, he could still not comprehend it. But in his belly, where nausea and dread roiled into a terrible, noxious brew, he finally knew what war was.

The knowledge was unwelcome.

* * *

Only his speed had saved him thus far, but Archangel was tiring. He let off another flurry of wingknives, desperately hoping that several might slip past Deathbird's enhanced body armor and tag her face or hands. The paralyzing effects of the knives might be his only chance. They cut the armor, but apparently did not make it all the way through. Several times, he'd cut her wings, but the paralyzing chemicals in his wingknives seemed to have no effect there. Archangel had bombarded Deathbird with so many, they jutted from her body armor like the quills of a porcupine.

Each time he would launch a new barrage, she would block and then attempt a physical attack. And each time she would fail. With her need to keep her arms extended, her every blow was telegraphed long before it would reach him. With his far superior speed, Warren was not an easy target. Each time Deathbird attempted to strike and failed, she would go into a dive. Twice he had tried to get her during these moments, but she recovered in time to go at him again. She'd almost had him last time.

Where he was growing tired, slowing down, it seemed as though she could keep up the battle forever.

"Your attack has only proven that I was right all along," Deathbird squealed, madness in her eyes. "Lilandra and the cripple Xavier are plotting my downfall. They have sent you to test my mettle. You will find me more difficult to defeat than you imagined, X-Man. I will send them that message with your corpse!"

She lunged at him again. This time, Warren wasn't fast enough. Deathbird's closed fist caught him a glancing blow in the back of the head. Dazed, Warren began to fall, thinking dimly about how lucky he was that she'd struck with closed hand rather than her talons. Otherwise, his brains would have spilled out in mid-air.

Screeching, Deathbird dove after him. Warren didn't really see her coming, but he could hear her. It was the sound of the reaper come to claim him, but Archangel wasn't ready yet. He shook off his disorientation, and switched direction in an instant.

"That's it!" he shouted. "Now you've really pissed me off!"

At three times the speed with which she was diving toward him, Archangel flashed upward at Deathbird. With all his speed and strength, he flew toward her, then turned away at the last moment. His left wing lashed out, lightning fast, and sliced open her body armor. Deathbird shrieked in pain, reaching for the eight-inch-long wound that had suddenly appeared in her side.

And, lowering her arms, she began to fall.

After a moment, she recovered. But the tyrant was wounded, now, and Archangel was filled with rage and a thirst for vengeance. He did not so much embrace the things Apocalypse had wanted of him when he'd received his new wings. Rather, he took up the reins of the savagery within him, and wielded it as the most terrible of weapons. He did not become the fury, he mastered it.

Further maddened by pain, yet slowed and confounded by her wounds, Deathbird was no match for him. Again and again, Archangel attacked, lured her into committing herself to a lunge for her throat. Then he struck. Once, twice, three and four times, he slashed through her body armor.

Finally, she went down.

Warren was triumphant, not merely over his enemy, but over himself. He was proud of both victories. Archangel had not struck to kill, but to incapacitate. And despite her poisoned soul, the depth of her evil, he would not let her fall to her death. In mid-air, he snagged Deathbird around the waist.

Suddenly, Archangel was blinded by the glare of a powerful light from above. The courtyard and the outside of the Capitol Building lit up as if it were day. Shielding his eyes with one hand, Warren saw that it was not merely one light, but several that spotlit the building.

The *Starjammer* had arrived.

* * *

The Imperial Guard was almost beaten. But Cyclops knew that, as the Beast was fond of saying, almost only counted in horseshoes and hand grenades. Gladiator was still standing. It wasn't over yet.

Cyclops stood with Jean and Rogue, who carried the unconscious, severely injured Gambit over her shoulder. The Kree rebel leader, Kam-Lorr, and the Starjammers came up to stand with them. Corsair laid Candide's ravaged corpse at his feet, and stood to shake his fist at Gladiator in defiance.

"You're just following orders, right?" Corsair screamed. "I know that's what you're going to say, Gladiator. You're a good soldier, aren't you? Well, old friend, I've heard it all before."

Gladiator did not fly so much as float from the balcony, slowly dropping to the rubble-strewn floor. He landed perhaps twenty feet from them, but did not approach.

"I am sorry you have lost your friend, Corsair," Gladiator began, "but she was a political prisoner. She knew what she was getting into here. It is war, after all. Even the innocent are sacrificed to the machine of war."

Corsair hung his head, and Cyclops felt his father's pain.

"How can you so blindly follow the orders of a ruler you know is despicable?" Corsair demanded. "How can you simply let all of this happen?"

"I am not blind," Gladiator said coldly.

"Which is all the worse!" Corsair cried. "If you were simply ignorant, at least I could pity you. But you have a soul, you have a conscience. You are not blind, no, not at all. You simply choose to close your eyes."

Corsair paused, and Scott looked over to see a ferocity in his father's countenance that he had never before witnessed. Disgust, rage and agony, all were clearly visible in every twitch, every motion. He crossed the space separating him from Gladiator, a mere human face to face with one of the most powerful beings in the galaxy.

"You pride yourself on your honor," Corsair sneered. "But you have none. You are a coward, Gladiator. Afraid to have a will of your own. Afraid to express principles that might differ from those you so ignorantly consider your betters."

Gladiator stiffened, breathed in slowly, then spoke through gritted teeth.

"I order you all to surrender," he said. "You will not be allowed to leave Hala."

Corsair stepped even closer, and Scott winced. Gladiator could kill his father with one blow. But Corsair was not to be deterred. He leaned forward so that his forehead was nearly touching Gladiator's.

"Get out of my way, Praetor," Corsair said. "You have caused enough death and misery this day."

The words cut deep. Gladiator blinked, twice, and a look that spoke of uncertainty, even regret, crossed his face.

Then the room glaring white light bathed the room, and they all turned toward the huge window shattered by Archangel's clash with Deathbird long minutes earlier. After a moment, that pair returned through the window. They looked far different now, however, than when they had gone out.

"Warren?" Jean murmured at Scott's side, and Scott was taken aback as well. For Archangel carried the tyrant Deathbird under one arm, like a sack of groceries. Blood flowed from the injured despot, and Warren's wings spread to their full sixteen foot span as he landed several feet from the blazing but unconscious Starbolt.

Unceremoniously, he dropped Deathbird to the ground near Starbolt.

"Let's go X-Men," Archangel said, breaking the silence that had descended upon the room. "Our ride's here."

"Is she dead?" Gladiator asked quietly, and for once, Scott could not read his tone.

"Certainly not," Warren replied. "But she may well be if she does not get attention soon."

"Scott," Jean said softly. "I scan a whole host of minds massing outside the building. Reinforcements, getting ready to storm the place."

The loud crack of devastating weapons fire punctuated her words.

"Surface-to-air weaponry, that is," Hepzibah said.

"Time to go, folks," Rogue added.

"I cannot allow you to leave," Gladiator said, staring, unmoving, at the bleeding form of Deathbird.

But his heart wasn't in the words. Cyclops knew that, and stepped forward to confront him, but without the anger that his father had shown. Instead, he felt only sadness. He laid a hand on Corsair's shoulder and, much to his surprise, Corsair turned away and went back to where Candide's body lay.

"Gladiator," Cyclops said in a comforting voice. "You are one man, yet I think it very possible you could actually prevent us from leaving here. But not without further death.

"You know that, despite your orders from Deathbird, this is not what your Majestrix would want. There is no one here to see that you follow your Majestrix's wishes over her mad sister's orders, which is as it should be were it not for governmental etiquette. Let us pass."

Behind them, Corsair lifted Candide's corpse and handed it to Kam-Lorr.

"Take her," Scott heard his father say. "Bury her with the people she fought to avenge. But go now before your escape is cut off. But know this, Kam-Lorr. She willingly gave her life for your cause. I have seen the results of your war with the Shi'ar, and though I blame you both, I cannot live with the thought of Deathbird poisoning your planet further. Something must be done before you are all dead.

"As a great Terran soldier once said, 'I shall return.'"

"That would be unwise," Gladiator said quickly, and it took a moment for the meaning of his words to sink in.

He was not going to stop them.

"Tend to your injured, Praetor," Cyclops said. "We will tend to ours and bury our dead."

Gladiator glanced around the room, a sad but bemused expression on his face.

"It is very strange," he said, to no one in particular. "For a moment I thought I heard someone speaking to me."

Cyclops turned to find the rest of the X-Men and the gathered Starjammers staring at him expectantly. Kam-Lorr had already disappeared with Candide's corpse, and Cyclops realized he hadn't known the woman long enough even to mourn. He could, however, grieve for his father, who had lost a friend that day.

"What are you waiting for?" he asked. "We can't use the front door, so we go back to that marble staircase."

They ran for the stairs that had brought them up from below, and Cyclops hoped they would go to the top of the building. Warstar was nearly rebuilt, but Oracle and Titan were still unconscious, and Starbolt and Deathbird were gravely wounded. The last thing he saw before he followed Rogue, who was still carrying the unconscious Gambit, up the stairs, was Gladiator lifting Starbolt and Deathbird and heading for the front door.

A few moments later, as they pounded up the stairs,

he heard Gladiator's shouts of command.

"Quickly!" Praetor cried. "The prisoners are escaping! After them! You there, help me tend to the Viceroy!"

Cyclops smiled. Either Gladiator had had a change of heart or, more likely, he wanted to be sure none of the soldiers would even be able to conceive of the idea that he might have let them go. Among the many things the X-Men had learned in the past day, one of the most shameful had been that Gladiator was far more intelligent, and far more noble than any of them had ever given him credit for.

Several minutes later, with blaster fire and shouted voices echoing through the winding stairwell beneath them, they emerged in a short hallway that led to a single door. Without waiting for the X-Men to remove it with their natural mutant abilities, the Starjammers obliterated it in an assault with their own weapons.

"Nice digs," Archangel said, whistling in admiration.

"Must be Deathbird's private aerie," Corsair observed. "Y'know, I feel like trashing the place, but I'm just too damn tired."

"Alas, we have not the time," Raza said grimly, "or 'tis certain I wouldst trash the place with mine own hands."

"Ch'od," Corsair said, tapping the comm-badge on his breast.

"Aye, Captain?" Ch'od responded.

"Glad to see you made it in one piece, my friend," Corsair said wistfully. "Now let's just hope we can all make it out. We're near the top. Look around for our blaster fire as we clear ourselves an exit."

The long, beautifully appointed outer wall of the aerie, with arched windows that looked down on the courtyard, was completely incinerated by blaster fire and optic bursts. Seconds later, the *Starjammer* hovered in place of the disintegrated wall, its side hatch open and a short ramp extended out.

They hustled aboard, the shouts of soldiers getting closer and closer. As Ch'od closed the hatch, Shi'ar warriors burst through the door and began firing on the ship. Such small arms fire was no match for the *Starjammer*'s hull, however.

Cyclops helped Rogue get Gambit strapped to a medi-slab. They rigged his lifesign monitors. Only when they went to strap in with the rest of the passengers, and saw Raza assisting a staggering Hepzibah, did Cyclops realize his father's lover was also injured. He admired her courage, for Hepzibah had never uttered a word of complaint.

Just as Scott snapped his belt into place, Corsair appeared in the door to the cockpit.

"Bad news, team," he said grimly. "Warp engines are out. Even if we make it out of Hala's orbit, we'll never outrun the armada up there. We have to use the stargate."

"But Earth's sun can't take too many 'gates in such a brief period," Jean said. "You know that, Corsair. It becomes unstable."

"Nothing is certain, Jean," Warren argued. "From everything I've read or heard the Professor and Hank say, I think it would have to be a high concentration of stargates over a long period of time to actually destabilize the sun. That's what they were afraid of when the Shi'ar originally placed the stargate there. This is different."

"Is it really, Warren?" Cyclops asked, brow furrowed with concern, brain muddled with exhaustion. "Twice was bad enough, but now a third stargate in less than a day? As you said, nothing is certain. We can't take that chance."

"So what are you sayin', sugar?" Rogue asked. "We just give up and let 'em shoot us out of the sky? That doesn't get my vote."

"A handful of us versus the whole population of Earth, the planet itself, Rogue," Jean added. "We can't risk that."

"Look," Warren snapped. "It's like this. We use the gate, there's a slim possibility that we may endanger Earth. We don't use it, we are absolutely going to die. No contest."

"Corsair!" Ch'od called from the cockpit. "My ruse with the hyperdrive has allowed us to elude the armada this long. We have perhaps a few seconds before they find us. We need that time to reverse the process, or there's no way we'll make it to the stargate. The argument would be moot, at that point."

"Decision is out of your hands, X-Men," Corsair said. "I'm the captain of this vessel. My ship, my conscience, my choice."

He breathed deeply, then turned and strode into the cockpit. From where he sat, Cyclops could see his father drop into the co-pilot's chair and strap in.

"Punch it, Ch'od," Corsaid said. "Hit the hyperburners and let's get out of here."

"Aye, Captain," Ch'od replied.

Scott couldn't see the reptilian alien, but he knew Ch'od had followed Corsair's instructions, because moments later they were all pressed against their seats as the hyperburners kicked in.

Several times as they left orbit, surface to air weaponry strafed the ship. It rocked, and Cyclops thought he heard something pop and fizzle. Perhaps an electrical short, he thought. He smelled sulphur, something burning.

"Is that fire?" he asked, not ready to panic yet.

"Stay in your seats!" Corsair yelled. "We'll deal with it when we're through the gate. We've got to slow down to get through, and that's when the armada's going to get their shot at us."

With an abrupt jolt, Scott was thrown forward in his seat. He knew they were still moving, but it almost felt as if they had come to a complete stop.

"Oh God!" Jean cried next to him as an explosion on board the *Starjammer* threw them together. It must have been the armada, firing on them. Which meant they were entering the stargate.

"Just a few more seconds," Scott said, but he was as unnerved as she was. As he imagined they all were. Sparks were flying somewhere off to his right, and there was definitely a fire on board, perhaps more than one.

They were hit again, and the ship seemed to drop with a nauseating suddenness. Scott's stomach lurched. The interior lights went out, and the backup lights came on for a moment, then flickered out as well. The only light within the cabin came from the flicker of flames.

In silence, they all braced for another hit. They prepared themselves for what they expected would be the final strike against the *Starjammer*. You didn't have to be a star pilot to know the ship couldn't take much more. Scott thought he heard someone praying, a male voice, but he couldn't begin to think about who it might be.

Every muscle in his body tensed, waiting for that last hit.

But it didn't come.

"We're in!" Corsair shouted. "Now put those damn fires out!"

Cyclops, Raza and Archangel went to work immediately, dousing the flames with chemicals kept on board for that specific purpose. Minutes later, the fires were out and the emergency lights had been restored.

"We're coming out of it, folks," Corsair said quietly. But there was something in his tone. A hesitancy that Scott found particularly unsettling.

"Dad?" he asked, though he did not usually use the term in front of others. "What is it? What's wrong?"

Corsair stepped into the cabin and scanned his passengers. Finally, he looked at his son. Scott studied his father's expression, his handsome, rugged features. He'd seen the look on Corsair's face before. For a moment, Scott was a boy again, back on that burning plane with his brother Alex and his parents. But he'd lost his father once before. He was no longer a boy. He was a man now. No matter what, Scott Summers was not going to bail out again.

"What is it?" he asked again, and hearing the concern in his voice, they all froze, looking to Corsair for an answer.

"We've emerged into the Sol system, as planned," Corsair said. "We're almost home, people. But we're not going to get there."

Nobody moved, nobody spoke. Cyclops didn't think, at that moment, that any of them even remembered to breathe.

"What are you saying?" he asked, finally.

"The only thing still functioning on this ship is

backup power and life support," Corsair answered, a hard set to his jaw.

"The *Starjammer* is drifting. For all intents and purposes, this ship is dead in space."

EPILOGUE

From the window of his study, Charles Xavier watched with extraordinary relief as the *Blackbird* descended through the night sky over his home. He'd spoken to Val Cooper half a dozen times in the previous two hours, but there had been no word regarding Magneto, the Acolytes, or the Sentinels. The last time they'd spoken, Val had informed him that it might be some time before they would be in contact again. Washington, unsurprisingly, was in an uproar.

And the public had no idea. Not a single clue as to what was really happening. Certainly, the press had been spouting wild theories all day and night, but the truth had not yet been revealed. Xavier knew from experience that, if at all possible, the government would want to keep it that way. Keeping secrets . . . creating secrets was one of Washington's favorite pastimes.

Charles psionically monitored the X-Men's arrival in the hangar. When they had all emerged from the *Blackbird*, he stretched his mind out to touch each of their minds.

Welcome home, X-Men. Please hurry to the ready room immediately. We must prepare for Magneto's next move, whatever it may be.

• • •

Fifteen minutes later, they gathered in the ready room. The mood was grim. Video monitors in the wall were tuned to the major networks and CNN, hoping that some news would be forthcoming. Xavier had the comm-system constantly dialing and redialing Val Cooper's number, without luck. He didn't expect an answer any time soon.

Storm had given the Professor a full accounting of the events that had taken place in Colorado. After which, a thoughtful silence descended upon the room, broken only by the chatter of television broadcasts.

"What do we do now, Professor?" Bishop asked. "We can't just wait around for Magneto to make his move."

"I'm grieved to say that is probably our singular option," Hank sighed.

"It don't sit well with me, but I got to agree with Hank," Logan admitted.

"Hey, guys," Bobby said, getting the team's attention. "Are we forgetting who we're dealing with here? Whatever Magneto's got planned. We won't have to wait very long. What worries me is, between him, the Acolytes, and the Sentinels, we're going to need every bit of help we can get."

"Which brings us to the rest of this team," Storm said. "What of them, Professor? Any word from Cyclops?"

Xavier knew that he should have told them when they first arrived. But he simply had not wanted to think about it. Now, though, there was no avoiding it. His eyes narrowed as he considered his words.

"Professor, what is it?" Hank asked, and Xavier could sense his concern.

"I communicated with Lilandra a short time ago," Xavier answered. "The Shi'ar hierarchy is in an uproar. Deathbird has been badly injured, and both the Starjammers and the X-Men escaped into the stargate. Of course, I was forced to deny any knowledge of the X-Men's actions."

"That's phenomenal news, Professor!" Bobby said excitedly. "Not that I ever doubted they'd pull it off, but . . ."

"There's more to it than that, Iceman," Xavier interrupted. "Whatever happens with Magneto, you must be prepared to face it without your teammates."

Professor Xavier swallowed. He could not have missed the anxiety that now filled all of the gathered X-Men, even without his psi powers.

"It has been several hours since the *Starjammer* entered the stargate, nearly that since they ought to have emerged," Xavier said. "Yet, I have not been able to contact the vessel, nor have I received any communication from them."

"Where are they?" Storm wondered aloud.

"God knows," Xavier responded. "And I hope that he watches over them."

Once more, silence draped the room like a sodden blanket, heavy with apprehension that was quickly evolving into dread. Xavier wished he had the words to comfort his friends, his former students, his X-Men, but for once, he could not think of a single thing to say.

"Professor," Hank murmured, breaking the silence. "Professor."

Xavier looked up. *What is it, Hank?* he thought, using telepathy to ask the question.

"Increase the volume," the Beast whispered, and only then did Xavier notice that Hank was not looking at him, but past him, to the bank of video monitors on the far wall.

Professor Charles Xavier turned, and was startled to see the face of his oldest friend, and his greatest enemy, staring back at him from all four of the monitors.

"Eric," he mumbled to himself.

Then all they could do was listen.

". . . am jamming all cable feeds and network broadcasts and supplementing them with my own signal," Magneto said.

His face filled the screen. Framed by his crimson helmet, Magneto's eyes glared with intensity under winter-white eyebrows that ought to have made him appear kindly. Instead, they made him look cruel and, somehow, sad as well. Or perhaps that was Xavier's interpretation, for he knew Magneto to be both of those things.

"Two roads diverged into a wood," Magneto began, using a quote from Robert Frost that made the moment all the more surreal. Xavier remembered that Eric Magnus Lehnsherr, the man who would become Magneto, had always loved Frost.

"Humanity has ever chosen the easy path. Like animals to the slaughter, you brainlessly trod together down the path of intolerance, bigotry and hate. All along, you might have chosen another path, and this day might have been averted. But perhaps you are animals after all. Perhaps you are without true awareness or nobility.

"For many years I have fought to make the world a safe place for my people, for mutantkind. Recently, I determined to create a haven, or sanctuary, where mutants could live undisturbed by the fear-inspired predations of the human animal.

"As of this moment, I have the means to create this haven here on Earth. And there's nothing you can do to prevent it. The choice has been taken from your hands. I have forced the world onto the road less traveled, and you will find it a hard road indeed."

The camera panned back to reveal two Sentinels, hovering in the air some distance behind Magneto. Beyond them, the skyline of New York City.

"Dear God," Xavier said in astonishment.

"As of this moment," Magneto continued, "Manhattan island is in my control. It is a haven for mutants, which will serve as the template for the world of peace that I have worked so long to bring about. All mutants are welcome, as are all humans. But mutants will rule here. No human being will be harmed so long as they adhere to the laws of the mutant government. Those who wish to leave will be allowed egress and relocation. The new laws, and the boundaries of the haven, will be enforced by the Sentinels, by my Acolytes, and of course, by myself.

"Manhattan island is the financial and cultural center of North America. Yet it is only the beginning. Very soon, the Mutant Empire will spread throughout the world.

"Earth will be at peace, or it will be destroyed. That is my promise to you."

Magneto disappeared from the screens, and they erupted with a panicked meltdown of news coverage. As the X-Men began to discuss strategies, and looked to him for direction, bile rose in Xavier's throat. For decades, he had dreamed of harmony between mutants and humans.

Xavier's dream was about to be put to the ultimate test.

CHRISTOPHER GOLDEN is the author of eight novels, including *Of Saints and Shadows*, *Angel Souls & Devil Hearts*, and the Daredevil novel *Predator's Smile*. Golden has recently entered the comic book field with work on such titles as *Wolverine* and *Vampirella Strikes!* He has written articles for *The Boston Herald*, *Hero Illustrated*, *Flux*, *Disney Adventures*, and *Billboard*, among others, and was a regular columnist for the worldwide service BPI Entertainment News Wire. His short story appearances are present in *Forbidden Acts*, *The Ultimate Spider-Man*, *The Ultimate Silver Surfer*, and *Gahan Wilson's The Ultimate Haunted House*. Golden was born and raised in Massachusetts, where he still lives with his family. He urges everyone to check out his WorldWideWeb page at http://www.oneworld.net/sf/authors/golden.htm.

* * *

RICK LEONARDI was born in Philadelphia. He started working at Marvel in 1980 and set himself up as one of their premiere fill-in artists, providing issues of *Daredevil*, *Uncanny X-Men*, *The New Mutants*, *Amazing Spider-Man*, *Excalibur*, *Spectacular Spider-Man*, and many others. He broke the trend by becoming the regular penciller on *Cloak & Dagger* and *Spider-Man 2099*.

* * *

RON LIM got his start on the alternative press comic *Ex-Mutants*, then moved on to prominence as the artist on Marvel's New Universe book *Psi-Force*. He has since lent his artistic talent to a variety of comics for Marvel, including *X-Men 2099*, *Spider-Man Unlimited*, *The Silver Surfer*, *Nightwatch*, *Venom: Nights of Vengeance*, and many more. He is also pencilling *They Call Me . . . The Skul* for Virtual Comics, and provided chapter-heading illustrations for the Spider-Man novel *The Venom Factor*.

* * *

TERRY AUSTIN is the Eagle, Saturn Alley, and *Comics Buyer's Guide* award-winning inker of such comics as *The Uncanny X-Men*, *Detective Comics*, *Star Wars*, *Dr. Strange*, *Batman vs. Predator II*, and the prestigious *X-Men/New Teen Titans* and *Green Lantern/Silver Surfer* team-up books. He has also written issues of *Cloak & Dagger*, *Power Pack*, *Uncanny X-Men Annual*, *What if . . . ?*, *Excalibur*, and, most recently, the adaptation of *Star Wars: Splinter of the Mind's Eye*. His current complaints include his inability to get the theme song for the Saturday morning cartoon *Freakazoid* out of his head.

All-New, Original Novels
Starring Marvel Comics'
Most Popular Heroes

__FANTASTIC FOUR: TO FREE ATLANTIS
   by Nancy A. Collins   1-57297-054-5/$5.99
Mr. Fantastic, the Thing, the Invisible Woman, and the Human
Torch—the Fantastic Four—must come to the aid of Prince Namor
before all of Atlantis is destroyed by the fiendish Doctor Doom.

__DAREDEVIL: PREDATOR'S SMILE
   by Christopher Golden   1-57297-010-3/$5.99
Caught in the middle of a battle over New York's underworld,
Daredevil must combat both Kingpin, his deadliest foe, and
Bullseye, a master assassin with a pathological hatred for Daredevil.

__X-MEN: MUTANT EMPIRE: BOOK 1: SIEGE
   by Christopher Golden   1-57297-114-2/$5.99
When Magneto takes over a top-secret government installation
containing mutant-hunting robots, the X-Men must battle against
their oldest foe. But the X-Men are held responsible for the takeover
by a more ruthless enemy...the U.S. government.

—COMING IN JULY 1996—
THE INCREDIBLE HULK: WHAT SAVAGE BEAST
® ™ and © 1995 Marvel Entertainment Group, Inc. All Rights Reserved.

SPIDER-MAN

SPIDER-MAN: CARNAGE IN NEW YORK by David Michelinie & Dean Wesley Smith 1-57297-019-7/$5.99
Spider-Man must go head-to-head with his most dangerous enemy, Carnage, a homicidal lunatic who revels in chaos. Carnage has been returned to New York in chains. But a bizarre accident sets Carnage loose upon the city once again! Now it's up to Spider-Man to stop his deadliest foe. *A collector's first edition*

THE ULTIMATE SPIDER-MAN   0-425-14610-3/$12.00
Beginning with a novella by Spider-Man cocreator Stan Lee and Peter David, this anthology includes all-new tales from established comics writers and popular authors of the fantastic, such as: Lawrence Watt-Evans, David Michelinie, Tom DeHaven, and Craig Shaw Gardner. An illustration by a well-known Marvel artist accompanies each story. *Trade*

SPIDER-MAN: THE VENOM FACTOR by Diane Duane
1-57297-038-3/$5.99
In a Manhattan warehouse, the death of an innocent man points to the involvement of Venom—the alien symbiote who is obsessed with Spider-Man's destruction. Yet Venom has always safeguarded innocent lives. Either Venom has gone completely around the bend, or there is another, even more sinister suspect.

® TM and © 1995 Marvel Entertainment Group, Inc. All rights reserved.

Payable in U.S. funds. No cash orders accepted. Postage & handling: $1.75 for one book, 75¢ for each additional. Maximum postage $5.50. Prices, postage and handling charges may change without notice. Visa, Amex, MasterCard call 1-800-788-6262, ext. 1, refer to ad # 563

Or, check above books	Bill my:	☐ Visa	☐ MasterCard	☐ Amex	
and send this order form to:					(expires)
The Berkley Publishing Group	Card#				
390 Murray Hill Pkwy., Dept. B					($15 minimum)
East Rutherford, NJ 07073	Signature				
Please allow 6 weeks for delivery.	Or enclosed is my:	☐ check	☐ money order		
Name		Book Total	$		
Address		Postage & Handling	$		
City		Applicable Sales Tax	$		
		(NY, NJ, PA, CA, GST Can.)			
State/ZIP		Total Amount Due	$		